LIAR'S TEST

Also by Ambelin Kwaymullina

The Things She's Seen

LIAR'S TEST

AMBELIN KWAYMULLINA

Alfred A. Knopf
New York

THIS IS A BORZOI BOOK PUBLISHED BY ALFRED A. KNOPF

Visit us on the Web! GetUnderlined.com

Educators and librarians, for a variety of teaching tools, visit us at RHTeachersLibrarians.com

Library of Congress Cataloging-in-Publication Data
Names: Kwaymullina, Ambelin, author
Title: Liar's test / Ambelin Kwaymullina.
Description: First edition. | New York : Alfred A. Knopf, 2024. | Audience: Ages 12 and up. | Audience: Grades 7–9. | Summary: In a competition where seven girls from different guilds vie for the throne, Bell Silverleaf, a reluctant fifteen-year-old contender with a hidden talent for deception, intends to win and overthrow the kingdom, but finds she is not the only competitor with secret plans.
Identifiers: LCCN 2023034344 (print) | LCCN 2023034345 (ebook) | ISBN 978-0-593-57178-1 (hardcover) | ISBN 978-0-593-57179-8 (library binding) | ISBN 978-0-593-57180-4 (ebook)
Subjects: CYAC: Fantasy. | Contests—Fiction. | Ability—Fiction. | Kings, queens, rulers, etc.—Fiction. | LCGFT: Fantasy fiction. | Novels.
Classification: LCC PZ7.K9759 Li 2024 (print) | LCC PZ7.K9759 (ebook) | DDC [Fic]—dc23

The text of this book is set in 11-point Scala.
Interior design by Ken Crossland

Printed in the United States of America
10 9 8 7 6 5 4 3 2 1
First Edition

For the Grandmothers
Spiky and strong
Fierce and proud
Warriors all
Survivors all

We who came after
remember

Seven will come
Two will die
Two will sleep
Two will serve
One will rule

1

I slammed into the altar of the sun and howled as something broke. Well, something *else*. The high priest had been beating on me for a while. Lots of things were already broken.

It hurt to scream. It hurt to breathe. It hurt.

Please. Stop. I tried to say the words. They wouldn't come out. My mouth was full of something salty and hot. Blood. I spat it out. It sprayed onto the gold of the altar. Only it wasn't so gold anymore. Everything was coated in red. Who'd have thought I had so much blood in me? And more was coming. Filling up my throat. I was choking.

I was dying.

I was dead.

Except I still hurt, and it seemed like being dead should mean no more hurting. But the pain was fading, the high priest had vanished, and everything had gone shadowy and gray.

Something soft brushed against my skin. The wind? It smelled of trees and whispered with a thousand voices. Okay, *not* the wind. This was the Ancestors.

The last of the pain disappeared, along with all of my fear. There was no need to be scared now. Not when I was out of the sun-temple and with my kin, who'd look after me the way Ancestors always did. They lifted me up to carry me away, and I knew I was going home. Away from the sun-priests and the moon-sisters. Back to other Treesingers. To family and green and life.

But instead the Ancestors brought me to an empty space. White light and nothing else. No trees. No life. No— Wait.

There was a blue spark, floating in my direction. Feelings that weren't mine flowed over me. Shock. Confusion. Fear.

The spark was *alive*. Some kind of spirit?

"Hello," I said. "I'm Bell." But the spark (Blue, I decided to call them) didn't seem to understand me.

The Ancestors spoke: *Long seasons, he's been lost here.*

Poor Blue. I'd been lost ever since I'd been taken into the sun-temple, except I'd always had the Ancestors. Blue didn't seem to have anybody.

A leaf appeared in the whiteness. It was followed by another and another, until there was a long line of them leading off into the distance.

"Look, Blue! That's got to be the way out!"

But he didn't seem to understand that either. Words didn't work on him. Only feelings. So I sent him exactly what he'd sent me. *Shock—confusion—fear.* Telling him that I'd felt all those things too. That I understood.

For a moment nothing happened. Then Blue drifted closer. He was listening.

I radiated out my own presence. Trying to say *I'm here* and *I won't leave you.* Because I knew what a difference it made, not to be alone.

Blue went all shimmery. I got the impression he was . . . thinking? Then new feelings came. First a bitter, freezing cold. Then a sense of a hand closing over mine, and the cold disappearing. As if someone had reached out to draw me into a warm room.

Oh! I knew what he was saying. *Found.*

"That's right, Blue. You're found." I took off after the leaves, slow at first to make sure he'd follow, and then quick once he came after me. We soared together, flowing along the trail the Ancestors had made until we were out of the white void.

And the pain tore me apart.

Someone was making wet choking noises. *Me. That's me.* I was back in the sun-temple, and not dead after all. Just close to it.

The wind stirred my hair: *Holdonholdonholdon.*

In the next minute something buzzed through my body. A wave of fizzing, zapping energy. Blue. He was helping me. He was *healing* me, although I didn't think he could make me all the way better.

But I knew I was going to live.

Then everything went black.

I shot up in the bed, gasping for air. Drowning in pain. A scream tore out of my throat. I slapped a hand over my mouth to cut it off.

Shut up, Bell Silverleaf. You're not hurt. Not now.

Pathetic whimpering noises leaked out from between my fingers. I sank back down, curling into a ball as I waited for my body to catch up with what my mind already knew.

It had been four years since high priest Alasdar had nearly beat me to death. Four *long* years, and all of them spent here in the sun-temple as the so-called blessed ward of the sun-priests and moon-sisters. Being trapped in this place was still real. But being nearly dead wasn't, and Alasdar had never hurt me that bad again. The priests and sisters wouldn't stand for it, although they happily overlooked bruises and the odd broken bone. ("Blessed ward," my arse. Some guardians they all were.)

I tried straightening out my legs. Only they wouldn't unbend, because they thought they *couldn't* unbend.

"You're not all smashed up," I growled at myself. "It's just a memory."

Except there was no "just a memory" for a Silverleaf. My family were memory-walkers, able to visit moments in our past and experience them as if they were happening right *now*. But we weren't supposed to do it by accident! I hadn't fallen into a memory since I was a little kid. And now this one wouldn't quite let me go. The pain had begun to fade, but my heart was pounding and my breath was coming too shallow and too quick.

I hauled myself up, switching on the glow-orb by the bed and staggering over to my mirror. It helped, sometimes, to see myself in the *now*. So I studied my own face. Brown skin. Round cheeks. Short dark curls. Fierce eyebrows. I had Mum's eyes, but the rest of me looked like Granny, except I didn't have her dimple, the one that only came out when she smiled (so hardly ever—my granny wasn't a smiley sort of person). And I was fifteen, not eleven.

My breathing eased. My heartbeat slowed. I abandoned the mirror for my window, opening it up to lean out into the cool of the night breeze. And thought of Blue.

He'd been with me ever since the day I'd saved him and he'd saved me back. Until two months ago, when he'd disappeared. The invisible presence that had been at my side for so long had just . . . vanished! I kept trying to find him (even in my dreams, apparently, because that had to be why I'd memory-walked tonight). But I had no idea where he was, or why he'd gone, and without

4

him I felt—well, a bit lost. And horribly afraid that something bad had happened to the only friend I had here.

My blood hummed, beating out a gentle rhythm under my skin. The Ancestors. Telling me the same thing they'd been telling me since Blue disappeared, which was that everything would be all right. I got the strong sense that they thought I should just be patient and wait for events to unfold. Except I didn't want to. I also didn't have to, because there *was* a place I could look. A secret place here in the temple that was connected to Blue. And, okay, I'd looked there before, more than once. But it couldn't do any harm to check again.

I climbed out the window and darted into the night.

I swerved left and then right, following familiar twists and turns as I wound my way onward. The sun-temple was a confusing mess of buildings, but after four years I knew this place better than most of the priests. And it was a good night for sneaking. There was no moon in the sky, which meant it was about as dark as it ever got. It still wasn't totally black, because the temple (like the rest of the city-kingdom of Radiance) was built out of brightstone. That horrible golden stuff had been a gift from the sun-god himself, and it was always shining. But tonight the shine was weak, not like how it was when the moon was full or the sun was up.

My run gradually became a jog and then a walk. Okay, a stroll. That memory had taken more strength from me than I'd thought. I kept on going anyway, until I came to a tall, narrow building in an out-of-the-way area. Then I launched myself upward, hands and feet easily finding the gaps and bumps I needed. The moment I reached the roof, I grabbed for the tiles, pushing them out of the way to make an entrance into the room below.

I dropped onto a heavy bookcase, scrambled down to the floor, and hit the orb in the wall to light the space. It looked the same as always. Desk, a couple of armchairs, and a thick rug on the floor. No door, and no windows. But you could see where they'd once been, before they'd been blocked off and this room had been forgotten by everyone but Blue. He'd led me here not long after I'd recovered from nearly dying. This was *his* room. Or at least it had been two centuries ago, when he'd still been alive. When he'd lived here, in the sun-temple.

When he'd been a god.

And, yeah, hadn't *that* been a surprise?

There were four gods in total—Tomas the sun-god, Allora the moon-god, Elodie the dawn-god (Tomas's sister), and Ronan the twilight-god (Tomas's baby brother). It was Ronan who was Blue. I could still remember how shocked I'd felt when I'd realized that the spirit I'd rescued was related to the sun-god I hated. But Blue wasn't anything like his brother. He'd never convinced a bunch of folks to worship him or led those same folks across the seas to invade Mistfall, the Treesinger homeland.

The story of the gods, their followers, and us Treesingers goes something like this: There were once some folks living in happy ignorance of gods until Tomas and Allora came down from the skies to "raise them up." The newly enlightened folks called themselves the Risen, and they went on to lead much less happy lives as the gods' chosen people. Then about a hundred and fifty years ago Tomas got it into his head to raise up Treesingers, so he and Allora set sail with a Risen fleet to land on our shores. My people told them where they could stick their enlightenment, and the Risen attacked, slaughtering half of Mistfall before Tomas got hurt bad in a battle with our trees. He slunk back to Radiance, and Allora and the Risen followed after, dragging a bunch of Tree-singers along with them.

But none of it was Ronan's doing, or Elodie's either. She'd fought the sun and moon gods with us until she'd mysteriously disappeared, which probably meant Tomas had killed her. He'd certainly killed Ronan, decades before then. My Blue. Dead because of a book.

I crossed to the shelves, running my hand along the spines. The gods each had their own special books, or as they called them, testimonies. Tomas's *Testimony of the Sun* was twelve volumes devoted to his own greatness; Allora's *Testimony of the Moon* was all cold science; and Elodie's *Testimony of the Dawn* was about peace, love, and equality. But Ronan's testimony was filled with such terrible "blasphemous falsehoods" that Tomas had murdered him and destroyed every copy of his work.

Well. *Almost* every copy.

I pulled the twilight testimony from the shelf and carried it over to the desk. Then I flipped it open and waited for it to recognize me. This book was a little bit alive, enough to hide itself from the wrong reader by pretending to be a volume of the *Testimony of the Sun*. After a moment, the words on the page shifted, becoming the first of the "lies" that had gotten Blue killed: *There's no such thing as gods.*

Turned out, the so-called gods weren't gods at all. They were visitors from another world, and while they could do some amazing things, there was nothing holy about them. Ronan and Elodie had tried to tell the Risen that, but none of them had wanted to listen. So Ronan had written the truth down in the hope that someday, someone would believe. And I guessed he'd realized that anyone who did would have to be good at deception to evade the sisters and priests (not to mention Tomas and Allora), because most of his book was a manual on lying. Which had been hugely helpful to me. Of course I'd already been a liar when I'd come here, on account of speaking truth to the Risen being bad for Treesinger health. But Ronan had made me a better one.

I pressed my hand onto the page, hoping to feel . . . something. This book had given Blue a voice, at least in my head. He spoke only in buzzes of energy, but after reading his words, I knew what he sounded like. Clever. Sarcastic. And always making fun of himself or the world. Every time Blue buzzed, it'd been Ronan's laughing voice I heard, and the two of us had mocked the powerful together. But he wasn't really in this book. He wasn't anywhere.

I'd actually had an idea for a while now about what might have happened to him. An idea I'd been ignoring. Hiding from, really. But as Ronan himself had taught me, true liars don't lie to themselves. I sighed, letting go of the *Testimony*. And faced the thing I didn't want to face.

Blue was a spirit, and spirits didn't stay in one place forever. At least, Treesinger spirits didn't. After we died, we were born into the world again as a human or tree or bird or some other life. Not always right away (some of us stayed spirits for a long while and became Ancestors). But Blue was no Ancestor. I'd known from the start that he wasn't much older than me. He'd been twelve when he died, and I didn't think he'd started growing again until he left the void. But after that, he'd seemed to age as I had.

Which meant that maybe he'd gotten old enough to become something new. To move on to his next incarnation.

Maybe he was really gone.

It *hurt* to think that. Pain spiked through me, making me gasp for breath. I gritted my teeth and let myself feel it, knowing

I couldn't keep looking for someone who might not be there to be found.

Then I felt something else. A sense of . . . presence.

I'm here.

I gasped for a different reason. *Where? Where are you?* But there was no answer to that. Or if there was, it wasn't one I could hear. My awareness of him was faint, like he was a very long way away.

I focused in on that distant hint and listened as hard as I could. Until, finally, there was something else. A promise I'd once made to him, echoed back to me.

I won't leave you.

My legs went trembly in relief, and I sagged against the desk.

I still didn't know where he was, or why he'd gone so far that even now I could barely find him at all. But he wouldn't break that promise.

Blue was coming back to me.

2

I woke up slow, forcing open eyes that were sore and gummed together. It felt like I'd only crawled into bed a moment ago. But it had to have been a few hours, because the sun was streaming in to light up the brightstone. That wasn't what had woken me, though. There was a scent in the air, coming through the window I'd left open last night. Something soft and sweet. Starblooms!

I got up and went over to the window, leaning out to breathe in the smell. The only place that starblooms grew was Many Flowers grove. That was where my uncle Dar lived. I hadn't seen him or any other Treesinger since I'd been brought to the temple, but sometimes the wind (or maybe the Ancestors) would bring a grove to me. My people had grown the groves after we'd been dragged here all those years ago, using seeds brought from Mistfall to create six living worlds of green amongst the hard shine of Radiance. We'd never go back to Mistfall now (the knowledge of how to find it was long lost), but we had a part of our far-off island with us in the groves.

I leaned out a bit farther, realizing as I did that I could hear voices and footsteps. But not from outside. People were hurrying about the infirmary building (which was where I lived in the temple, along with the eighteen moon-sisters who looked after the priests when they needed medical attention). Seemed like something significant was going on. Maybe someone important got hurt? With any luck, Alasdar had finally choked to death on his own ego. Unlikely, but a Treesinger could dream.

Except when moon-sister Jodie threw open my door, I knew whatever was happening had nothing to do with the high priest. Because that mixture of adoration and terror on her face could mean only one thing. *Crap. High priestess Bernadise is here.*

In the next moment, she confirmed it. "We are being honored by the presence of Her Reverence! She wishes to see you. Make haste!"

She rushed off, and I got dressed quick as I could. Then I sat on the bed and focused on turning myself into the Bell I showed to Bernadise.

Ronan had said that when you were telling an untruth about who you were, you should "inhabit the lie like a comfortable set of clothes." It was good advice, although I'd found I needed more than one set of clothes. Different lies, for different people. The outfit I wore around the high priestess was that of a Treesinger changed by Bernadise's cruel (sorry, *firm*) guiding hand. A girl who'd come to appreciate the value of the moon-sisters' important scientific work and definitely had no interest in fighting their downright creepy obsession with studying me and my people. . . . Okay, I was slipping into truth.

It was hard to keep hold of my real feelings around Bernadise. Because that icy bastard of a high priestess was the reason I was in the sun-temple in the first place.

11

She'd gotten interested in me after a sickness had struck down my grove. The illness had begun in our Birth tree and spread out from there, getting worse and worse until the only thing Falling Leaves could do was go dormant. Animals, plants, trees, people— the whole of the grove was locked into a deep, frozen sleep. All except for me.

Bernadise found it *fascinating*, and back then she'd been living in the sun-temple because she was the boss of the infirmary. But everyone had known she'd be the leader of the moon-sisters one day, so Alasdar had been happy to bring her the only Falling Leaves Treesinger still awake (he needed powerful people to owe him favors, what with his total lack of a winning personality). When she finally got the top job and bugged off to the moon-temple, I'd hoped to be let go. But by then Alasdar had gotten fond of having a Treesinger to kick around, and besides, Bernadise hadn't totally given up on learning something from me. She still showed up now and then to ask questions she'd asked before. Which was probably why she wanted to see me now.

I gritted my teeth, forcing myself into my Bernadise deception until I lived it completely. Then I went to see her.

The entire third floor was set aside as a place for her to stay whenever she dropped by the sun-temple. I climbed the stairs and found her in a big reception room, sitting in one of the armchairs that surrounded a low table. As always, she was dressed in a crisp, snowy robe (sisters wore white, priests wore yellow, and all of them wore sun-and-moon medallions hanging about their necks). She looked much the same as when I'd last seen her, hair a little shorter maybe, and with a bit more gray amongst the black. But her dark gaze was as sharp as ever, and her mouth still turned down at the corners in an expression of perpetual displeasure. And (depressingly) she was hefting a teapot to pour a stream of brown liquid into two cups. Bernadise brewed her own medicinal tea, and it tasted awful.

"Greetings, Bell." She gestured toward the other chair, sliding a cup over to me as I sat.

I took a cautious sip. It was surprisingly pleasant. Or at least, not immediately gag-inducing. "A new blend, Your Reverence?"

"Yes. Something designed to invoke clarity." She picked up her own cup, casting a contemplative gaze at the contents, then at me. "I came past Falling Leaves grove on my way here. It remains the same, of course." By which she meant it was surrounded by spiky vines that kept her or anybody else from poking around my sleeping home. "It is always upsetting," she continued with a sigh, "to see it in such a state."

I would've liked to tell her where she could stick it for pretending that one of the worst things that had ever happened to me meant anything to her. Instead I let my gaze go all distant and sorrowful, like I was contemplating the terrible fate of Falling Leaves. (And it was terrible. But it was my pain, not hers.) Then I shook myself like I couldn't stand to think about it any longer.

"Will you be here long, Your Reverence?" *Inquiring Treesingers want to know.* It'd tell me how long I had to do the work of lying to her smug face. And it *was* work. Bernadise was mean all the way down to her bones, but she wasn't stupid.

"Not very long, no. This is just a quick visit."

I made my mouth turn down and quickly flattened it back out, like I was disappointed she was leaving so soon but was too much of an obstinate Treesinger to show it (Bernadise thought of my

13

people as tricky and wild, and she would never believe that I'd totally transformed into a "civilized" girl). Then I took another sip of tea. And another.

This tea was *delicious*! I couldn't stop drinking, and the more I drank, the happier Bernadise looked. She even smiled. Vaguely it struck me that I should be worried about that. But it was hard to think of anything beyond the tea.

She spoke again as I slurped up the last drop. "Bell? Why don't you tell me what you think of the high priest?"

"He's a bastard."

My hand flew to my mouth and I set the cup down with a clatter. *How* could I have said that out loud? I mean, okay, Bernadise would never believe I actually *liked* Alasdar, but she'd still expect me to be respectful of him. I braced myself for a blast of disapproval and an inventively cruel punishment.

But all she did was nod. "I quite agree. A brutal dullard of a man. Although useful, on occasion."

I giggled. *What the heck?* I didn't giggle! At least not around Bernadise. I pressed my lips together to stop any more embarrassing sounds from escaping. Words came out anyway. "He'd be very angry if he knew you said that!"

"I expect he might. But he won't hear about it from you, Bell. You won't remember any of this."

I *would*. Silverleafs always remembered. But before I could tell her that, she said, "I'd like to discuss the grove sickness. Why were you the only Falling Leaves Treesinger who recovered?"

"You know already. I've told you before." Something very weird was happening. I knew it but I couldn't seem to make myself care about it. Or anything, really. Until my gaze fell on Bernadise's still-full cup, and then all I could think about was getting hold of that tea. My hand crept across the table.

Bernadise slapped me away. "You can have a little more in a moment. *If* you tell me why."

I rolled my eyes. "Only Falling Leaves Treesingers got sick." Like I hadn't already explained this to her a thousand times over! "Because the sickness came from the grove. So my granny unbonded me from Falling Leaves."

She frowned. "But your granny was the grove Matriarch, Bell. Responsible for everyone. Why didn't she unbond every Falling Leaves Treesinger? Save you all?"

I'd told her this before too. But she seemed to need to hear it again, and I *really* wanted that tea. "Unbonding is hard. And Granny had already used up lots of strength trying to help the grove. So she could only unbond one of us, and that was me."

Bernadise leaned back in her chair with a disappointed shake of her head. "So you *have* been telling the truth, all these years. You were never cured of the sickness. Just . . . released from it."

I reached for the tea.

"Just a sip," she warned as I raised it to my lips. I nodded. Then I tried to guzzle down the lot. But I only got in a few good swallows before Bernadise was standing over me, wresting the cup away and sending tea splashing everywhere.

"I *said* a sip!" she snapped, shoving the empty cup onto the table. "You will make yourself ill, you greedy girl."

There was some tea on my hands. I sucked at it, eyeing her sullenly as she sat back down. I didn't believe for a second that too much would make me sick. Um. Except maybe that's exactly what it *was* doing? I felt strange. All fuzzy and floaty. Like I could just drift away. Plus, I could hear humming, and that couldn't be right—the only other person here was Bernadise. Who did not hum.

She spoke again. "Bell, you've told me before that the reason your granny chose to unbond you was because you were her granddaughter."

I nodded. I had told her that. Then I looked around for whoever was humming.

"But," Bernadise continued, "I find it difficult to believe a Matriarch would put the needs of her family above the needs of the grove. Surely there were others of more value who could have been spared. You were just a child." She rapped her hand on the table to get my attention. "Look at me, Bell! Why *you*? What was so special about you?"

I opened my mouth to answer. And started to shake.

The humming was coming from *inside* of me and it was vibrating through my body, sending every tiny part of me rattling against every other part. I couldn't get a word out past the sudden chattering of my teeth. I couldn't hear Bernadise anymore either, although I could see the shape of her lips moving (saying my name?) as she sprang to her feet.

My mind went very cold and very clear.

Crap, was I ever in trouble. Bernadise had dosed me with some kind of truth tea and if the Ancestors hadn't just intervened, I would've told her I'd been saved because I was a memory-walker. If things had gone how they were meant to, I'd have been with the Treesinger healers all these years, walking my memories to give them every tiny detail of what happened to the grove so they could find a cure. But if Bernadise ever found out I was the living record of the sickness, she'd subject me to every horrible scientific test she could imagine and never, *ever* let me go.

The humming was fading. Seemed like the Ancestors were getting to the end of what they could do for me. I had to get myself out of this and I had no idea how. My thoughts darted in all directions, zapping about like firebugs and getting nowhere. Until I remembered. Ronan had written about this! Well, he'd written about substances that make it hard to lie. And he'd said you could still fool someone, but I couldn't remember how. . . . No, wait, I could.

He'd said to tell your interrogator something that was true but not the truth they were looking for.

True, but not the truth. I could do that.

"Bell! Bell!" That was Bernadise, kneeling at my side. She grabbed my head, holding it tight in a painful grip. "Answer me! Why did she free you?"

True but not the truth. True but not the truth. Which meant there was really only one thing to say.

"I'm a Silverleaf."

That was exactly the same as saying memory-walker, because all Silverleafs were memory-walkers and *only* Silverleafs were memory-walkers. But Bernadise didn't know that.

Her mouth went all twisty and sour. "She *did* release you because you were her granddaughter."

No. And yes, but not in the way she thought. I'd fooled her, but I didn't feel happy. I didn't feel anything. Everything seemed to be fading away, like this was all happening to someone else.

Bernadise cast a frowning glance at my face and hurried over to the other side of the room, opening a drawer to pull something out. She came back with a small bottle in her hand, pressing it to my lips. "I do hope you survive, Bell. The antidote is usually effective. But you must drink all of it."

That seemed like a lot of effort. Everything seemed like a lot of effort. But I drank, one small swallow at a time, until I'd managed to finish the bottle. Whatever was in it made me feel warm. Sleepy.

My blood hummed again, and the humming became a beat. *Thump, thump, thump.* Like a heart. Like *my* heart.

It sounded slow.

I slid off the chair and into darkness.

3

I woke to find the gods looking at me like I owed them something.

It wasn't really them, of course. The actual sun and moon gods had bugged off back to the skies not long after the Mistfall invasion. I was staring at a painting on a ceiling. *Treatment ward. I'm in the treatment ward.* And still alive.

I sat up, glancing around. The ward was empty. No sick or injured priests. No moon-sisters. Just one victorious Treesinger who hadn't been slain by truth tea (and wouldn't *that* have been a disappointing way to go). I sucked in a long, deep breath, then another, just to feel myself breathing. *It's okay. You're okay.* Well, I was a bit achy and weak. But that was nothing, considering how close I'd come to maybe dying. Or to giving myself away, which would've been almost as bad. Um. As long as I *hadn't* given myself away. . . .

I went over the conversation with Bernadise in my head, the one she'd thought I'd forget. (Ha! Silverleafs never forget.) *It's all right. You didn't tell her anything.* Although it'd been close. I was lucky she hadn't dosed me with that tea before I'd found the twilight testimony. Guess she hadn't been willing to risk killing me, back then. But . . . why had she risked it now?

Something's changed. It must have, because Bernadise didn't take chances—at least, not without a good reason. And I'd better figure out that reason quick so I could avoid any more life-threatening surprises. *I need to talk to Eldan.* The wily old chief archivist was the closest thing I had to a friend amongst the priests, and he'd helped me out a lot over the years, starting with making me his "junior librarian" (a job that consisted of eating cake, engaging in philosophical discussions, and generally hanging about the archives where I was out of Alasdar's way). Only problem was, I'd have to cross the temple to have a conversation, because the archives were a long way from here— Oh. No, I wouldn't. Eldan would come to me, like he always did when I ended up on the ward (thanks to Alasdar, I was here a lot). All I had to do was wait.

I flopped back on the bed, letting the day drift past me until the quiet was finally broken by a cheery whistle heading in my direction. I sat up and scrambled into my Eldan identity—curious, smart, and even a little snarky, provided any barbed comment was directed at something he despised (like ignorance, dry cake, or Alasdar). In the next moment the man himself came in, carrying a pile of books and looking as rumpled as always, with his white hair sticking out in all directions and his robe in dire need of being pressed.

He put the books down on the bed nearest the door and came over to sit in a chair at my side. "I do hope you're feeling better, Bell. I don't know how many times I've warned Bernadise that someone would have a reaction to her dreadful teas one day!"

So that was the tale she was spinning. "I'm much better, thanks." Then I went silent, making space for him to fill up with words. Eldan collected knowledge the way pebbler-mice collected stones, and there was nothing he enjoyed more than showing off his stash. If he knew something, he'd say so.

And he did. "Great things are afoot, Bell. And they involve *you*."

Ha! "Such as?"

But instead of answering, he steepled his fingers together, regarding me over the tops of them. I recognized the signs of him settling in for a chat and bit back a sigh.

"You know, of course," he said, "that a significant event is about to occur."

Well, yes. The stupid Queen's Test. The Risen picked a new ruler every twenty-five years by making seven girls compete in pointless challenges, and the next Test was only a week away. But Treesingers weren't a part of it. "What does the Test have to do with me?"

"To answer that, I must ask you something else. How familiar are you with the places assigned to each class?"

Oh, for— Just tell me what's going on! But he was building up to something and wouldn't appreciate being hurried along. So I answered: "Knights have three places in the Test, traders two, and crafters and workers one each." Which pretty much reflected the Risen social hierarchy—workers at the bottom, knights at the top, and crafters above workers but below traders. The Risen liked to say that anyone could be Queen, which was technically true. But with three places out of seven, the knights usually won.

"You are quite correct. Or at least, you *were* correct. But matters have changed." He paused, and it was obvious from his air of suppressed excitement that there was a big announcement coming. *Finally.*

"The Queen has brokered a deal with the knights. They're giving up one of their places in the Test."

I flat-out gaped. I mean, I *still* didn't see how it connected to me, but it was a startling thing for the knights to do, and Eldan obviously expected me to be astonished by it.

He let out a laugh. "Yes, my reaction was much the same. I cannot understand why they've given up such an advantage. I suppose . . ." He broke off, shaking his head. "But the why doesn't matter now. What's important is *who* the place has gone to. A new guild has been formed, to nominate a new candidate." He leaned forward, studying me with shrewd, dark eyes. "I wonder if you can fathom who that guild belongs to."

Okay, well, each of the four classes had their own guild to represent their interests. Which meant that, what, the Risen had made *another* division in their already divided society? Except . . . maybe not. Because *something* about all this connected to me. And there was a big group of people living in Radiance who weren't a part of their social order and who'd never had a guild.

"It's us, isn't it? It's Treesingers."

He beamed. "Just so! And . . ." His smile grew wider. "They've named their candidate for the Test."

Everything came together in my head, and my stomach lurched in something that was maybe excitement or maybe fear or maybe both. I knew now why Bernadise had been willing to risk killing me with that tea. She was about to lose control of me altogether.

I was getting out of the temple. But I wasn't going back to a grove.

I only had a moment to bury my confused feelings about that too deep to show before Eldan said: "It's *you*, Bell! You're the Treesinger candidate! You're going to the Queen's Test!"

On the outside I let my mouth fall open. Widened my eyes in shock. Then curved my lips upward into a huge grin.

But on the inside my heart and mind were racing. The stupid Queen's Test, where girls *died*? Treesingers had always thought the whole thing was senseless and cruel. *Why* would my people have agreed . . . ? *Oh.*

They hadn't been given a choice. This was the Queen's doing, it had to be. Like the two Queens before her, she'd pushed hard to make things better for Treesingers. She must think it was a stroke of genius to give us a shot at the crown. It wouldn't matter to her that Treesingers had never wanted to rule a kingdom we hadn't asked to come to in the first place.

Eldan was looking puzzled and a little put out. He'd made me a gift of life-changing knowledge and I wasn't being sufficiently appreciative. *Guess I didn't bury those feelings deep enough.* . . . But then his face lightened and he exclaimed, "You're worried about Alasdar, of course! But you needn't be, Bell. He won't stop you from leaving."

Okay, I hadn't been thinking about Alasdar, but I was now. "The Queen has asked him to release me before," I pointed out. She'd asked *lots,* without any success. Maybe she'd fail this time too, which would be . . . bad? Good? Bad, since I desperately wanted to leave. Except the idea had been to get out and go *home,* not get out and get killed in a meaningless Risen competition.

"Ah, but matters are different now," Eldan replied. "Choosing candidates is guild business. If Alasdar tried to stop a candidate—any candidate!—from fulfilling her duty to compete, he'd be threatening guild authority, and they won't stand for it. He must release you to the Test. And"—he sprang to his feet—"I've brought you a present, to help!"

He hurried back to where he'd left the books, ferrying them over until he'd laid them all out on the bed next to mine. Now that they were closer, I could see the titles: *The Queen's Test: A Short History*; *A Kingdom and a Crown*; *The Girl Who Would Be Queen* . . .

I looked at Eldan, who was smiling in a smug kind of way, all puffed up with how very thoughtful and generous he'd been. My own mouth tugged upward in response. My almost-friend was more than a little self-absorbed and a lot in love with his own cleverness. But he was trying to help me in the best way he knew how.

"Don't take this the wrong way," I said, "but I'd *really* like you to go now."

"Of course, of course! You've got reading to do!" He strode to the door, pausing in the doorway to look back at me. "The high priest assumes you will fail. I expect him to be *very* surprised."

I managed a grin. "Count on it."

He left.

And I put my head in my hands and tried to make sense of a world that had upended itself around me.

A storm of emotions was raging through my body, all mixed up and fighting with each other. I was happy I was getting out. Angry I wasn't going home. Scared I was going to die.

Really scared I was going to die.

Get a hold of yourself, Bell! I lifted my chin, reminding myself that I'd survived worse than this. I mean, I'd never been in a Queen's Test before, but the odds weren't so terrible. Only two candidates actually died. And, okay, another two did end up in a weird, unnatural sleep—but that wasn't going to be me either. I was going to be one of the three girls left standing at the end, alive and awake. Maybe I'd even be Queen.

Impossible. Except yesterday I'd have said it was impossible for one of my people to even be in the Test. *You don't want to be Queen!*

No Treesinger does. And I didn't. Or at least, I didn't want to rule the Risen. Wreak a little havoc upon them, though? That was something else entirely.

My blood thrummed, unpleasantly sharp. *Yeah, I know.* That was not a Treesinger thought. We were a peaceful people. And Mum had told me a thousand times over that we had to resist the Risen in ways that didn't mean losing ourselves. For the first time, it occurred to me that she'd said that so often because she'd sensed I was capable of some un-Treesinger-like behavior. But Mum was sleeping. She didn't know I'd been taken away from everyone and everything I loved by two selfish bastards who'd gotten away with it because I was a Treesinger and they were powerful Risen.

Uncle Dar said that when someone hurt you, being happy was the best revenge. But I was thinking something else.

I was thinking revenge was the best revenge.

But to save Falling Leaves and get any kind of revenge, I had to survive the Test.

I grabbed *The Girl Who Would Be Queen* and started reading as if my life depended on it.

Because it did.

4

I'd escaped the temple! And landed in a Test where I might possibly die (but hopefully not).

The Queen's Guard had collected me from the sun-temple about half an hour ago, escorting me through the shiny Radiance streets to the enormous Testing Hall (three levels high, and with a big round tower that spiraled to the clouds). I'd been taken through a maze of hallways and put in a room with instructions to "await the arrival of the other candidates." So now I was sitting on a bench and awaiting.

My leg jiggled. I clamped my hand down on it. Then my fingers started tapping. I stopped that too. The rest of the candidates would be here soon and I didn't want to look nervous in front of them. But I *was* nervous. I was also more than a little giddy with relief at finally getting out of the temple. And this weird mix of jumpy and fizziness was *not* a good thing to be feeling when I had to focus on the Test.

I took in slow, calming breaths and let my gaze wander around the room. It was dominated by the statues of Tomas and Allora that stood on either side of the arched entrance, painted to seem as lifelike as possible. (Creepy. Very creepy.) Otherwise all that was in here was a bunch of benches lined up to face the gods and a whole lot of words. Every wall was etched with the refrain of the Queen's Test, repeated over and over: *Seven will come / Two will die / Two will sleep / Two will serve / One will rule.* Having spent the last week reading Eldan's books, I had a much better understanding of what that all meant.

The Test was made up of challenges set by the sisters, the priests, and the guilds. Everything happened here inside the Hall, specifically in the Glass (guild challenge), the Cave (sister challenge), and the Bubble (priest challenge). Since the priests, who weren't famed for their big imaginations, had done the naming, I figured the Glass was a room with lots of windows, the Cave was a room with no windows, and the Bubble was . . . Yeah, I didn't know. A room with something round and transparent in it? Guess I'd find out soon enough.

We'd do each challenge twice over. Which was okay when it came to the guild challenge, because that was all speeches and persuasion but no actual danger. The only thing I'd have to do there was make a good impression on the guildmasters. A really *good* impression, because they were the ones who actually chose the Queen, voting for their favorite out of the three girls left at the end of the Test. The remaining two candidates would become trusted advisers, although it didn't take Queens long to get rid of advisers they didn't like (the current one had made her "two will serve" into ambassadors and sent them off to lands afar).

I wasn't so pleased about going twice into the Cave for the sister challenge or into the Bubble for the priest challenge. The sisters put the candidates into a deep sleep from which two of us wouldn't wake until we were *twenty-five years* older (the sleepers were woken by the sisters when the next Test began). But at least that challenge was supposed to test willpower, which I had plenty of. The Bubble worried me more, because that was where two girls died in a trial of faith and strength.

Faith I was confident I could fake. But strength? The books said the challenge could take the form of a battle against "forces of ignorance and doubt," and I didn't like my chances of winning a physical fight. I had to improve my odds, and it seemed like the only way to do it was through teaming up with somebody else. And since we were going into the Bubble tomorrow morning, that didn't give me long to find an ally.

My thoughts got interrupted by voices headed in my direction. The other candidates! In the next moment they came trailing in, each one dressed (like me) in a yellow shirt and pants with a guild symbol embroidered onto the sleeve (mine was a leaf). Most had the classic Risen looks of dark eyes, straight black hair, and pale skin, though a few had the blue eyes or lighter hair that indicated ancestry from one of the surrounding kingdoms (it only took one parent from Radiance for Risen girls to be eligible for the Test—well, that and being born and raised here). But none seemed like much of a prospect for an ally.

First, the knights. The one with the white-blond hair sat herself down as close to the statues as she could get, clasping her hands together and gazing adoringly upward. I named her Worships and we'd never be friends. Anyway, I was betting it was the other girl who was the knights' shining hope for a win. Shiny had short, dark hair, slashing black brows, and the easy grace of the very well coordinated. Confidence radiated out of her like warmth from a fire (this girl had never failed at anything and wasn't going to do so now).

I offered her a smile. She didn't quite smile back, but she looked like she was thinking about it before she sat herself down next to Worships. Okay, so I hadn't won her over. But it seemed like maybe I *could*. And at least she didn't seem to resent me for taking a knight place in the Test, which was more than could be said for the tall trader girl.

Spite was alternating between casting mean glances *at* me and whispering mean things *about* me to the crafter candidate. And the crafter was copying Spite's every gesture and joining in the meanness with enthusiasm (I named her Mimic). *Definitely no allies there.* The second trader candidate was ignoring me and everyone else, sitting apart and staring at the wall with a contemplative dark gaze (Loner). That just left the worker candidate, who . . . wasn't here. Although I could hear footsteps approaching, so she must be on her way.

But it wasn't the worker who came through the arch. It was Alasdar.

He was dressed in the glittering finery of his formal attire, a sun headdress perched on his graying hair and a trailing robe wrapped around his lanky body. Both headdress and robe were impossibly shiny, on account of being covered with tiny brightstone chips (sewn on with gilt embroidery, no less). The high priest stood between the gods with his narrow chest puffed out, dazzling the room as he waited for everyone to scramble to their feet. Then he realized there was a candidate missing.

He stormed out, stomping off into the distance to yell at someone to "find the worker and make sure she catches up with the rest!" By the time he returned I'd sunk deep into my Alasdar lie, becoming a girl who was as stupid as she was devout. The stupid was so he'd never know I was continually plotting his downfall (and anyway he just assumed Treesingers were stupid), and the devout was to give him less excuse to punish me. Not that he needed an excuse, but hurting such a *good* Treesinger made him look bad in front of the priests who weren't as filled with hate as he was.

Alasdar cleared his throat and spoke. "Welcome to the Queen's Test. Three of you will rise up"—his gaze fell on the traders and knights—"and one will be Queen"—he focused on Worships. No prizes for guessing who was his choice for the win. Then his gaze flicked to me. And I *knew* that spark of anticipation in his eyes. It was the one I saw right before he hit me.

I locked my body in place to stop myself from ducking. He couldn't actually hit a Queen's Test candidate. But something was coming, and it wasn't going to be good.

"Each of you will be familiar with the usual progression of the challenges of the Queen's Test," he continued. "But"—he paused to savor the moment, then finished the sentence—"a Queen must be prepared to deal with the unexpected."

He's changing the order of the Test. Could he even do that? But I supposed he could, because he *was* and I didn't see anyone around to stop him. And there could be only one reason for him to mess with the order. My heart thumped against my ribs, painfully hard, in the same moment that Alasdar said, "The Test will begin with a challenge of strength and faith."

He was sending us to the Bubble, where girls died. Where he thought *I'd* die, since he was forcing me in there before I'd had a chance to form an alliance, putting me at a big disadvantage when it came to strength—or, actually, no. He thought I'd fail the faith part of the Test. Because I was a Treesinger and not worthy of his god.

The other girls murmured at the change. Alasdar ignored them, looking only at me. He smiled, a single cruel twist of his lips. Then he strode out, commanding everyone to follow.

I wanted to rip that smug grin from his face (possibly by making him eat that stupid headdress). But it was useless to be angry. It was useless to do anything except hurry after the rest and figure out a way to survive. Maybe I could catch up to Loner or even Shiny and try to form an alliance? That was one heck of a long shot, but it seemed like the only shot I had. Except before I could do anything I heard someone approaching at speed. The worker candidate was sprinting in our direction.

Well, well. I might just make it through this after all.

This girl had Sierran heritage—I knew that from her brown skin—and the Sierrans had a lot more in common with Treesingers than they did with the Risen. They loved their deserts like we loved our trees and got sneered at for being "sand nomads" just like we got sneered at for being "nature worshippers." She was absolutely my best prospect for an alliance, and I certainly wasn't complaining that she was also a lot bigger than anyone else. Long, dark hair fell over wide shoulders and arms bulging with muscles, and there was a lightness to her step that suggested she'd be quick as well as strong.

I pasted a huge smile on my face as she approached. She grinned right back, adjusting her long stride to match my shorter one.

"I'm Tamsin," she whispered.

"Bell," I said, and smiled even wider. So did she. And a jolt of recognition shot through me. *I know you.* Except I didn't. I'd never met her before today. So why did she seem familiar?

But before I could think more about it, everybody stopped walking.

We'd arrived at a narrow set of stairs. The high priest swung around and drew himself up to his full height (which was a lot higher than usual owing to that headdress). "Candidates! We are about to begin our ascent to the Bubble."

He peered at everyone in a way that was probably supposed to be heavy with meaning, but that I thought made him look constipated. Then he spotted Tamsin at my side and his lips tightened in anger. He'd expected me to be alone and was not at all pleased to find I wasn't. *Buck up, Alasdar. A high priest must be prepared to deal with the unexpected.*

"As we rise up the tower," he continued (sounding distinctly grumpy), "I urge you to use these moments to reflect upon your life's journey. For one of you, this is where the Queen's Test will end."

Of course he looked at me when he said that. So did everybody else. Then they disappeared.

Okay, they didn't *actually* disappear. But Tamsin had edged protectively in front of me, and her impressive height and breadth blocked my view. I peeked around her to see Alasdar turn away with an annoyed frown, reaching for a lever in the wall. He pulled it, and the stairs began to move. *A stepper.* One of the many conveniences bestowed upon the Risen by Tomas the Incandescent, expert swindler that he was. *Here's some things that'll make your lives easier, it'll only cost you your souls. . . .*

We all piled onto the too-narrow moving passageway, the seven of us stuck standing in a line spiraling up the curving walls.

It was a relief to look out the windows, which gave a view across Radiance as we got higher and higher. I drank in the sight of the Treesinger groves, the only splashes of green amongst the gold. When my people first came here, they'd been shocked to find that the Risen didn't have any trees (although they'd also thought it explained a lot).

Everything outside the groves was just a shiny mess to me. But I knew that somewhere out there were the infirmaries where people got healed and prayed to Allora, and the altars where people got blessings and prayed to Tomas. There were the artisan halls where crafters crafted, the exchanges where traders traded, and the conclaves where knights politicked. Plus the factories and foundries, where workers shaped brightstone and did any other job that the other classes were just too special for. Guess I'd be boss of them all when I was Queen, although they had no part in picking me. That job got left to their guildmasters.

Another trip around, and an arched opening came into sight. We walked off the stepper and onto a platform that hugged the walls to make a circular path, with only a low railing between us and a deadly fall to the bottom of the tower. But I wasn't looking down. I was looking *up*. Because floating above me was the Bubble.

A massive sphere bobbed gently in the air, rainbow colors swirling across its glassy surface. That thing was half the size of the infirmary building and it was just . . . hanging there. *It's an overgrown bauble with some flashy colors.* But true liars didn't lie to themselves and I had to admit the Bubble was a little bit impressive. Maybe even a lot impressive. And I wasn't the only one who thought so. Everyone was staring at it with their eyes wide and their mouths hanging open.

Alasdar preened, delighting in our amazement at the shiny thing his god had made. Then he gestured grandly across to where seven redstone boxes were sitting on the platform. "Locate the box marked with your name and retrieve your gift. Quickly, please!"

This'll be the guild gifts. Each candidate was entitled to a present, which according to the books was usually a weapon (although I wouldn't be getting one of those because Treesingers were forbidden to own them). Everybody rushed forward except for Tamsin and Loner, who both inched their way along as close to the wall and as far from the drop as they could get. *Scared of heights.* I wasn't, but I didn't move quick either. Because I was scared of something else.

What if my box held some meaningless Risen thing that showed my people didn't care about me anymore? What if they'd named me as their candidate because if someone had to die in a stupid competition, it might as well be the girl no one had seen in years?

What if they'd abandoned me?

You know *they never would!* And I did, sort of. But I'd been away from the groves for a long time. Blood hummed, beating out a gentle reassurance. But not even the Ancestors could stop the whisper of these poisonous doubts in my mind.

I'd reached my box. I gritted my teeth and flipped open the lid.

And was so relieved I had to bolt my knees in place to keep myself upright.

A Traveling. They sent me a Traveling! I picked up the little sprig that ended in a spray of blue flowers. She was a girl, I knew that from the white lines on her limbs (like Treesingers, plants could be girls or boys or neither, and wore markings to show who they were). And the softness of her leaves told me she was young, although she was a part of a much older and larger tree. Travelings sought adventure by sending parts of themselves out into the world, and it was a big honor to carry one. It was also a message. My people and the trees believed in me. They trusted me to care for the little Traveling and bring her and myself safely back to the groves. I hadn't been abandoned or forgotten. They'd made me their candidate to bring me home.

Unexpected tears stung my eyes.

"Well, would you look at that," someone drawled. "The Treesinger's been given a twig."

I looked up, blinking. It was Spite who'd spoken. She laughed at her own joke, and Mimic and Worships laughed right along with her. Shiny and Loner shifted uncomfortably. And Tamsin glared at them all. I gave her a quick shake of my head to stop the angry tirade she was so obviously about to launch into. There was a better way to handle this. A Treesinger way.

I held up the Traveling and spoke in a reverential tone. "This comes from a tree that honors Tomas the Incandescent with its beauty. The blossoms have blue petals and a yellow heart like the sun in the sky, although of course no mere flower can truly reflect his glory."

The laughter cut off so fast that Worships got her breath caught in her throat and started coughing. Tamsin made a choking sound too (but only because she was trying not to giggle). And I lowered the Traveling, gazing down at her as if I really was contemplating her resemblance to the sun. The reality was, trees were liars.

Back on Mistfall, a Traveling's flowers were a lovely purple-black. But in Radiance, our groves overflowed with flowers and leaves and fruit in shades of white (moon-god) or yellow and orange (sun-god). The god colors had helped to persuade the sisters and priests that

Treesingers and our plants honored Tomas and Allora, even though they weren't our gods and never would be. In a moment of inspiration, the Watcher trees had even grown leaves that underwent a slow shift from a bright yellow to a soft amber-gold. The priests had been thrilled when we planted stinky Watchers at the entrance of every grove, and so far as I knew, it still hadn't dawned upon them that those trees only released their gut-curdling scent to warn us when a Risen was near.

I lifted the Traveling to my hair as Tamsin made her way over to her own box. The little branch wound her way into my curls, and pictures flashed through my mind: a leaf falling from a tree into the path of a sun-priest, who slipped on it and tumbled over as the leaf whirled into the air to rejoin her tree.

She was speaking to me in the green language. I was a bit out of practice after years of having no plants to talk to, but it still didn't take long for me to translate images into words: My name is Tricks!

"My name is Bell," I whispered, making pictures in my own head but saying the words out loud like I'd been taught. That was to help me focus, so I'd speak clearly and in sequence. Otherwise human minds tended to flit across a bunch of images and we made no sense at all to trees and other plants.

Tricks let out a cloud of zesty scent. A burst of confidence exploded through me and I lurched toward the railing, eager to find out what was inside that giant rainbow ball.

I sighed and stopped, turning my steps back toward Tamsin. A Traveling's scent was highly influential and they were notoriously reckless.

"The Bubble is dangerous," I murmured.

It will be a big adventure!

It wouldn't. But I couldn't tell her that because I'd reached Tamsin. She was holding a battered, *enormous* hammer with a word carved into the handle. No, not a word. A name. "Bashy?"

She hefted it proudly. "It belongs to my aunty Electra. Best hammer in the foundry!" Then her gaze went to Tricks and her eyes widened. "Is your plant *waving*?"

"No," I lied, reaching up to still Tricks's cheery hello. "This kind of plant is just very sensitive to tiny currents in the air. Moves all the time."

I cast a quick glance around and saw that everyone had got their gifts—the knights and traders were holding redstone swords, while Mimic had a whitestone dagger. Good thing Tamsin had Bashy. If we were only going to have one weapon between us, at least it was the biggest one.

Worships started back toward Alasdar. But he yelled at her: "Remain where you are!" Then he swiveled to face the Bubble, his features settling into his "I am a very holy and important man" face as he reached for his sun-and-moon medallion. He lifted it high into the air—

—and did absolutely nothing else.

Pausing for dramatic effect, Alasdar? You're going to regret that. As I'd expected, his arm soon started to tremble. The high priest's medallion was a truly gigantic hunk of brightstone.

"Glory ever after to Tomas the Incandescent!" he bellowed. "Let the challenge commence!"

Light poured from his medallion, slamming into the Bubble. Colors flashed and whirled, impossibly fast and impossibly bright.

And the Bubble shot out of the air and swallowed us all.

5

I gasped in shock and was relieved to find I could still breathe. But there was nothing here. Just me and Tricks and bright yellow light. Where was everybody else? Where was *anything*?

The rainbow ball has eaten us!

Tricks seemed to think this was hugely exciting.

The light winked out and a world appeared, along with the rest of the candidates. We were standing in . . . *a desert?* Blue sky stretched out endlessly above a flat red plain dotted with rocky hills. I swallowed. The Bubble was big, but nowhere near big enough to hold all this. Yet it did. *Tomas is not a god,* I reminded myself. But in this moment I was finding it easy to understand why the Risen thought he was.

Tamsin came striding over, hefting Bashy and looking around for an enemy. The others had their weapons raised too. But there were no "forces of ignorance and doubt" to fight. Just hills. Rocks, scattered across the ground. Little holes . . . Wait.

Holes.

They were everywhere, and the dirt around them was trembling faintly. As if there was movement below. Like something was coming . . . *up.*

I grabbed Tamsin's arm and pointed toward the nearest hill. "We've got to get off the plain. *Run!"*

We sprinted for the rocks, feet pounding across the hard earth. There were shouts of alarm from behind us, and I looked back to see white wormy things shooting from the ground. They started out small but got big quick, turning into fat tentacles that reached for the candidates.

My foot landed on something cold and squishy. I put on a new burst of speed and Tamsin swung her hammer, clearing our way of worms as we pelted onward. We'd almost made it to the hill when a monster tentacle exploded up to seize hold of Bashy, sending it soaring into the distance.

Then two more tentacles wrapped around my ankles and pulled my legs out from under me.

I slammed into the earth, coughing and spluttering as I barreled across the ground. I was being dragged toward a hole that had appeared out of nowhere. Red sand trickled into a big, dark nothingness. *The Bubble really is trying to eat me!*

Tamsin turned to run for Bashy. "You'll never reach it in time!" I wheezed. But she wasn't going for the hammer. She was going for the hill.

Tamsin was leaving me behind.

Hurt flared, which was just stupid. *Get a hold of yourself!* I tried to shift into a sitting position so I could reach the worms but ended up sprawling in the dust. Tricks released a cloud of scent, sending strength surging through my body, and I lurched upward, scrabbling for rocks. I grabbed on to a couple and used them to stab at my wormy captors. But my rocks were too little and too blunt. And the hole was getting closer . . . closer . . .

A boulder came soaring through the air.

It landed on the worms with an almighty squelching sound, exploding them into pieces. A big arm reached down, closing around mine to haul me to my feet.

Tamsin hadn't left me to die. She'd just gone to find a really big rock.

A smile tugged at my lips as we ran to the hill. She was still a useful ally. And that was why I was smiling and not because it felt good to have someone on my side or even because I might like Tamsin a bit. And, okay, I knew I was lying, but I was in the middle of a life-threatening situation and sometimes even true liars have to pretend. I certainly didn't have time to process inconvenient feelings now.

We reached the hill and kept going, both of us breathing hard but neither of us stopping until we'd made it to the top. Tricks was laughing in my mind. *Too fast for you, rainbow ball! Can't catch us!*

Tamsin leaned over to rest her hands on her knees as I checked my injuries. I was bruised. My chest ached. And blood was leaking from a bunch of scratches. But compared to being eaten by a mysterious sphere created by a fake god? This was nothing.

"You okay?" Tamsin asked.

"Yeah. You?"

"I'm good." She straightened and shaded her eyes with her hand, staring out over the plain. "Looks like nobody's dead yet."

I followed the direction of her gaze to find that everyone had made it to higher ground. Shiny and Worships were standing on one hill and Spite, Loner, and Mimic on another. They all had weapons raised (except for Worships, who'd lost her sword). Only there was nothing for them to fight. The worms had vanished.

Tamsin said what everybody must be thinking: "What are we supposed to do now?"

"I don't know!" So far this seemed to have been a trial of strength. Would faith be next, or had that been part of what had happened already? But I didn't see how. Except . . . this whole situation felt familiar. It reminded me of something. Maybe something I'd seen?

No. Something I'd *read*.

I opened my mouth to speak, but before I could get a word out, the hill beneath us started shaking.

Then it started sinking.

In the same moment, worms came boiling up from the earth, multiplying fast until there were tens . . . *hundreds* of them waiting for us on the plain below. And we weren't the only ones in trouble. The other hills were sinking too.

Tamsin pointed to where her hammer was lying on the ground. "I'm going to make a run for Bashy!"

"Don't! We have to pray."

I dropped to my knees. She gaped at me. "What are you doing? Get up!"

Words rushed out as I tried to explain. "This whole thing is from the *Testimony of the Sun*. There's this bit about how Tomas continually tries to soar on the wings of his aspirations into the clear skies of his potential. But lesser minds keep dragging him back to the arid earth of mediocrity, until he believes in himself and *ascends*. We have to show we believe in him, and we'll ascend too!"

"Are you sure? I don't remember that part!"

"Trust me, it's there." I wasn't surprised she didn't remember, what with its being an obscure passage from the third volume. But I knew *all* the words of *every* volume. I'd literally had them beaten into me.

I began to recite the first of the one hundred prayers of the sun: "Holy Tomas, look down upon your unworthy servants. . . ."

After a moment, Tamsin dropped down beside me and joined in. But the hill kept sinking, and it was obvious why. Her voice was shaky and unsure. Filled with doubt.

"You have to sound more confident, show you really mean it," I said. But she looked at me with fear in her eyes. And I knew.

Oh, no. What a time to discover a fellow unbeliever. Tamsin wasn't any more of a follower of Tomas the Incandescent than I was. But unlike me, she wasn't an expert liar, and if she didn't get better at deception fast we were going to be food for worms.

Think, Bell! Lying to the Bubble couldn't be that much different from lying to people. You just had to *sound* like you believed. Which she didn't, at the moment. . . . Okay. I knew what she had to do. But I was afraid to say it out loud in case the Bubble was somehow listening.

"I know you want to go get your hammer," I said, reaching across to squeeze her arm. "But it *was* the worst hammer in the foundry." I squeezed twice. "You said so yourself." Twice, again, because she'd know she'd said exactly the opposite. *Once for truth, twice for lie.* I raised my eyebrows at her.

She nodded. She got it.

"We don't need the hammer. We just have to focus on what we believe in most in the world." I squeezed once (truth). "That will be Tomas the Incandescent, of course." Twice (lie). "So think about what you believe, and pour everything you're feeling into the prayer." Once (truth).

Her eyes lit up and she nodded again.

There were wet noises from below. I looked down to find we'd gotten way too close to the earth and the worms were making hideous sucking sounds. *"Do it now, Tamsin!"*

And she did. I had no idea what she actually believed in, but she started speaking that prayer with so much conviction she could've passed for a moon-sister.

I did as well. I was thinking of trees.

With every word we spoke, the hill sank slower and slower until it shuddered to a stop. For a second it didn't move at all.

Then it began to rise.

Blue petals exploded around my head in a burst of color and scent. I shared a grin with Tamsin, but I didn't stop praying, and nor did she. The two of us just kept on groveling to a god neither of us believed in, and that hill kept on ascending into the blue skies of *our* potential. And right now that potential felt limitless, because we were going to survive this.

I brushed petals out of my eyes and looked around to see what had happened to everybody else.

Worships was praying, only her hill was still sinking because Shiny wasn't. But as I watched, Shiny cast a long look in our direction and fell to her knees beside Worships (she'd seen it work for us). Spite, Loner, and Mimic were running and fighting the worms as they went, although I wasn't sure where they thought they were running *to*. But in the next moment Loner veered off, heading toward Worships and Shiny. She must've spotted that their hill was now rising. Only she didn't get far before a worm got hold of her leg and dragged her to the ground.

She still had her sword, which meant she could have stabbed the worm and gotten away. But in her panic she screamed something out. A cry for help, to a higher power. Except the god she called out to was Elodie.

And just like I'd feared, the Bubble was listening.

The earth rumbled and the wind roared, rushing across the ground to send a storm of red dust swirling around Loner. Then the earth went quiet, the wind dropped away, and the dust settled.

Loner was gone.

And everything disappeared into yellow light.

For a while there was only the light. Then it vanished and I tumbled onto a hard surface. I rolled to my feet, head swiveling left and right as I tried to see what was coming next.

But there was no next. The Bubble had spat me back into the tower.

I looked around for Tamsin. She was sitting with her back against the wall and a woozy expression on her face. All the candidates and the weapons were here too, except for Loner (I guess the Bubble kept what it took). Everyone looked terrible, and I understood exactly how bad they were feeling because I felt the same. My legs were weak, my stomach was heaving, and my vision had gone blurry around the edges.

I blinked and breathed, trying to settle my stomach and clear my sight. And trying *not* to think about a girl vanishing into dust. *Sorry it had to be you, Loner.* I knew now why she'd kept herself apart. She was an Elodian. A lot of the Risen were, what with Elodie's "let's all hold hands and be friends" philosophy gaining popularity over the years. But you didn't admit to believing in someone who'd told people to "worship not gods, but the kindness in your hearts" around priests and sisters. Or inside a faith-testing device created by Tomas.

A disbelieving voice spoke from behind me. "You're *alive*?"

Alasdar. I turned to face him, and all the anger I'd felt before came surging back. He'd tried to kill me, and it'd almost worked, and another girl *had* died for no other reason than not loving Tomas best. And even though I knew it wasn't smart to provoke him, I just couldn't help myself.

I lifted my eyes to the heavens, clasped my hands together, and spoke words guaranteed to make him furious. "Tomas the Incandescent has found me worthy."

He drew in a hissing breath. I dropped my gaze to his to find his features had twisted into a familiar, ugly expression. He wanted to hit me. But the only thing he could do was glare.

I stared back. Piously.

There was a long, tense silence. Then he let out a growl and stalked over to the stepper. He pulled a lever to send it going down the tower before spreading his glare across the rest of the candidates. "You may all follow me to your quarters. There will be no further challenges today."

I'd bet there wouldn't. He'd changed the order to get rid of me, and instead a Risen girl had died (and a trader, no less). The high priest was going to have some questions to answer from the guilds.

I began to move toward Tamsin, only to find she was making her way over to me.

"You all right?" she asked as she got near. "The high priest seemed really angry with you."

Oh, she had no idea. "I'm fine." Better than fine. I'd defeated the Bubble. And Alasdar had helped me do it by making me memorize the *Testimony*, which was hilarious in a grim kind of way. It was so funny that it was hard not to laugh and laugh. . . . Okay, I might just be having a little bit of a reaction, what with nearly dying and all.

I grinned at Tamsin. "Let's get out of here."

We followed the others onto the stepper. Afternoon had turned to evening while we were in the Bubble, and I stared out the windows at the soft glow of Radiance, wondering if any of my people were staring back at me.

Voices murmured from below, one of them sounding kind of whiny. *Spite.* She was complaining to someone (probably Mimic). In the next moment her whininess got louder, rising up the tower: "It's not *fair*. It should've been *her*. Everyone knew the Treesinger would die first!"

Tamsin growled. And Tricks let out a gleeful chuckle. Not this Treesinger!

I reached up to tangle my hand in her leaves and whispered, "Not *any* Treesinger."

Not anymore.

6

So this was my room.

Big window. Comfy-looking bed. Drawers full of candidate clothes, thick rug on the floor, and a little bathroom to myself. All of it golden and shiny and *very* fancy. *Seems more like the kind of place they'd give a knight.* . . . Oh. It *was* that kind of place. The rooms must be as identical as our candidate clothes, and since they weren't going to stick a knight with the sorts of bedrooms lived in by ordinary folk, the rest of us got the knight standard.

My bag was sitting in the corner. I was pleased to see the Queen's guards had kept their promise to return my stuff, although there was only one thing in there I cared about. I went over and dug out the *Testimony of Twilight* (safely disguised as the sun testimony). Then I sat, hugging the book against me and trying to sense Ronan. But all I got was the *very* faintest hint of him. He still seemed to be a long way away, and I wasn't sure he was aware of me. *He's coming back,* I reminded myself. But probably not soon. Maybe I could try . . . maybe I could . . .

But I was too tired to think up ideas. My brain was foggy and stupid with exhaustion. I needed to sleep, especially with there being another round of the Bubble tomorrow, *and* the Cave, *and* the Glass. Tricks released a sweet, heady scent that made my eyelids droop. She thought I needed sleep too.

I dragged myself over to the bed, dropping onto the puffy softness and drifting into darkness.

Then the darkness cleared and I was somewhere else.

I was *someone* else.

My world had grown small. The whole of my existence was confined to the curving walls of the tree in which I made my home. Soon I would fall into the sleep from which there might be no waking.

My world had grown silent. There were no singing birds, no scurrying animals, and no laughing children. Not even my own child. Bell didn't laugh anymore.

I watched her as she sat, weaving a basket. I wanted to tell her the words spoken at the passing of every Treesinger: *Everything returns to the earth. But everything returns from the earth too. We will all be here again.* To remind Bell that we came back, and in whatever form we lived next, we were always connected to those we loved and who loved us. But I knew my daughter would find no comfort in us being together in that way.

I hummed a tune at her. Bell rolled her eyes. She found my made-up song to be ridiculous. But she still sang the silly rhyme that went with the melody:

> *One step, two steps, three steps, four*
> *Turn to the right and step some more*
> *When you reach the place of eight*

Step left and left and then step straight
Now you're almost done, my love
Just once more left and then above

One day she would understand what the words meant. Once her gift truly woke, she would know what to do. If indeed she was the one to do it. My mother thought so. But my mother had always asked much of my daughter.

"Come sit with me, Bell. Tell me a story."

She crossed the room to nestle at my side. "What kind of story?"

"Tell me about how Treesingers are strong. Tell me about the Beneath."

She brightened. This was a tale she loved. "When Treesingers first got here, we weren't allowed to leave our groves, not unless a moon-sister came with us."

"That's right. We weren't free to move around Radiance for over a hundred years, until the Queen changed the law."

"They thought they had us trapped! But the Tangler trees knew what to do. All the Tanglers in all the groves sent their roots down into the ground, deeper than any other roots had ever gone. They found the crystal caves. We called those caves the Beneath, and they stretch under half of Radiance! Which means we can move between the groves without the Risen knowing anything about it."

"Yes, we can." I tightened my hand on hers. "Because the Risen don't see the connections that link us together. But that doesn't mean we aren't connected. They don't see how we resist. But that doesn't mean we aren't resisting."

Bell hunched her shoulders. My child didn't value the hidden ways as much as she should. I sighed. "There are many ways to be strong, Bell. You must remember that, when I am not here to remind you."

"You won't be sleeping for long! The healers will use my memories to fix the grove, and everything will be okay again."

"I'm sure it will. But remember anyway."

I kept my voice steady. Calm. She was uncannily good at detecting an untruth. And she didn't know, she *couldn't* know yet, that her memories of the "sickness" would do nothing.

What people called the sickness was in truth an infection in the Birth tree, one caused by the foreign substance that had been pushed into her veins. The rest of the grove had gone frail and weak because she was drawing on us to fight it. But she could not overcome the effects of the strange stuff called pathway. Nor could any healer cure her of it. Only one person could: *the* Silverleaf. The one we'd waited for, ever since Alethea Silverleaf herself had set our bloodline on this long journey. That might be Bell. Or it might not. And if not, it would be her daughter, or granddaughter, or another Silverleaf after that. But I feared what Bell would do if she discovered these truths too early. The person my Bell was now would never accept that she wasn't *the* Silverleaf. She'd destroy herself seeking a victory that might not be hers to claim.

There was a sound outside, loud in the quiet of the grove. Dar was coming. I pressed Bell close, hugging her against me so she wouldn't see the worry in my face. I was handing my daughter over to someone who knew no more than she did of the responsibility carried by the Silverleaf line. But it was not for me to tell him. Silverleaf secrets were for Silverleaf women and Silverleaf trees. And as Bell grew, as her gift grew, the memories would teach her what she needed to understand. It would be enough. *Surely* it would be enough.

Dar appeared in the doorway. He said nothing, for we'd already said all there was to say. He just smiled his big, gentle smile, enveloping us both in the warmth of it.

I pressed a kiss to Bell's head. "Love you, little warrior."

"Love you, Mum."

Dar held out his hand. Bell walked over and took it, looking back over her shoulder for one last glance at me as he led her away.

Her footsteps grew fainter and fainter. Until there was nothing.

My world was small.

My world was silent.

I shot bolt upright with a gasp. What the *heck?*

A happy voice burbled in my mind. I have woken your gift!

I drew up my knees, resting my pounding head on top of them. "My gift was already awake!"

Not *enough.*

"What is that supposed—" But I stopped, because I knew exactly what she meant. I'd always been able to walk my own memories. But never other people's.

"It was just a stupid dream," I muttered. A stupid, *very* realistic dream. . . . Okay, I was lying to myself. I knew what a memory felt like. But I wanted it to be a dream, because if it wasn't, my mum had lied to me. And I'd been wrong about everything I'd thought I was supposed to do.

Her words echoed in my mind. *She couldn't know yet that her memories of the "sickness" would do nothing.* . . . How could that possibly be true? And what was this about an infection? I'd never heard the sickness called that before! I pressed my feet down onto the bed, just to feel something beneath me. Because it seemed like everything I'd thought was real and solid had been torn away.

Tricks burbled again. Now you can walk the pathway!

The pathway? That had been in the dream too. I lifted my

head, forcing myself to think past my shock and confusion. "You mean . . . the stuff that's infected the Birth tree? It sounds like some kind of poison, Tricks! How exactly am I supposed to 'walk' it?"

No answer. I sighed. "You don't know, do you?"

I know many things. In other words, she had no idea. I was told, *Wake the gift so the guardian can walk the pathway.*

"Told by who?"

Silverleafs.

"You can't have been. Mum and Granny are sl—" But then I realized she didn't mean Silverleaf *humans*. She meant Silverleaf *trees*. Those lovely, tricky trees that my family was named for held all sorts of knowledge, although they were choosy about what they shared to the point of being downright mysterious. "Did the Silverleafs tell you anything else?"

I didn't need to be told anything else! It was a great responsibility to wake your gift. A responsibility for a special, *thoughtful* Traveling, not a silly sprig who'd be distracted by the shine and noise of the world.

Which I was sure was what the Silverleafs had said to her when they'd given her this job. Sounded like those trees had been as cagey as always, and there was no point in pressing Tricks for information she didn't have. Instead I reached up to pat her leaves. "You are a special Traveling."

I know. She sounded satisfied but tired. I am the *most* special Traveling. We will do big things! Songs will be sung. . . .

Her presence faded from my mind. Tricks had gone into the plant equivalent of sleep.

I threw back the blanket and got up, pacing back and forth in the soft brightstone glow. I couldn't be still right now, not with all these feelings surging through me. I was bewildered, and hurt, but mostly I was just plain furious at Mum for lying to me. *How* could she have let me believe my memories would save the grove, all these years . . . ?

Okay, in fairness, she hadn't done that last bit. She'd expected the Silverleaf gift to show me the truth. *I got kidnapped by sun-priests,* I growled at her in my mind. *I've been shut up in the temple for four years.* Where I hadn't done a lot of memory-walking, because I couldn't go wandering about the past when I had to survive in the present. My gift hadn't grown like it was supposed to, and I'd learned nothing.

There was no way for Mum to have known that would happen. But I was still angry with her, and Granny too, for not trusting me with the truth. Although I supposed Granny might've intended to tell. She'd taken a sudden turn for the worse, so maybe she'd fallen asleep before she could reveal that my family had spent generations waiting for some special Silverleaf who was supposed to do . . . I didn't know, something! Deal with the "strange stuff called pathway," whatever it was? But that couldn't only be it, because Mum said it was *Alethea* Silverleaf who'd started us on this journey. My great-great-great-grandma, one of the Treesingers taken from Mistfall by the Risen, and the first of our line with the memory gift. But Alethea couldn't possibly have known there'd be a sickness—sorry, *infection*—in the grove years after she was dead.

Also, what was it that the trees were going on about? *Wake the gift so the guardian can walk the pathway?* That made no sense. For starters, I wasn't a guardian. Silverleaf women had been once, but what we'd guarded were the Nexus trees, and every last one of those big, beautiful trees had been murdered in the Mistfall invasion, right along with the women who'd fought to protect them. Alethea alone had survived, and from her onward there'd been only one child born in each generation, making me the last

Silverleaf and the guardian of nothing. Plus, it surely wasn't possible to "walk" a poison. Although there might've been a mix-up with the words, being as Silverleaf trees weren't the best communicators. Perhaps "walk" meant something else, like "cure."

Maybe the song could help? The stupid song Mum had insisted on teaching me that apparently had some hidden secret meaning. *One step, two steps* . . . Huh. Now that I was thinking about it again, it almost sounded like directions. Maybe I had to *actually* walk somewhere to get rid of the pathway stuff and the song was telling me where to go! Except it was a bit on the vague side. I mean, "Turn to the right and step some more"? How many steps, exactly? And what was the "place of eight"?

I heaved a frustrated sigh. I was trying to put together a puzzle without all the pieces. *You should have told me, Mum!* But my anger at her was ebbing. Because whatever this "long journey" was, Mum had felt the weight of it, as if the expectations of generations were pressing down on her shoulders. This was much bigger than her and me. This was something . . . Silverleaf. Something we had to protect with everything we had, and I hadn't been as strong as I'd thought, back when the grove got sick. Because Mum was right—I hadn't valued the hidden ways like I should. But I knew better now.

And . . . maybe *I* was *the* Silverleaf? It seemed like Granny had thought so, and she wouldn't have believed that just because I was her granddaughter. Her faith had to be earned. Which meant I could still save the grove! Just not in the way I'd thought.

But, wow, did I need those Silverleaf memories.

I closed my eyes and concentrated *really* hard on pathway, trying to trigger a memory. *Come on, tell me what it is. Tell me how to save the Birth tree from it. . . .*

Nothing happened. All I felt was a faint, fragile stirring, like a small plant uncurling its leaves to the sun for the first time. I knew what Mum would say. *Wait. Have patience. New things need space and air to grow and flourish.*

Except I didn't have time to wait. Maybe I could dream what I needed instead? I buried my head in my pillow, willing my gift to show me something useful.

I dreamed of nothing.

7

I woke the next morning with no new knowledge, which was deeply frustrating. And now I had to stop thinking about Silverleaf things, at least until I'd survived the day. If the books were right about day two of the Test, we should be going into the Bubble this morning, the Glass this afternoon, and the Cave this evening. Which meant that by tonight, one of us would be asleep and one more would be dead.

I'd just finished getting dressed in my yellow shirt and pants when there was a knock at the door. I went to open it, arranging my face into a timid expression (as befitted the humble Treesinger candidate).

But I abandoned that look altogether when I saw who was on the other side. *"Eldan?"*

He grinned. "Hello, Bell! I hope you're not too disappointed, I know you must have been hoping to see Alasdar"—he heaved an exaggerated sigh—"but I'm afraid you'll just have to make do with me."

I grinned back, matching his sigh with an even more exaggerated one of my own. "Well, of course I was hoping to see Alasdar." I let my gaze grow soft and unfocused, as if contemplating a pleasant memory. "The look of crushing disappointment on his face when I survived the Bubble is a moment I will cherish forever."

Eldan scowled. "*Nobody* knew he'd changed the order of the Test. It only serves to demonstrate what a colossal fool the man is, to believe that Tomas wouldn't favor you." He nodded down the hallway in the direction of the other candidate rooms. "We don't have long to chat, I'm afraid. I'm here to take everyone to the dining chamber."

They'd sent *Eldan* to escort candidates to breakfast? Or, no, they hadn't, because he was way too highly ranked to have been given that job. "I'm okay, you know."

He sniffed. "I never doubted you would be."

Which was a lie, but I let him pretend he hadn't come here to check on me. "How much trouble is Alasdar in?"

Eldan chuckled gleefully. "Rather a lot! He's been up half the night explaining himself to the Queen and the guilds. They appear to have latched onto the idea that the change in the sequence was a deliberate insult to them, since the guildmaster challenge was supposed to be first."

I eyed him knowingly. Sounded like Eldan had seized the opportunity to strike a blow for his side in the priest war, not that any of the priests would admit there *was* a war. But the temple was split between two factions—the Metaphorics (who believed that the sun testimony was a series of allegorical tales) and the Literalists (who thought it meant exactly what it said and nothing more). Eldan led the Metaphorics, Alasdar the Literalists, and the two of them absolutely loathed each other. "I don't suppose the guilds had any encouragement from within the priestdom to, ah, latch onto that idea?"

He affected an affronted expression. "My dear girl, what are you implying? *I* certainly never spoke to them!"

"Who did you talk to, then?"

He put his hand on his heart. "Not a soul." Then: "Well, if you *must* know . . ."

"Oh, I must."

"I *may* have expressed some thoughts aloud, which *may* have been overheard by initiate Lander, whose uncle's sister is the trader guildmaster." He bounced on his feet. "I expect we'll have the numbers amongst the priestdom to vote Alasdar out very soon."

I opened my eyes wide. "And then you will finally realize your dream of becoming high priest. How you'll enjoy presiding over all those tedious—I mean, *important* ceremonies. . . ."

He laughed. "Bah! You know I have no interest in that job. Too much pomp and no time to read. No, I've chosen someone else, a promising, um . . ."

"Minion?" I suggested.

"*Scholar* from amongst the younger priests." His tone was stern, but he was still smiling. "An old student of mine. We must end the chaos of Alasdar's rule and turn our attention to more critical matters." His mouth quirked into a sour twist. "You know the influence of the temple is not what it should be."

Yeah, that was on account of the gods bugging off. The Risen just didn't believe in Tomas and Allora the way they had when those two had walked amongst them. I personally hoped the influence of the temple would shrink to nothing, but of course I wasn't going to say so to Eldan (who thought that while I rightfully hated

Alasdar, I had nothing against the *good* priests). "I won't forget my friends. When I'm Queen."

"And on *that* subject—I'd like to believe Alasdar wouldn't dare to interfere with the Test again. But I didn't think he'd do it the first time, and I cannot dismiss the possibility that he'll attempt something worse. If anything worries you, anything at all, ask to see a moon-sister for medical treatment. You know they can't refuse that, if you say you're not feeling well."

I did, from reading the books. I also knew that no one would ever ask because a candidate would basically have to be dying before being willing to admit to a vulnerability. I adopted a doubtful tone. "The others will think I'm weak."

"They think it anyway, my dear. But you and I know different. And I've made an arrangement with the sisters. They'll see to your safety and get a message to me."

Now that was a surprise. He would've had to bargain with Bernadise to arrange it, and he was already in her debt. Eldan had some kind of wasting sickness and the only treatment was a medicinal salve that Bernadise had invented. Like most of her medicines, it seemed to be deeply unpleasant (I'd overheard him complain about how it was constantly burning his skin). He must have hated asking her for more help. But he'd done it. For me.

He's not your friend, I reminded myself. Just some old priest who wasn't as much of a bastard as the others. Supporting me now was nothing more than a sensible investment for him, because if I got to the final three, the Metaphorics would have a friend in the court (or so he'd think). I still felt a little bit grateful. Which was just stupid.

But since I did feel it, I wasn't above using it. I allowed some of my embarrassingly genuine affection for the old man to leak into my voice. "Thanks, Eldan. That means—um. Just thanks."

He went pink and shuffled his feet. Finally, he managed: "Hmph. Well. The Test must be fair. Can't have the high priest breaking the rules." Then he looked down the hall and heaved another sigh, a real one this time. "I'd best be getting on with escort duty. They'll be expecting me back at the temple."

I leaned in closer and affected a conspiratorial whisper. "Good luck overthrowing the high priest—not that I think you need it."

He winked at me. "Good luck winning the Queen's Test—not that I think you need it either!"

And he hurried down the hallway to gather up the other candidates.

Within a few minutes the lot of us were following Eldan through a bewildering array of passages. I tried to memorize the layout, but it made absolutely no sense. The Risen had obeyed Tomas's command to "build, build from my most holy stone!" with great enthusiasm but little concern for architectural logic (there were no less than twenty-seven stairways to nowhere in the suntemple). And neither Tomas or Allora had cared about the confusion. They'd just wanted a kingdom of brightstone. That was the payoff for their god con, because brightstone drew a bit of energy from everyone who lived in Radiance and channeled it to the sun and moon temples, where Tomas and Allora had fed on it. So Ronan said. Except the energy hadn't been enough to give them their hearts' desire, which I suppose was why they'd eventually bugged off. Because what they truly wanted was to be actual gods.

All-knowing. All-seeing. All-powerful. And all-round bastards.

We reached the dining chamber. Eldan waved us in with a cheery order to "eat as much as you like" and left.

The chamber was a big, bright space (a little too bright, thanks to the windows in the far wall that were letting in the morning sun). Once my eyes adjusted to the shine of the brightstone, I could make out round tables covered with (of course) gold table-cloths. *Empty* tables. . . . Then I spotted a long table against one wall that was full up with food. Not just any food, either. Pastries, baked eggs, potato cakes . . . the breakfast was knight standard, like the rooms.

There was a general rush forward. I loaded up a plate and sat down with Tamsin. The others sat at a table on the other side of the room and talked about me. Or at least Mimic, Spite, and Worships did (that much was obvious from the frequent hostile glances in my direction). Shiny wasn't speaking at all. She seemed to be trying to hold herself apart from the rest. *Interesting*.

"Do you know anything about that dark-haired knight?" I asked Tamsin.

She shook her head. "Sorry. I've been too worried about getting here to do any research on the others. My stepdad almost kept me out."

"He doesn't want you in the Test? Why?"

"Because he hates me." Her mouth twisted. "He was trying to get me replaced with another worker, right up until yesterday— that's why I was late. But"—she grinned—"not even the guild-master can stand against *all* the other workers. They think I'm their best chance to win, and they wouldn't let him kick me out."

Well, well. Tamsin's stepfather was the worker *guildmaster*. And from the sounds of it, a seriously unpleasant person. He'd have to be, to hate Tamsin. She was not at all hateable.

She was also staring at me *really* hard.

I raised an eyebrow at her. "Something you want to say?"

"Um. Yes. That is, I wanted to ask you something. But you don't have to answer if you don't want to. Although . . . I think you should. As long as you're comfortable with answering, that is."

Okay, now I was really curious to know what had got her so tangled up. "Ask away."

"It's about yesterday. After we all got out of the Bubble, and you were talking to the high priest. It's just . . . the way he was looking at you . . ."

I didn't know why she was finding this so hard to say. Unless she somehow thought I didn't realize that Alasdar was no friend of mine?

"Yeah, he doesn't like me much," I said cheerfully, stabbing my fork into a potato cake. "And he'd have kept *me* out of the Test if he could. Guess that kind of gives us something in common."

"I guess it does," Tamsin said. "Except not really, Bell. Because my stepdad might not like me much, but he doesn't hit me."

I stared at her, fork paused halfway to my mouth. "How did you know?"

"It's just . . . a thing I can do." She leaned closer and spoke in a low, urgent tone. "It's not your fault, Bell. It was never your fault."

"Well, *of course* it's not my fault. He's a total bastard. What do you mean, a thing you can do?"

She was staring hard at me again. Whatever she saw seemed to reassure her, because the tension drained out of her shoulders. "I can't really explain it. But when someone is hurting someone else, I always know." Her mouth pressed into a firm line. "And I do something about it, if I can."

Huh. Useful sort of understanding to have. Except I couldn't have her trying to do something about Alasdar. "He can't hurt me now that I'm a Queen's Test candidate."

"But he hurt you *before*."

"Yeah, but—"

"And changing the order of the challenges was about you as well, wasn't it? Was he trying to get you killed?"

Okay, now she was getting a little too insightful. "The point is, I didn't die. And it's not like you can do anything to him."

She leaned back in her chair, gazing contemplatively into the distance. "Can't I, though?"

"Tamsin! He's the *high priest.*"

"He's a bastard. You said so yourself." Her gaze went to my hair. "Your plant is waving again."

I put my hand up to still Tricks and opened my mouth to growl at Tamsin some more. But before I got a word out, I realized that I could hear something. Someone was . . . singing? I tried to work out where the sound was coming from, but I couldn't pin it down. It was getting loud enough to make out words, though. Something about a sapling, growing all alone far from the forest. . . .

I bit back a gasp as it dawned on me what I was hearing. How had I missed seeing it? Except I had seen it. I just hadn't understood. But it was obvious to me now why Tamsin had seemed familiar when we first met and why I'd been so hurt when I'd thought she'd abandoned me.

I leaned across the table and hissed, "You're a *Treesinger.*"

8

For a second she seemed to stop breathing. Then she bent closer to me and whispered, "I wanted to say something, but I didn't know how, or even if you'd believe me!"

"Treesingers can recognize each other. I should've realized yesterday, but—well, I've been away from plants for a long time. My senses are a bit rusty."

She made a strange, choked noise. *She's crying.* Actual tears were streaming down her face. If anyone saw, it'd draw attention that we absolutely didn't need. I kicked her under the table. "Get a hold of yourself!"

She sniffed, wiping at her eyes. "I'm sorry. It just . . . it means a lot. To be recognized as one of you."

Any Treesinger she got close to would have known what she was, and a lot quicker than I had. "You've never met another Treesinger?"

She shook her head.

I am Tricks!

She was talking to Tamsin, who couldn't hear her and wouldn't have understood if she did. It was going to take a while for Tamsin's own Treesinger senses to wake up, and even longer for her to learn the green language.

I gestured toward my head. "This is Tricks. She's a Traveling, a part of a tree that seeks out new experiences. She *was* waving at you, before."

Tamsin's eyes went huge. "Is it okay to speak to her?"

"Go ahead."

She straightened up, giving Tricks a nod so deep and respectful it bordered on a bow. "Hello, Tricks. I'm Tamsin. It's a great honor to meet you."

It is, isn't it?

Tamsin looked at me. "Do I need to make her an offering or something?"

What's an offering?

To Tamsin, I said, "She doesn't even know what that is." And to Tricks, I explained: "The Risen give offerings to their gods. Gold and stuff."

She thinks I'm like the gods? Tricks sounded horrified. Tell her I'm not!

I tried to explain. "The trees and plants . . . they're family. No one wants offerings or anything like that. Everyone in the grove—humans, trees, animals, everything—just does their best to keep the grove in balance, so all the life can grow and be happy."

A panicked expression crossed Tamsin's face. "I don't know how to keep things in balance!"

"It's okay. You'll learn." Granny said being a Treesinger was about two things: the blood and the ways. Tamsin had the blood, sure enough, but she didn't know anything about the ways of living in a grove. But she would. I'd teach her, and so would her grove Matriarch and all her Treesinger relatives. "Do you know who your family is?"

"No. I don't know much, really. The people who could have told me—my granny and my grandpa—they're gone. My mum too. Most of what *I* know comes from Grandpa Jak. Except he's not really my grandpa at all, at least not by blood. . . ." She sighed. "Maybe I better start at the beginning?"

I nodded, and she launched into the story. "My grandma was an Elodian. Except—she didn't really get on with a lot of the others. She thought they did a lot of talking and not a lot of doing. She also thought that if she really wanted to help Treesingers, she should ask them what would be helpful. Only . . . that wasn't easy." She added quickly: "I should say this was all happening a little way into the reign of the Queen before this one."

Okay. Back then, the moon-sisters were still trying to keep Treesingers isolated from everyone and everything so they could study us in our "natural state" (like there was anything natural about being forbidden to leave our groves and constantly spied on by them). It wouldn't have been easy for a Risen to have a conversation with a Treesinger.

"My grandma stole a moon-sister robe," Tamsin continued, "and got herself into a grove. That's where she met my grandpa Laken." She fixed a hopeful gaze upon me. "Do you know that name?"

"It's a common name. Do you know his tree name, or what grove it was?"

She shook her head, looking miserable.

"It's okay," I said. "The grove Matriarchs will be able to figure it out. Tell me what happened next."

"They fell in love. So they planned to run away."

"Where to? Sierra?"

She nodded. "They thought they could be happy there."

Well, it'd been a solid plan. They certainly couldn't have stayed here, what with relationships between Treesingers and non-Treesingers being against Risen law at that time. And Sierra had offered Treesingers sanctuary, sending guides and supplies to help us reach the desert kingdom. Except not many of us had ever gone. No matter how bad things were (and they'd been very bad for a while), most Treesingers just couldn't bear to leave the groves. "I'm guessing they never made it."

"They never even got far out of Radiance. My grandma's dad caught up with them, and he was—well, he was no Elodian. It was night, and there was a chase along the cliffs. My grandfather went over the edge and died."

Tricks flattened herself into my hair, and a doleful melody sounded in my head.

I went quiet, letting her sing the mourning song through. When it faded, I said, "But that's not the end of the story, is it? Your grandma was pregnant."

Tamsin nodded. "When she realized, she went to the Sierran guide who had tried to get them out of Radiance. Jak agreed to let her pretend the baby was his."

That was a solid plan, too. Because they certainly couldn't have risked the sisters finding out about a baby born from a Treesinger and Risen, not back then (they weren't keen on the idea now either, but they couldn't do anything about it since the Queen before this one changed the law that made it forbidden).

"The baby was your mum? Your dad?"

"My mum. Except Grandma got really sick, and the baby was

born early. Grandma died, and Mum was never strong. The sisters couldn't ever do much to help her."

Treesinger healers might have. "She never tried to find her Treesinger family?"

Tamsin sighed. "You have to understand, my mum—she got raised by her grandparents. Grandpa Jak stayed in her life as much as he could. He travels back and forth between here and Sierra, but he'd come to see her whenever he was in Radiance." Her mouth twisted. "Great-Grandpa had to let him, because they kept pretending he was the dad. They thought it was shameful to have a Treesinger in the family. Not that they much liked being related to Sierrans either."

I was starting to understand. "Your mum grew up hating Treesingers."

"She grew up scared. Of—well, basically everything, including being a Treesinger. I think she was happy for a while, after she met my dad. But he died in a foundry accident when I was little." Her mouth flattened out. "Then she met my stepdad."

The worker guildmaster who'd tried to keep his own step-daughter out of the Test. "He knows, doesn't he?"

"In a weird way, that's why he married her. He expected her to be grateful, and she turned herself inside out trying to make up for being a Treesinger." Tamsin sighed. "But she passed last year. So now it's just me."

"No, it's *not*," I growled. "You've got a family, Tamsin. I don't know who they are yet, but you've got lots of family. And trees. And a grove." *You're not alone. Treesingers are never alone.* "And me."

Her eyes had gone all misty again.

I would've liked to leave it there. But I had to say this next bit. "Except . . . you can't tell anyone you're a Treesinger yet."

"Why not?" she demanded indignantly. "I've only been keeping quiet because I didn't know how Treesingers would feel about me. I don't care what the Risen think. I'm proud of being a Treesinger!"

"Keep your voice down!" I hissed. "And listen to me, would you? We're in the *Queen's Test*."

"So?"

She hadn't seen it. But I did. "So when your mum was born, relationships between Treesingers and non-Treesingers were illegal. And the sisters could use that to get you thrown out of the Test."

"You think they'd do that?"

Yes I did, and they'd be helped along by Alasdar, who'd want to hurt Tamsin for no other reason than that she'd allied herself with me. "They've only just let a Treesinger into this thing. Once they know you're one too, they might not see you as the worker candidate anymore. More like a second Treesinger sneaking in." In fact, I knew exactly how this would play out. "I bet they'd give your stepdad permission to replace you with another worker, even though the Test's already started. And with the sisters and the priests and the worker guild in agreement, it—"

"Stop!" she interrupted. "I understand. I won't say anything."

Her voice was shaky with panic, and I knew it had nothing to do with losing a chance at the crown and everything to do with leaving me alone here. She might not have grown up in a grove but she had the Treesinger instinct for looking after our own. I would've panicked at the thought of leaving her too.

Tamsin suddenly stiffened, staring at something behind me. I twisted to see Alasdar walking into the room, trailed by a couple of priests.

There were dark circles under his eyes and a gray tinge to his skin. And he was avoiding looking at me, focusing all his attention on the other table. I didn't understand why until I realized the other priests were wearing their sun-and-moon medallions beneath their robes. That meant they were Metaphorics (the Metaphorics had started wearing medallions next to their skin soon after I'd come to the temple, something about keeping Tomas close to their hearts). And from the way those two were glowering at Alasdar, they were here to keep watch on his behavior.

Eldan was definitely winning the priest war.

Alasdar cleared his throat and spoke. "Candidates! As there was a challenge of strength and faith yesterday, there will be none today."

Well, that was a bit disappointing, because I was confident the Bubble wasn't stronger than Tamsin or sneakier than me. I glanced over to check her reaction. And was immediately relieved that Alasdar wasn't looking our way.

Tamsin had leaned back in her chair, stretching her long legs out in front of her. Her fingers tapped a steady beat on the table as she eyed the high priest with a focused, speculative stare. Like she was considering how to take him apart a piece at a time.

I spoke out of the corner of my mouth. "Stop looking at him like that!"

She ignored me.

Alasdar spoke again. "When you have finished your breakfast, you will find priests waiting outside to escort you back to your rooms. You will spend the day in quiet reflection before joining the guildmasters in the Glass. I will see you all again tomorrow."

He swung around and strode out, closely followed by his

Metaphoric minders. I leaned across the table to jab Tamsin in the arm. "You can't stare at the high priest as if you want to kill him!"

"Oh, I'm not going to kill him." She picked up a mushroom with her fork and swallowed it down. "I'm just going to hurt him. A lot."

A delighted chuckle echoed through my head. *She is a fierce Treesinger! I like her.*

She was a reckless Treesinger who was going to get herself in trouble because she didn't know what she didn't know and she wasn't listening to me like she should.

I liked her too.

9

Quiet reflection, my arse.

The only reason we'd been sent to "reflect" was that the day was supposed to have been taken up with the Bubble challenge that we'd already done. I filled in the hours by rehearsing the speech I'd deliver in the Glass. Every candidate had to give a little talk to the guilds on why she should be Queen. Mine had something for everybody, encouraging them to vote for me because they thought they could push me around, or because they wanted to raise up a poor Treesinger girl (who'd be eternally grateful for the opportunity), or even because they believed in equality (you never knew your luck). And if I couldn't get their votes, maybe Tamsin could. Except . . . she wasn't really trying.

I'd tried to talk to her about votes when we'd been let out of our rooms for lunch. But she'd just looked at me blankly, and I realized that she hadn't thought much further than getting into the Test and meeting another Treesinger. Oh, and surviving until the end, of course. But I wanted more than that for her and me. I wanted one of us to win. And it didn't matter which. I might've come into this Test to get that crown for myself, but that had been when I was competing against Risen girls. Treesingers didn't compete with each other. The two of us would wreak havoc on Risen society together, no matter who wore the crown. Okay, I hadn't had the chance to tell her about the havoc part yet, but I knew she'd be for it. Like Tricks said, Tamsin was a *fierce* Treesinger.

It seemed like forever until the sky outside began to darken into the blue-gray of late afternoon. My escort would be turning up shortly (all the candidates were being taken to the challenge by Queen's Guard trainees). So I got ready. Which was to say, I put on a stupid dress. We'd all been given one at lunch, a gift from the Queen to the candidates.

I eyed myself in the mirror as I pushed my feet into the gold sandals that had come with the gown. "What do you think, Tricks?"

You are very shiny.

I certainly was. The dress was gold and made of never-wash fabric, so if I spilled anything on it, the stain would dry out and vanish pretty much instantly. It was also covered with enough gilt embroidery to make Alasdar jealous. In fact it didn't look unlike a priest's robe, with a high neckline and long sleeves. Although instead of going straight down, the dress flared out at the bottom. There was a *lot* of fabric swooshing around my legs. The huge skirt made me seem smaller. I thought of Tamsin's impressive bulk and sighed. I looked just like Mum and Granny, and Silverleaf women were plenty round but not overly tall.

I practiced expressions to use at the Glass: "humble Treesinger, overwhelmed by the honor of being part of the Queen's Test"; "humble Treesinger, easily manipulated by the Risen guilds";

"humble Treesinger, who thought the person I was talking to was so powerful—beautiful—smart . . . whatever."

Those are funny faces!

"They're lying faces." I reached up to brush my hand against her leaves. "There'll be lots of people at this next challenge, Tricks. So don't go waving at Tamsin."

Will it be like the rainbow ball?

"Nope. It's kind of a talking challenge. Don't say anything to me unless you really need to, okay? I probably won't be able to answer without someone overhearing."

What if I need to warn you that squishy worms are trying to eat you?

"There won't be any squishy worms. The Glass isn't going to be anything like the Bubble."

A disappointed sigh ran through my head, followed by a sense of Tricks withdrawing. The Glass wasn't exciting enough to hold her attention.

Another few minutes, and there was a rap at the door. I opened it to find a boy a little older than me and a little taller (so, not very tall). He had dark eyes, pale skin, and black hair, and he was wearing a trainee uniform (gold, of course). That much was just as I'd expected.

But.

His hair was disheveled. There was a button missing from the sleeve of his uniform, and the whole thing was rumpled. He looked—well, vaguely disreputable, which I supposed was about right because escorting the Treesinger candidate was likely a punishment for some form of misbehavior. And his eyes . . .

His eyes were focused on mine, wide and shocked. He breathed, "It's you."

That was a very weird thing to say, and there was no harm in showing I was confused by it. Anyone would be.

I blinked at him and adopted an uncertain tone of voice. "Have we met?"

I knew we hadn't, but better to say that than ask him what he was talking about. Knights generally didn't take well to being challenged, and this boy had to be a knight. No one else would get away with being so careless with his uniform.

He swallowed. Took a breath. And spoke again in a light, quick torrent of words. "My apologies, my mind was elsewhere, I'm always leaving it places! I am Kieran, the very bravest and noblest of trainee guards."

He swept a bow with fluid grace. Like Shiny, he was extremely well coordinated, although there was a mocking edge to his movements. But it didn't feel as though he were laughing at me. More as if he were laughing at the world. And when he looked up with a smile tugging at the corner of his lips, I could've sworn he was inviting me to share the joke.

This was *not* the escort I'd been expecting to deal with. But a true liar adjusts to context. I looked him over and sniffed disdainfully. "Bravest and noblest, maybe. But *definitely* not the best dressed."

His smile widened. Good, I'd got that right. In my head I was constructing a new set of clothes: feisty Treesinger girl with nothing better to do than mock social conventions with scruffy Risen boy. Scruffy, *bored* Risen boy, protected by his privilege and playing at rebellion. He probably thought he was hugely daring for turning up to work with a button missing.

I held out my hand, turning the gesture into one of exaggerated grandeur, as if I really were Queen. "You may escort me to the Glass, bravest and noblest guard trainee."

He took my hand and tucked it into his arm. As we left the room, his features shifted, settling into an expression of amused indifference. Which meant he was a good liar, because his arm was trembling faintly beneath my fingers and I could see the pulse jumping in his throat. He hadn't gotten over whatever had surprised him about me when I'd first opened the door. And I had no idea what that was. Maybe he'd mistaken me for someone else? Except the only people who looked like me were Mum and Granny and . . . Oh.

He'd mistaken me for another Treesinger, someone of around the same age who didn't look like me at all. The Risen never could tell any of us apart. Although it did make me wonder who the Treesinger was, and why he'd been so shocked to see them.

Kieran spoke as we started down the hallway after the others. "It's three hundred and thirty steps from here to the Glass. Which doesn't give us long to talk."

He sounded serious, as if he actually wanted to have a real conversation. But that didn't seem likely. I tossed my head and spoke lightly. "What shall we talk about?"

Kieran cast a quick, assessing glance at me, then responded in a tone that matched mine. "We could talk about the public lecture the high priestess gave last week. It was all about the rescue of Treesingers from Mistfall. You would have found it . . . interesting."

That comment seemed like sarcasm, but I couldn't be absolutely sure, because a lot of Risen still bought into moon-sister lies. But then he continued. "I'm sure you'll agree that it was very

good of us Risen to 'save' some of you from the chaos and devasta-
tion that we created."

Okay, he *was* being sarcastic, which made it safe to be a little
sarcastic in return. "Oh, but Treesingers don't know what's best
for ourselves."

"You and the high priestess are in complete agreement."

I laughed at that, and something like delight flashed across
his face. It pleased him to make me laugh. Before I could figure
out why, he spoke again. "The high priestess told quite the tale
of peril and salvation. It makes you wonder who's the more dangerous: the Risen soldiers who slaughtered half of Mistfall or
the priests and sisters who made it all okay. My money's on the
priests and the sisters. Unfortunately, though"—he gave a regretful shake of his head—"we simply can't do without them. Because if we *weren't* following the will of the gods when we invaded
Mistfall, we'd all just be killers. Kidnappers and thugs, too."

My mouth wanted to fall open and I let it. No harm in showing
a real reaction to *that* little speech, which was breathtakingly blasphemous even for an Elodian. And he had to be one, except . . .
maybe not. Because while Elodians were more than happy to go
on about the terrible crime of the Mistfall invasion, they seemed
to think it was a crime that had nothing to do with them (apparently every Elodian's ancestors had been home drinking tea while
Treesingers were being murdered).

I decided to just come right out and ask. "You're an Elodian?"

"I'm . . . an agent of change, let's say. But we've already walked
sixty-two steps. That leaves only two hundred and sixty-eight to
tell you everything you need to know."

He might be making up how many steps we'd walked, but I

didn't think he was. And I was seriously upgrading my assessment of his ability to deceive. Beneath that faintly bored expression he was taking in every detail of what was happening around him. "What do I need to know?"

"For starters, the Cave is malfunctioning."

"It is? Malfunctioning how?"

"Apparently the whole thing relies on vapors that rise up from deep in the earth, and they're not rising as they should. Which has come as a dreadful shock to the sisters." He gestured to our surroundings. "This was all built long ago. I'm not sure the sisters and priests really understand how any of it works."

I was sure they didn't, because if Alasdar had any idea *how* the Bubble tested faith, he'd have realized I was practically guaranteed to pass that bit. "What will they do if they can't fix it?"

"Try to come up with an alternative, I suppose."

I shrugged, as if I wasn't worried (although of course I was, especially with Bernadise's talent for cruelty). "Well, we can be sure of one thing. Whatever happens, they'll say it was part of the gods' divine plan all along."

He grinned. "Two hundred and thirty-three steps now. The head of the crafter guild has Elodian leanings. Not committed yet, but I'd say she's quite enchanted with the idea of being the kindly Risen savior of your people."

That was information I could really use. I began planning how, and Kieran broke into a laugh. "Oh, that's very good! I bet the priests and the sisters love it when you look at them in just that way."

For a second I had no idea what he was talking about. Then I realized that my expression had slipped into "humble Treesinger grateful to be saved from my terrible plight." And, yes, the priests and sisters *did* love that look. But I should never have put it on by accident. It dawned on me that I felt oddly comfortable around this boy. And I didn't like the way he was watching me now with a curve to his lips and a warmth in his eyes that seemed to light up hints of hazel brown amongst the black. I *really* didn't like that I wanted to smile back.

But I did anyway in order to keep this useful source of information on my side and for no other reason, or at least none I cared to examine too closely at the moment. Or ever. "What about the other guilds?"

"You'll never get the workers. Their guildmaster is the type who needs other people to feel small so he can feel big. He'll never cope with the notion of a Treesinger higher in the social order than he is."

Sounded like he liked Tamsin's stepdad about as much as Tamsin did. "I'm thinking the traders might blame me for their candidate dying?"

"A little, but there's also a great deal of anger at the high priest. If you can redirect their rage toward him instead of you, the trader vote might not be completely out of your reach."

We'd arrived at a set of stairs, wide and deep and decorated with golden circles that I supposed represented the crown. We must be near to the Glass. No stepper, though. Just as well, because my swooshy skirt could've easily gotten caught between the moving steps. I bunched some of it up in my hand so I didn't get tripped up.

Kieran kept talking as we began to climb. "As for the knight guildmaster—Sirius Daylon is almost as smart as he is ruthless. He'll generally do whatever he perceives to be in his best interests, but he plays a long game. Sometimes he does things that are hard to make sense of in the moment, because he's looking ahead."

Was that why he'd given up a place in the Test? Because he was looking into the future? I would've liked to know what he'd been looking *at*.

We'd reached the top of the stairs. There were double doors ahead, and I didn't need Kieran's muttered "Ten steps left" to let me know we'd almost reached the Glass. He'd been exceptionally helpful and I didn't think he'd been lying to me. Which made me even more curious about the Treesinger he'd thought he'd recognized when he saw me. And once we went through those doors, there'd be people to meet and lies to tell. This might be my last chance to ask, so I took it.

"Who did you mistake me for, when we first met?"

His expression of amused indifference disappeared. In its place was a complicated mix of emotions I couldn't name, except that one of them was sadness.

He said in a raw, low voice, "I could never mistake you for anyone else."

And the doors opened onto the Glass.

10

In the next moment the mask of indifference was back on Kieran's face and we were walking through the doors.

I sucked in a steadying breath, trying to slow my stupidly racing heart. I didn't know what to make of what had just happened. I didn't know what to make of *him*. But I couldn't allow myself to be distracted. Not when I had votes to win and Risen to deceive.

The Glass was a huge, round room that was dominated by an *actual* lake. The big circle of water was clear and still and—well, glassy (of course). A brightstone path stretched across it, leading to a platform in the middle that held a table set with golden glasses. *Six glasses. Six candidates.* I was guessing that was where we were going to make our speeches. My gaze wandered to the high-backed chairs that sat at the edge of the lake, facing toward the platform. There were six of them too, although one was much grander than the others. *The five guildmasters and the Queen.* Except . . . there was a lot of distance between the chairs and the platform. What were we going to do, shout at them across all that water? Guess I was going to find out.

I took in the rest of the room as we walked onward. Above us floated massive glow-orbs, rotating around each other in a gentle dance. The walls and floor were emblazoned with circles, as were the curtains that covered the windows. And there was another set of doors at the other end of the room. As I watched, they opened up and the guildmasters entered in a line of red robes.

I craned my neck, looking for my own guildmaster. It was supposed to be Granny Faran, the Matriarch of Many Flowers grove (or so Eldan had told me before I left the temple). But I couldn't see her anywhere.

A voice spoke from behind me. "I'm afraid Granny Faran is feeling unwell."

I swung around, and froze. Because I was facing the Queen.

She was tall and stern. Dark hair fell in shining waves to her shoulders, and she was wearing a golden dress in the same style as the candidates' (except hers was embellished with so many chips of brightstone they could've switched off the orbs and used her gown to light the room). And atop her head was the crown. Just a thin golden band, like in all the pictures in the books. But it radiated power.

"A replacement representative is being sent," the Queen continued, "but they will be a little late. You need not fear for Granny Faran—I am told she will recover."

I let my shoulders relax, like I was reassured. The truth was that no reassurance was needed. Granny Faran was as tough as Tangler roots. But she never hesitated to come over all frail when it suited her purposes to do so. She was up to something.

The Queen's attention shifted to Kieran. "Be elsewhere, please, nephew. I wish to have a word with the candidate."

Kieran was the Queen's *nephew*? That seemed like something he could've told me before, although judging by the way he was looking at her, they didn't get on very well. He leaned closer to me and murmured, "Don't let her talk you into anything you don't want to do." Then he executed another of his mocking bows and sauntered away.

She made an exasperated noise. "My nephew does not value the crown. But . . ." She looked me up and down. "You do, I think."

My first instinct was to fall into the role of a humble Treesinger who longed to be Queen but didn't dare to dream that she could be.

My second, better instinct was that a *humble* Treesinger was not what the Queen was looking for.

I straightened my shoulders and lifted my chin. "Yes."

Her dark eyes glinted in approval. *Second instinct was right.* "Walk with me, my dear. We have little time and much to discuss."

I fell in at her side, plastering an expression of awed respectfulness on my face because we were being stared at by basically everyone. Or, rather, *glared* at, in the case of Worships, Mimic, and Spite. Especially Worships. Both she and her escort shot me identical resentful scowls before putting their heads together in an intense conversation.

The Queen saw it too. "Be wary of her. That one is from a religious family, as is her escort. It is unfortunately not possible to keep *all* the zealots out of the guard, although I do try to ensure they don't make it past the trainee stage."

Oh, did she just? I returned my attention to a Queen who was being a lot more forthright than I'd expected.

"I will be speaking to each candidate tonight about the great responsibilities of the crown," she continued. "You can tell the others that is what we spoke of too."

"What are we *actually* talking about?"

"The limits of power. I worked for years to free you from the temple. Do you know why I didn't succeed until recently?"

That was easy. "You didn't have the support of the guilds."

"Just so." Her mouth twisted into a bitter line. "Queens rule for all of Radiance. But the guildmasters advocate for their classes. Which means that the workers, the crafters, the traders, and the knights will *always* put their faith in their guildmasters before the crown. Because guildmasters put the interests of their classes first." She stopped walking and turned to face me. "It is exceptionally difficult to convince any of the guilds to act in a way that costs them, even if it is ultimately beneficial for all."

"But *you* did," I pointed out. "You got the knights to give up a place in the Test."

"Ah, but their guildmaster was farsighted enough to understand that the other guilds would have joined together to take that place from them eventually. There has been *much* dissatisfaction with the knights' dominance of the Test. I simply persuaded Sirius Daylon to recognize the strategic advantages of yielding the place now, rather than having it wrested from them later." Her eyes narrowed into an assessing gaze. "I wonder if you can tell me what those advantages were."

I thought about it for a moment. "Well, if the knights give something up, they can say they're being generous. But having something taken from them makes them look weak."

She inclined her head. "There's also the matter of *who* the place went to. If the other guilds had taken the place, it would have been assigned to the crafters. And a crafter Queen would have then been in debt to the workers and traders for helping their guild to obtain an extra position. That would cause a power shift, which is not in the knights' interests."

"But," I said, "since Treesingers don't have any alliances with other guilds, we're in no danger of shifting power. So . . . the knights have given something up they were going to have to give up anyway, but in a way that causes them the least possible disadvantage."

"I see you understand the matter." She leaned in closer to me. "You have an opportunity, but you will need the guilds to govern, Bell. So you must learn to persuade. To bargain. To push, sometimes. But never so fast or so hard that you risk them turning upon you."

"You're talking as if I've already won the Test."

"I would like you to do so, although I cannot guarantee the outcome of the final vote. But . . ." A cold smile touched her lips. "I *can* help you to succeed in the Cave."

My mouth wanted to fall open. I didn't let it. We were still being watched, and besides, it wasn't the right reaction for the Queen. *Excitement, not surprise. Ambitious Treesinger girl who'll grab hold of any advantage.* I made my eyes sparkle in anticipation. "I'm listening."

"When you enter the Cave, you will fall asleep and dream. They will be dreams you don't wish to leave—perhaps of people you've lost, or of secret aspirations achieved. However, if you concentrate hard enough on *leaving* rather than *staying,* a way out will present itself. You must take it."

I worked my way through all that. "The candidates who keep sleeping are the ones who don't leave the dreams?"

The Queen nodded. "The sisters are testing the ability to resist temptation. To deny oneself what one wants." Her lip curled. "I doubt any of them could succeed in it. But *you* will."

That sounded more like she was ordering me to succeed than saying she had faith in me, but okay. I drew myself up and met her hard gaze with a determined one of my own. "I'll be seeing you at the end."

"I expect nothing less." She heaved a sigh. "Now I must speak to every other candidate, which will be extremely tedious." Her gaze drifted over my head, focusing on something behind me. "You will have a better time over the next little while than I will, I think. Go to your guild, Bell Silverleaf."

The Queen strode away. I took a moment to try to force down the bubbles of exhilaration rising up inside. I knew how to get through the Cave! And I'd tell Tamsin, which meant she'd get through too, and—

—and I could not be thinking about this right now. I stomped on all the happiness until it stopped being so . . . fizzy. Then I turned to see which Matriarch had come in Granny Faran's place.

But it wasn't a Matriarch who'd come through the doors.

It was a man, tall and broad but a bit bowed down, like his years were weighing heavy upon him. He was wearing a red (well, reddish) robe made of the leaves of a Dancer tree, and as always his shaggy hair was falling over his face. I knew what Granny Faran had been up to now, and I loved her for it.

She'd sent me Uncle Dar.

I didn't stop to think or to scheme or to worry about how the Risen would react to what I was about to do. I bunched up my skirts and ran, tearing across the room to fling myself into his arms. For a long moment we stood there, holding each other.

Then I pulled back, staring at him just as he was staring at me. Both of us catching up with the changes in the years we'd missed.

He looked so . . . *old*. Worn-out. What had happened to him? But I knew. I'd been taken by the priests. And there was no one that would have been harder on than him. Because Uncle Dar wasn't really my uncle. I just called him that because Silverleaf daughters are raised by Silverleaf women.

Uncle Dar was my father.

He spoke, in a voice so filled with pain and desperation it hurt to hear it. "I tried to get you back. We all did. I'm sorry, Bell, I'm so sorry."

This broken-down man was *not* my uncle Dar. I jabbed at his arm. "Don't be stupid. You know what Granny says about Tree-singers who blame ourselves for what the bastard Risen do to us. We're supposed to report to the healers to get our minds fixed. And you *are* a healer, so you should know better."

That made his mouth turn up a little, but it quickly shifted into a twist of pain. "How did they treat you? In the temple?"

I'd never been more grateful to Ronan for teaching me to be a better liar. I adopted a disgusted expression. "The sisters kept asking me about the sickness for ages until they *finally* realized I didn't know anything. And the priests insisted on giving me a religious education. They made me read the *Testimony of the Sun*." I made sure to sound outraged, as if this was the absolute worst thing that could ever happen to a person. "Over and over."

The heaviness in his face lightened. He believed me. And I *would* tell him about Alasdar eventually. But not now. Those stories were things to be talked about by the flicker of a fire in the quiet dark and the safety of a grove.

I tugged at his arm, drawing him even farther away from everyone else and toward an empty corner of the room where we could be absolutely sure of not being overheard.

"How's Jeffry?" I asked as we went. Jeffry was the love of Dar's life, and a Falling Leaves Treesinger, or at least he had been once. But he'd left long ago to join Dar in Many Flowers grove.

"He's well. He misses you. We all do. Every Treesinger from every grove would've been here to see you, if they could have. Listen, Bell—"

But he got interrupted. I am Tricks!

Dar reached out to brush her leaves. "Hello, Tricks."

We are winning the Test! We will be Queen!

"About that . . ." He pushed his hair behind his ear and whispered, "Look."

Dar was wearing a vine earring with a small, striped berry hanging from it.

"You know what it is?" he asked.

"A sleeper seed?"

"Yes! You have to eat it. Swallow it down, right now, while I'm here."

We'd reached the corner, and I stopped, turning to stare at him in confusion. Sleeper seeds were a healer's tool. They sent Treesingers into a state that was a lot like dormancy, buying a healer time to figure out how to cure a difficult illness or injury. If I ate that thing, I'd have no heartbeat and no breath. "Everyone will think I'm dead!"

He beamed at me. "That's right! And they'll give what they believe is your body to me. I'll be able to take you back to Many Flowers!"

"And what happens after I wake up? I hide in the grove

forever?" Because I certainly couldn't show my face in Radiance after cheating my way out of the Queen's Test.

"No. We're leaving. You, Jeffry, and me. We'll go to Sierra and live out our lives there. You don't have to worry—you'll be safe from the Risen."

I sighed. "Uncle Dar . . ."

"I know you don't want to move away from Falling Leaves, but this is the only chance we've ever had to get you out. We've been working on this for weeks! When we heard they'd sent you to the Bubble . . ." A shudder ran through him. "We thought we might have lost you. But you survived. And now it's time to go."

I blinked at him as the implications sank in. "Are you saying this was the plan all along? You were trying to rescue me?"

"Of course!"

Of course. And I saw it now. If things had gone as they were supposed to, I'd have gotten my guild gift (a Traveling to tell me I was coming home, just as Travelings always returned to their trees). Then I'd have come to this challenge, where I'd have eaten a sleeper seed, gotten pretend-dead, and been taken away without having to go anywhere near the Bubble or the Cave.

Dar was frowning. "You *can't* have thought we meant you to compete in the Test!"

"Actually, I did think that," I admitted. "Only I thought the Queen had forced Treesingers to join the Test."

He snorted. "I wouldn't put it past her. She didn't, though. But we only agreed to be part of it as a way to get you out. Girls *die* in the Test, Bell! We'd *never* allow a Treesinger to be put in that kind of danger."

Well, didn't I feel stupid. "What are you going to do about the next Test, then?"

He gave a rueful shake of his head. "We figure we've got twenty-five years to find a way out of it. But for now . . ." He reached for his earring.

"I can't go, Uncle Dar."

"Now, Bell, I know you want to help Falling Leaves. But I can study your memories in Sierra. Get word back here if I find anything that'll help."

Oh, Uncle Dar. This wasn't about Falling Leaves. Well, it was, but not in the way he thought. It was *me* and not my memories that would help the grove (assuming I was *the* Silverleaf, which was exactly what I was hoping for). And whatever it was that Silverleafs were supposed to do, the place for us to do it was here. Where the Silverleaf trees were. Where the groves that nurtured our gift were. Where there was something that Mum's stupid song led to, if it was directions.

Only I couldn't say any of that. Because Silverleaf secrets were for Silverleaf women and Silverleaf trees. Instead I said, "I can win this."

I'd never seen him look so horrified. "Why would you want to?"

So I can heal the grove and get revenge on the Risen. "So I don't have to go anywhere, and nor do you and Jeffry. Listen, I already know how to beat the Bubble, and the Queen herself just told me how to beat the Cave!"

"Why would she do that—" But he stopped, because he'd realized why. "She wants a Treesinger to win. Of all the . . . That's *her* plan for us, Bell. Not ours."

"I know that. But what does it matter, if it gets me through the Test? I'm not in danger, Uncle Dar, truly I'm not!"

"Of course you are, especially in the Bubble. A girl died there yesterday, and one will die tomorrow, and you're all alone—"

"But I'm not. There's another Treesinger in the Test."

"Another—" He broke off and looked over my head to scan the room, just casually as if he were taking in the splendor. Dar was a straightforward man but he was Treesinger; he knew how to lie when he had to. When his gaze returned to me, he said, "The tall girl isn't Sierran."

"Her name is Tamsin." I told him her story, finishing with "She doesn't know what grove she's from, or who—"

But Dar interrupted me. "Winding Vines. She's a Blackbark."

"Are you sure?"

He nodded. "My grandpa used to talk about Laken Blackbark. Took off in the night and left a note behind that he was going to Sierra. No one knew he was involved with one of the Risen." He sighed. "I'll tell the Blackbarks about her. And I can understand that you don't want to leave your friend. But you're in danger in a way that she's not, Bell. The priests and the sisters have an obsession with you that we've never understood."

Except they didn't want me anymore. *The high priestess dosed me with truth tea and now she thinks I have no value, and, yeah, Alasdar liked to knock me around, but he's about to be kicked out as high priest so he's got way too many problems to be thinking about getting me back.*

I couldn't say any of that either. It'd make him more worried, not less. "I'm not going anywhere, Uncle Dar."

"You're *not* staying here, Bell."

"I—" But I didn't get any further before Tricks interrupted me.

You said not to wave at her but she is waving at us!

I shifted to see that Tamsin was trying to attract my attention. And no wonder, because the other candidates and their escorts were either on the platform in the lake or heading toward

91

it. I looked around for my own escort, only to find he was having what seemed like a very unfriendly discussion with his aunt. As I watched, he snapped something at her and came striding in my direction.

I looked back at Uncle Dar. "I've got to go give a speech."

He watched me out of narrowed eyes. I knew he would've liked to just pick me up and carry me off to safety. Or maybe force me to eat that seed.

"If you try *anything*," I warned, "I'm going to start shouting that you're trying to interfere with the Test. They'll probably disqualify me, which means I might get sent back to the temple."

Dar growled in frustration. "We'll have a chance to speak again after the speeches. This conversation isn't over, Bell."

I didn't say anything, because he loved me and he'd come here to save me.

But it was over. He just didn't know it yet.

11

Kieran met me halfway across the room. "Sorry! Got a bit distracted." He offered me his arm with a lazy smile. But I could sense the anger coursing through him. Whatever he and the Queen had been arguing over, he was still furious about it.

I took his arm, and he added, "My aunt thinks you'll make a good Queen. But I must warn you, it's a terribly boring job."

Not going to tell me what that fight was about, huh? Okay. "I suppose it might be a little dull," I conceded, "but I daresay I'll manage to bear it. For the sake of the riches and the power, you know."

"Ah, but you have *no* idea how boring it is. It's even worse than being a guard trainee, and there's days when I've considered starting a small riot just to relieve the tedium. Wouldn't you rather be doing something else?"

I snorted. "Like being dead, asleep, or a Queen's adviser?"

"Those aren't your only other choices."

That was such a Risen thing to say, because they had options that Treesingers didn't. I felt a sudden spike of anger that he didn't know better than to make a comment like that. Which was stupid, because why would he be different from any other Risen?

"What else do you suggest I do?" I asked sweetly. You could never go wrong asking a knight to share their opinion (especially a boy knight).

"Run away."

That was way too close to what Uncle Dar had planned. I fought down a surge of panic. Had Kieran and his aunt somehow found out about it?

But then he added, "With me, of course. I'm *much* more fun than the queenship."

Oh, he was just playing. I looked up at him under my lashes. "Tempting, but . . ." I heaved a regretful sigh. "I still think I'd rather be Queen."

He rolled his eyes. "Be bored, then. But don't say I didn't warn you."

We'd reached the path and started down it. The others were milling about on the platform ahead, arranging themselves along the table with their escorts standing a few paces behind them. They were (of course) lining up in order of rank, which put my place on the end next to Tamsin.

I went and stood in front of my glass, which had a distinctive golden liquid inside. *Honeymelon juice.* No surprise there; the Risen thought of it as a sort of holy drink because it's what they'd offered Tomas when they first met him. Or so said the *Testimony of the Sun.* It couldn't actually be true because Tomas was supposed to have arrived "in the dead of winter," and honeymelons wouldn't have been available. He was more likely to have been offered sweetvine juice, but sweetvine wasn't an amber-gold color. So it was honeymelons all the way.

Tamsin bent over to whisper, "Everything okay?"

I had so much to tell her, and none of it could be said here. "Yeah. You?"

She grinned. "My stepdad is trying to be nice to me. It's hilarious. I think he's worried I'm going to make it to the end of the Test, so now he wants to be friends."

Oh, she was definitely making it to the end. We both were. But I couldn't tell her about the Cave with so many people around us.

I looked back across the water to find that everyone was settling into their chairs. The Queen was last, dropping into her seat in a pool of golden skirts. She tapped something on the arm of her chair, and an orange orb on a golden pole came rising up out of the floor in front of her. The Queen put her hand on it. "Candidates!"

I jumped, along with everyone else on the platform. It sounded like she was *right* next to us.

"For as long as I am touching the orb," the Queen explained, "my voice will reach you, and *your* voices will reach me and your guild representatives. Before we begin, I have an announcement to make. This will be the only challenge today. You will not be entering the Cave tonight."

There were murmurs of surprise from the other candidates. *Guess the sisters didn't get it working.* Which was a big disappointment now that I knew how to beat it.

"The six of you are here to compete for the crown," the Queen continued. "But it is no mere prize to be won. The crown is a responsibility. This is your first chance to persuade the guilds that you are the wisest candidate to bear it."

Those dark, cold eyes swept over us one by one. Even across all that water, I could feel her gaze press in around me, demanding that I become the Treesinger she wanted me to be. I straightened my shoulders, like I was determined not to fail her. But on the inside I made a rude gesture. Uncle Dar was right; these were her plans for Treesingers, not ours for ourselves. I was going to take whatever the result of this Test was and turn it into what *I* wanted it to be.

The Queen nodded at Shiny. "You may begin."

Shiny raised her glass high and took a big gulp of juice, swallowing it down. Then she launched into her speech. We were supposed to keep them short, which she did. But she managed to cram a heck of a lot of content into not a lot of time, outlining a comprehensive twenty-five-year strategy for Risen advancement.

Worships was next, and she unsurprisingly stressed the importance of a close relationship between the Queen and the sun and moon temples. Then came Spite, who delivered a flowery presentation that amounted to keeping everything just the way it was (guess it was working pretty well for her). Mimic was all about opportunities for the truly deserving to rise up the social ladder.

That made it Tamsin's turn, and I didn't like the spark of defiance in her eyes. I shot her a warning look. She looked back at me, heaved a sigh, and (much to my relief) delivered a measured speech about the need for all the guilds to work together as one. It definitely wasn't what she wanted to say, but it wouldn't attract the wrong kind of attention.

That just left me.

I took a step forward with my head lowered before raising my gaze to look at each of the guildmasters in turn (leaving out Uncle Dar, who would not be impressed by me putting on a show aimed at winning a crown that Treesingers didn't want). With any luck, that long stare at the guilds would convey a desperate desire to please, such that I'd be easily manipulated. I picked up my glass, making my hand tremble enough that they'd notice the movement from across the water. The kind of confidence the others had displayed wouldn't be well received coming from me.

I raised the glass high. And Kieran reached over from behind to take it from me.

"My apologies, Bell! But I really can't let you drink this." He moved as he spoke, stepping lightly around the table until he stood on the other side. "At least . . ." He looked across at Mimic. "Not until she tells me what she put in it."

"Nothing!" Mimic gasped. She cast a panicked glance at Spite, who stared downward, apparently suddenly fascinated by the embroidery on her golden skirt.

"I—I don't know what you're talking about!" Mimic stammered.

"No?" Kieran shrugged. "Then I suppose it's safe to drink."

He tipped back his head and swallowed the lot.

For a moment, he seemed to be absolutely fine. Until he started to cough. The glass slipped from his fingers to fall onto the table as he staggered backward. Fear flashed across his face, and his coughing turned to ragged gasps.

Then his eyes rolled back in his head and he fell into the water.

And I, the girl who rarely did anything without thinking about it, moved faster than I ever had to jump right in after him.

It was too deep for me to stand and the stupid dress was pulling me down. But I managed to get hold of Kieran, keeping his head above water as best I could. I knew I wouldn't have to do it for long. Sure enough, in another second there was an almighty splash and Tamsin was there. She *was* tall enough to stand, and she grabbed on to me and him both, dragging us back to the platform.

I lurched onto my knees, registering that the Queen and a whole bunch of guards were charging in this direction. But they weren't here yet, and all my attention was on Kieran. His eyes were closed and his skin was horribly pale. I put my hand on his chest, trying to feel if he was breathing. His eyes flicked open and he said something, but I couldn't make out what.

I shifted closer, turning my head to put my ear near his mouth. He spoke again, very soft but very clear. "Are you sure you won't reconsider running away with me? I have just saved you from certain death. Or at least a little nausea."

I jerked back. Kieran winked at me. And the Queen and the guards were upon us.

I scrambled out of the way and got tangled in my wet dress. Tamsin hauled me up. I clung to her, trying to get a grasp on what was happening—which wasn't made any easier by the sound of Tricks laughing herself stupid in my head. This is *much* better than the rainbow ball!

"It's not funny," I muttered at her, but the truth was, I would have liked to laugh too. I was angry at Kieran for scaring me, and happy he wasn't poisoned, and those mixed emotions wanted to escape in a hugely inappropriate fit of giggling. And the more I thought about the sheer artistry of his whole performance, the worse the need to laugh got. I made myself breathe through it and looked for Uncle Dar.

He was on his feet along with all the guildmasters, and the only reason every last one of them wasn't running over here was the burly guards in the way. I caught Dar's eye and tugged at my ear, a Treesinger gesture that meant "all okay." His shoulders sagged in relief.

A couple of guards lifted Kieran up, rushing him out of the

room to get him the medical attention that he didn't need. He had better make a miraculous recovery before the moon-sisters got a hold of him. The Queen followed them out, looking terribly anxious, which meant he'd fooled her too, or maybe she was as good an actor as he was.

That left everyone just standing around. Things on the platform got . . . interesting. The guard-trainee escorts apparently decided it was their job to keep the candidates where we were, because they bunched themselves together in front of the path that led across the water (totally unnecessary since there were actual guards at the other end of the path). Tamsin and I stood at one end of the platform, wringing out our skirts to help the never-wash dry quicker. Shiny, Worships, and Spite were at the other end, and Mimic was all alone in the middle.

She kept looking at Spite, who was still refusing to look at her. I'd bet that putting something in my glass hadn't been Mimic's idea. But she was the one who'd done it, and now she was the one who'd pay for it. Although I doubted much would happen to her—at least, not for trying to hurt me. Poisoning the Queen's nephew was something else entirely. And Kieran had known that when he'd staged the tumble into the water. Scruffy Risen boy was being very useful to me.

Shiny was staring across at Tamsin and me with an intense expression, almost like she was trying to communicate something, but I had no idea what. Worships was staring at us too—well, at me—but in a whole different way, like I was some dirt that needed to be cleaned up. Then Shiny suddenly shifted, moving away from the others as if she wasn't a part of their group. *What is going on with this girl?* But I didn't have time to figure it out before the Queen came storming back into the room.

She stalked up to the edge of the lake and flat-out shouted, loud enough that she didn't need the orb to reach us. "The crafter candidate will remain where she is. The rest of you may rejoin your guildmasters. Escorts—your presence is no longer required. Return to your barracks."

There was general confusion as everyone rushed forward. Shiny got ahead of the pack, tearing across the room to reach the tall, dark-haired figure of the knight guildmaster. Then she started talking, and from the way she was jabbing her fingers in the air to emphasize whatever point she was making, she was really worked up about something. Tamsin and I waited until everyone else was on the path before following along behind.

She bent down to whisper, "That's an interesting friend you've made."

There was laughter in her voice. She'd seen Kieran wink at me.

"He's not exactly . . . I mean, he's . . ." But I really didn't have the words. Although apparently Tricks did: He's like us!

"He's not," I said, waving my hand at my head so Tamsin would know who I was talking to. "He's basically a Risen prince."

He is a liar.

Well, she had me there.

We reached the other side of the water. Tamsin and I broke apart, heading for our guilds as the Queen and the crafter guildmaster stepped onto the path we'd just left, making their way to Mimic. I'd bet it wouldn't take long for her to confess, especially now that Spite had abandoned her (although I supposed she might return the favor and say it had all been Spite's idea).

The moment I got close to Uncle Dar, he enveloped me in a hug.

"The stuff in my glass wouldn't have really hurt me," I whispered. "Just made me a little sick. Kieran was exaggerating."

"I didn't know that, Bell," he growled. He let me go, scanning my face with an uncomfortably shrewd gaze. "You want to tell me what you're really doing here?"

"You know what I'm doing here!"

He said nothing, just watched me. But I knew better than to fall into the trap of filling one of Dar's silences with words. He'd gotten a few confessions out of me that way when I was a kid.

Eventually he gave up and spoke again. "Your friend. Tamsin. I'm thinking the Blackbark blood runs true in her."

I knew this tactic too. It was just like him to shift topics and approach whatever he was trying to say from a sideways angle. I eyed him warily as he continued. "You don't have any Blackbark trees in Falling Leaves, so I don't suppose you know much about them. But they provide shelter so other trees can grow up safe and strong beneath their canopies."

Oh. Well, that made sense. It also explained why Tamsin knew when people were being hurt. We all drew something from the trees we were named after. "You're saying Tamsin is a protector."

"That's who Blackbark people are, at their best. But at their worst, they take it too far. Become so obsessed with keeping people safe that they choke off opportunities to grow."

"She's not like that!"

"I'm not saying she is. It's you I'm worried about. Because I'm thinking the Silverleaf blood runs true in you, Bell. Maybe a little too true."

I had no idea what he meant by that. People *loved* Silverleaf trees. They looked gray and ordinary until they lit up from within with a pretty silver glow that appeared out of nowhere and vanished again just as fast. Children made a game out of waiting for them to shine.

"At their best," Dar said, "Silverleaf people are the most trustworthy of Treesingers, because they can hold things of value in a way that's safe and quiet, revealing them only when needed. At their worst, though . . ." He shook his head. "Silverleafs are secret keepers and show-offs."

"We are *not!*"

He gave me a long, steady look. I stared right back at him. I mean, okay, Granny and Mum had kept secrets, but that was because they'd had to. For reasons I didn't understand. But that didn't mean they weren't good reasons. And it wasn't for outsiders to be coming in and telling us our business. . . . Um. My thoughts were sounding like Granny.

"I'm not going to ask you why you're so determined to see this through," he said. "I don't think you'll tell me. But . . ." He bent down and whispered, "I want you to remember you've got my blood, too."

Dar was a Holdfast, a tree that held strongly to the earth and to other Holdfasts. He straightened up and added, "Don't let the Silverleaf love of secrets and big revelations stop you from reaching out for help when you need it. You seem to have friends here, and Holdfasts find strength in sharing."

That was Holdfasts at their best. He didn't say the other part, but I knew the Holdfast weakness. They were a tree that only grew in groups. At their worst, Holdfast people never got over losing somebody they cared about. It left a wound that grew and grew until it ate them up.

"Are you trying to tell me you can't lose me, Uncle Dar?"

"I'm trying to tell you that you're loved, my girl."

I rolled my eyes. "I know that."

"I hope you do. But sometimes when bad things happen to a person, they forget. They doubt." He reached out to take my hand. Warmth seemed to pour out of him, and I knew I hadn't fooled him about the temple after all. He'd just known I wasn't ready to talk about it, so he'd let me pretend.

"I want you to value yourself and your life as highly as I do," Dar said quietly. "As highly as we all do."

Something hard and bitter inside me seemed to unravel. *Tree-singers shouldn't blame ourselves for the things the bastard Risen do to us.* But I had, a bit, and it had led me into some seriously messed-up thinking. Like that my people would send me into the Test because they didn't care about me, which seemed such nonsense now. Dar was right. I hadn't valued myself highly enough.

That didn't mean I was going to leave, of course. It wasn't like I was staying to hurt myself. I was doing it *because* I was trying to be the Silverleaf I was supposed to be. But maybe . . . maybe it couldn't hurt to be a little bit Holdfast. I'd certainly have recognized Tamsin quicker if I'd been looking deeper for connections, the way Holdfasts always did.

"I can't leave, Uncle Dar. But I promise you, I'll look after myself. And I won't forget that I'm a Holdfast too."

Dar sighed. "I suppose I can't ask more than that."

I squeezed his hand tight. Then let him go.

The Queen's voice cracked across the room. "Guildmasters! Candidates! Attend to me, if you please."

She'd come back across the water with the crafter guildmaster, leaving Mimic on the platform. The guildmaster didn't look happy, and from the way she glared in my direction, she was *especially* unhappy with me. No hostility aimed at the traders, though. *Mimic didn't give Spite up.*

The Queen waited until everyone had gathered around her in a loose half circle before speaking again. "The crafter candidate has admitted her guilt. I hope I hardly need tell you all that what she appears to regard as a harmless prank could have had dire consequences."

"I trust your nephew will recover, Your Majesty." That was the trader guildmaster.

"He will. I understand that the substance would ordinarily only have induced vomiting, but he had an allergic reaction." She paused, gazing at each guildmaster in turn. "It now falls to all of us to determine how the crafter candidate should be punished. We will hold a vote on this matter. But my suggestion is that she should be disqualified."

That brought a storm of furious protest from the crafter guild-master. "Too harsh . . . relatively innocuous substance . . . didn't intend to do any real harm . . ."

And Tamsin's stepdad jumped right in. "I agree, that is much too harsh! I'd like to propose an alternative punishment."

But the Queen shook her head. "I think we should hear from all the guilds before we start considering alternatives. Treesingers, what say you?"

Dar rumbled, "The punishment is just. Treesingers will vote for it."

"Traders?"

The trader guildmaster heaved a mournful sigh, although she couldn't quite manage to stop her mouth from pulling up into a tiny smile. "It is a dreadful punishment, Your Majesty. But this is not merely a question of the potential physical harm that might have been done here, but of the moral character of a girl who would be Queen. I fear the traders must vote for disqualification."

Well, she was fooling no one. The traders had already lost one of their candidates and they were thrilled that another guild was losing a candidate too. And Spite was standing right beside her, looking all pious like *Oh yes, the guilty must be punished,* when I was certain she was behind the whole thing.

"Thank you, Gabie," the Queen said, turning her attention to Daylon. "Guildmaster? What do the knights say?"

For a moment, Daylon said nothing at all. He was staring at Shiny, who was looking . . . well, kind of fierce, actually. She lifted her chin, meeting him stare for stare, and it was clear that whatever she was challenging him on, she wasn't going to back down.

Daylon sighed and swiveled to face the crafter guildmaster. "I am sorry, Saranis. But if candidates believe that this kind of behavior is tolerated, where will it end?"

Saranis let out a gasp of outraged disbelief. So did Worships, who was staring at her guildmaster in astonishment. She opened her mouth to say something, but shut up when Daylon cast a warning glance at her.

"We all have a duty," he continued, "to ensure that the integrity of the Test is preserved. The knights vote for disqualification."

Three votes out of five. That was all the Queen needed. She didn't (quite) smile, but she was certainly radiating satisfaction as she nodded at the crafter guildmaster. "Saranis, I will leave it to you to remove your candidate from the Test."

Saranis stomped off toward Mimic, but not before casting a long, baleful glare at the knight and trader guildmasters, Uncle Dar, and me. Dar glowered back at her. I shrugged inwardly. Guess I wouldn't be getting that crafter vote.

Tamsin's stepdad was sharing glares around too. Then Tamsin herself caught my eye. She was mouthing something. After a second I realized what it was. *Five.*

She was right. We were down to five candidates. Not only that, but . . .

I knew how to survive the Bubble *and* the Cave. I'd found some unexpected allies. I'd gotten to see Uncle Dar again. My people loved me and always had.

I forced my mouth not to curve up. A humble Treesinger couldn't be seen to be pleased when another candidate was getting kicked out, even if that candidate had tried to drug me.

But this had been one heck of a good day.

12

The dining hall was just as bright as it'd been yesterday, and the breakfast was just as good. I piled my plate high and sat down at a table, getting on with the important business of eating. Food was energy, and today we'd have the Cave (assuming they'd got it working) *and* the Bubble.

The challenge yesterday had ended fast. Mimic had been carted off by her guildmaster; I'd said goodbye to Uncle Dar; and we'd all been taken back to our rooms. I hadn't gotten to deliver my speech, but the Queen said I'd be given extra time to address the guilds when we next went to the Glass. And it wasn't like I hadn't made an impression, what with bravely leaping into the water to save the life of a knight.

Another plate (piled even higher than my own) arrived at the table as Tamsin dropped into the seat opposite mine. She nodded at me, stabbing her fork into a roasted tomato.

This was the first chance I'd had since the Glass to properly talk to her alone. I leaned across and whispered, "I know who your family is."

She dropped the tomato. "Really? Who?"

"You're a Blackbark."

A huge grin broke out across her face. "A Blackbark! Tamsin Blackbark, of . . ."

"Winding Vines grove."

"Tamsin Blackbark of Winding Vines grove!"

Her voice was getting loud. "Hush! In fact, don't even say that again until we're through the Test."

She went silent. But I knew she was repeating the words over and over in her head.

"My uncle Dar is going to tell your family about you," I told her. "You'll be able to meet them once the Test is done."

Her smile faded. "Do you think they'll like me?"

"Course they will!" But she looked worried, so I added, "Uncle Dar said the Blackbark blood flows strong in you."

"He *did*?" The smile returned, even bigger than before. "How does he know?"

"Because Blackbark trees give shelter, so that other trees can grow up safe and strong. He saw that you were like that. A protector." I decided not to tell her the other part about being a Blackbark. She had plenty of time to learn about the different sides of the trees we were all named after. Besides, she *wasn't* overprotective, any more than I was a secret keeper and a show-off.

"A *protector*," she whispered. Her eyes had gone misty. But she was holding it together. Which was good, because I needed her to focus. I opened my mouth to explain everything the Queen had told me about how to beat the Cave. But before I could get a word out, Shiny came striding across the dining hall. Toward *us*.

Everybody stared at her as she approached our table—and, *wow*, were the others ever shocked. Especially Worships, who couldn't have looked more appalled than if Tomas himself had returned from the heavens to tell her he wasn't a god.

Shiny came to a stop and spoke. "Hello. I'm Sasha."

"I'm Bell," I answered promptly, curious to see what she wanted. "And this is Tamsin."

Sh—no, *Sasha* took that as an invitation, putting her plate on the table and sitting down. Then she looked from Tamsin to me and announced, "I've come to join your alliance."

Tamsin snorted. "What makes you think we want you?"

Sasha's mouth dropped open. "I—I—I'm a *knight*."

"Yes," I said. "We know." And I wasn't actually going to send her away. There had to be a third candidate who made it to the end, and she was a better prospect than Worships or Spite. But I was *very* interested to find out why she suddenly wanted to "join our alliance." So I turned my mouth down and let sadness leak into my voice. "It's just that you haven't been very friendly to us, so far."

"I *have*! I mean, not in the beginning, but I helped you yesterday." Words were rushing out of her in her eagerness to prove herself. "I told Guildmaster Daylon I'd find a way to throw the final vote if he didn't make sure the crafter girl was properly punished. I *forced* him to do what was right."

Tamsin made a disbelieving noise.

"I'm telling the truth!" Sasha said indignantly. "I'm not who you think I am, I promise! I'm—that is, I'm . . ."

She broke off, staring into space with a frown. Thinking. Then she focused on me. "When we were in the Bubble, you knew what to do. About the faith part of the challenge, I mean. But . . ." Her gaze switched to Tamsin. "You didn't. Because you didn't start praying as quick as she did. So . . . maybe you're not a follower of the sun-god?"

I spoke fast. "She's an Elodian." I didn't want Tamsin saying anything that so much as hinted that she was a Treesinger.

That answer seemed to please Sasha, who brightened. "And—what are you? I know Treesingers don't usually believe in Risen gods, but you were in the sun-temple, and—"

"What does it matter to you what she believes?" Tamsin interrupted. "Or me, either?"

But I thought I knew. Because this girl was happy Tamsin was an Elodian, and she'd been paying a lot of attention to how the Bubble went about testing faith.

Which was the kind of thing you might do if you were worried about *passing* a test of faith.

"I know the *Testimony* from being in the temple," I said. "But I'm still a Treesinger. We don't have gods." Sasha's shoulders sagged in relief. Definitely not a believer. "You want to tell us what you are now?"

She drew herself up and sucked in a deep breath, like she was about to say something significant. But what she actually said was "I'm a Gleaming."

I had no idea what that meant.

Tamsin didn't either. "I've never heard of Gleamings."

"No one has. We've kept ourselves hidden." Sasha's mouth twisted. "Except I don't think we need to anymore. And we should all just *stop* lying about who we are."

Well, that was an attitude I wanted to encourage. (Not in myself, obviously. But in other people.) "And who *are* you, exactly?"

"We're—well, it's kind of hard to explain, but we're . . ." She paused, chewing on her lip as she sorted out her thoughts. Then she said, "I'll start at the beginning. A long time ago—*before* the gods—there was a blaze of light in the night sky. That light was the Gleam, coming here from the stars. He sent out a call, and people answered it. They were the first to ever live here. And the Gleam spoke to them, sharing his knowledge. Except he didn't have an actual body. He was more like . . . a shimmer, speaking to us in our minds."

Tamsin spoke slowly. "You're saying that the Gleamings are who the Risen *were*, before the gods came?"

"That's right! Everything was different then. There was no hierarchy. No *ridiculous* destiny to keep on rising up." Her gaze drifted to the window. "No golden city, either. We made our home in caves of crystal. But we destroyed all that in Tomas's name when we built Radiance."

I blinked, working my way through that. The Gleamings were the "ignorant" society that the sun and moon testimonies talked about, the one that existed before the gods showed up. Who'd apparently lived in crystal caves. . . . Could those be the same caves our Tangler trees found for us? The Beneath? If so, those caves still existed under Radiance—not that I was going to tell her that. And their Gleam had been someone who came from the stars and spoke to people in their minds? *Another* visitor from elsewhere? I didn't know why they all kept coming here, but it'd be mighty nice if they stopped. "What happened to the Gleam when the gods turned up?"

"He left." Sasha hunched her shoulders. "We betrayed him, you see. At least, most of us did. Turned away from what he'd taught us and started worshipping Tomas and Allora. But," she added brightly, "we think he might have returned!"

I wasn't sure I liked the sound of that. The last thing Treesingers needed was a new other-worlder messing with our lives. "What makes you think he's back?"

"Some of us have been having these . . . moments. Like a flash of light, in our head. And they give us clarity. *I* had one, in the Glass. And I saw how I'd always gone along with what was expected of me, even when I thought I shouldn't." She drew herself up, lifting her chin. "So I didn't do what was expected. I did what was *right.*"

And wasn't she proud of herself? Although she deflated a bit when Tamsin muttered under her breath, "Well, aren't you special." But in this moment I wasn't as interested in what Sasha had done as I was in the actions of another knight. One who looked a long way ahead.

"Sasha, is Sirius Daylon a Gleaming too?"

"Yes! That's part of why he gave up a place in the Test. We Gleamings want to change things, you see. Make things better. Except . . ." She sighed. "He thinks we don't need to do anything else for a while." Her voice shifted into an excellent impersonation of Daylon. "It is for the Treesingers to make what they can of the opportunity now. We have done enough and need not risk ourselves any further."

Tamsin frowned. "How have you risked yourselves at all?"

"It's like I said before—we've kept ourselves hidden. We had to, in the beginning, because unbelievers were being killed by the people who'd converted. If we hadn't pretended to go over to the gods, we'd have died with the rest."

Huh. Seemed like the arrival of Tomas and Allora had been a heck of a lot bloodier than what was recorded in the sun testimony. But it didn't make sense to me that the Gleamings were *still* scared of people knowing who they were. "Yeah, but I can't see

Risen killing other Risen over the sun and moon gods now. No one's gone off slaughtering any Elodians."

"It's . . . well, it's . . . you see, the Gleamings, we tried to rise up as high as we could in the new social order. To acquire influence, because you can't change anything without influence. And we were successful. Most of the Gleamings are traders and knights."

That made even less sense. Why would people at the top of Risen society need to hide?

But Tamsin saw what I didn't. "You're not afraid of losing your lives. You're afraid of losing your *power*. Because traders make deals, and knights make alliances, and a lot of them are with people who truly are sun and moon god followers. And I bet they'd be real unhappy to find out you've been lying about your faith all this time."

"Well . . . yes."

Tamsin and I exchanged a long look. Then she said what we were both thinking. "Gleamings don't really want change. At least, not big change. You just want to say you do. But"—her lip curled in contempt—"you'll never do a thing that costs you too much *influence*."

Sasha flinched. "I know, okay? I know it's not right. But I'm done with that." She looked between both of us, eyes wide and shining. "I want to be a *real* Gleaming, one who lives what we say we believe, no matter the consequences. With me as Queen, and the two of you as my advisers, we'll be able to change everything!"

Of course she thought she'd be Queen. And I wanted her to go on thinking it right up until the moment when she (hopefully) wasn't.

Unfortunately, I didn't step on Tamsin's foot quick enough to stop her from speaking.

"What makes you think it should be you? And please don't say *I'm a knight.*"

Sasha blinked in bewilderment. "I suppose I just assumed. I'm the one best placed to understand the complexities of the governance structures, because . . ." She stopped. "Oh no! I *was* going to say, *Because I'm a knight!*"

She broke into a fit of giggles, all bubbly and infectious and entirely at her own expense. Okay. We could work with someone who could laugh at herself. Plus, it was clear the Gleamings were enemies of the gods (they weren't very good at it, but it was better than being a *friend* of the gods).

"We can worry about who's Queen later," I said, shooting Tamsin a look that I hoped read as *Trust me on this.* "For now . . . welcome to our alliance, Sasha."

Her gaze flew to Tamsin, who gave a grudging nod before shooting *me* a look, which I had no difficulty in interpreting as *You'd better know what you're doing.*

Then Alasdar entered the room and shouted at everyone.

13

The high priest's voice boomed through the chamber. "Candidates! It is time for a challenge of strength and faith. Follow me, please. *Now!*"

Forks and knives clattered and chairs scraped as everyone got up to scramble after Alasdar. I shoved as much food into my mouth as I could, then joined the general rush. The high priest was walking so fast that he was almost running, which meant we had to as well. At least, most of us did. Tamsin's legs were so long she just walked a bit quicker than normal.

"Why is he in such a hurry?" Sasha asked.

I couldn't answer because I was still chewing, so I just shrugged. Tamsin did the same. Then she raised an eyebrow at me. I nodded, knowing what she was asking. *Yes, he's probably still trying to get me killed.* Despite the fact that it hadn't worked before. But facts were no match for hate. Alasdar obviously remained convinced that his god would strike me down. Tomas just needed another opportunity, and his faithful high priest was going to give it to him.

Although from the way he was speeding everyone along, I didn't think he was supposed to be taking us to the Bubble. I'd bet we were meant to be going to the Cave (assuming they'd fixed it) on account of missing out on it last night. He was messing with the order of things *again,* so I could maybe get out of this by asking to see a moon-sister, like Eldan had suggested. Except I didn't see any point in delay. Tamsin and I had to go into the Bubble sometime, and what with our new ally, it might as well be now.

The high priest kept up the pace all the way to the top of the tower. Everyone ran for their weapons, barely getting hold of them before he raised his medallion and shouted the words that woke the Bubble. Once again, it swallowed us all.

We are back! Tricks trilled. Then, in a disappointed tone: This is not the same.

It certainly wasn't. We weren't in a desert. We were in a room.

A large, circular, empty room, lit by a huge glow-orb that floated above us. The walls were etched with a single sentence, repeated over and over. It was what Tomas had said when he'd met the people who would become the Risen: *Behold, I have appeared before you that you may know my glory and raise yourselves up from the wretchedness of your ignorance.* You'd think someone would've punched him in the nose, but apparently folks had been impressed (or so the sun testimony would have us believe).

An arch led out of the space, opening onto a passage that went curving away into the distance. I knew better than to go down it, though. I'd already realized what this room was about. But Worships hadn't. She went tearing off with Spite at her heels. I caught Tamsin's eye and shook my head. She nudged Sasha and mouthed, "Wait."

The three of us stood in silence until Worships and Spite had disappeared around the curve of the passage. Then I said, "I think this is all referencing the fourth codicil to the three hundred and tenth verse of the eighth volume of the *Testimony of the Sun*."

Tamsin and Sasha stared at me blankly.

Really, Alasdar would be appalled at the state of religious education in Radiance. "It's the bit where the ignorant masses travel a false trail seeking the light of the world, but only Tomas holds that light," I explained, waving at the big orb above us. "And the ignorant masses would see that, if they just *paid attention* to the glorious words of the sun-god."

Understanding dawned on their faces. "Whatever we're supposed to do isn't out there," Sasha breathed. "It's in here."

I nodded. "I'm thinking maybe one of these sentences is a bit different from the others? Let's split up and look."

We scattered through the room, staring at smug words. But they were all the same. I was starting to worry I'd gotten this wrong when Tamsin called, "I think I've found it!"

Sasha and I ran over to her. She pointed at the wall. " 'Behold' is written twice. Maybe we should press it?"

She pushed her thumb against the second "Behold." Nothing happened. I tried. Still nothing. Then Sasha.

And the third time must've been the one that did it, or maybe it had just been waiting for all of us to touch the wall, because *behold,* there was a blinding burst of light.

When it faded, we weren't in the room anymore. We were on a hill.

It was green and dewy and sloped gently downward to a field of white daisies. Warm, scented air swirled, carrying petals around us and up into the cloudless blue sky. It was all very pretty. Peaceful.

Really creepy.

Tamsin pointed to something in the distance. "There—do you see?"

I squinted. There was a statue of Tomas on the far side of the field.

"That must be where we're supposed to go," she said. "Except . . . all we have to do is stroll through some flowers? It can't be that easy."

"Got to be more to it," I agreed. "Especially since pushing against a tiny bit of wall is *not* a test of strength. That was faith. Which means . . ."

My voice trailed off as we all stared at the sea of blooms.

"Which means," Sasha concluded, "that there's something really dangerous in that field." She sighed. "And we could *still* be tested on faith. I think this place will just keep throwing challenges at us until someone's dead. If all our hills had risen up in the last one, there would've been something else."

Yeah, she'd really thought about this. But we had to be careful about how we talked about faith, because the Bubble had definitely heard Loner calling out for Elodie. I jerked my head up at the sky to remind them that *something* in here was listening and said in my most pious tone, "We all hold the sun-god in our hearts. He will protect us, just as he did before."

They looked up too, and nodded. They'd got it.

We made our way downward, slipping a little on the dewy grass. Once we got to the edge of the field, we stopped, just in case something was going to come storming out to kill us. Nothing did.

Tamsin cast a thoughtful gaze at the daisies. Between the blossoms and the leaves, we couldn't see much of the ground beneath. "Could be something hiding in there."

She swung Bashy. Sasha joined her, chopping at the flowers with her sword. But all they uncovered was dirt.

It really did seem like it was just a field. But it couldn't possibly be.

"Wait here," Tamsin told me. "We'll go a bit farther out."

I hated being left behind. But I didn't have a weapon.

"Be *careful*!" I called after her. And I was relieved to see that she was. She and Sasha moved slowly, taking a few steps, hefting their weapons in readiness of being attacked, and then going farther when they weren't. Before long they were a quarter of the way into the field, and everything was still weirdly peaceful.

Tamsin went onward, swinging Bashy through the flowers ahead. Sasha caught up, poking around with her sword. They weren't doing anything different from what they'd already done over and over.

But this time there was an almighty splintering sound. And everything broke apart.

I scrambled back onto the hill as the earth cracked into pieces, separated by . . . air? What had been a field was now just clumps of white flowers, floating in sky. No, not flowers. Clouds, and I was mightily relieved to find Tamsin and Sasha were sitting on top of one. *They're okay.* Except that Tamsin was crouched down and clinging to the surface (which looked misty but must be solid or they'd have gone right through). And I remembered, with a sudden, awful lurch, that she was scared of heights.

Oh no, no . . . this was bad. Because I could see now what we had to do.

The statue was where it'd been before, standing atop a patch of floating green earth. We'd have to jump from one cloud to another to reach it. *Moving* clouds that were drifting gently back and forth. It was going to take a lot of jumps to reach the statue, soaring through the air with nothing but that endless blue below. Guess the Bubble figured the strong would make it to their god.

But Tamsin wasn't going to be able to do it.

She knew it too. Even from here I could feel the terror rolling off her. I *had* to get to her, and then—okay, I had no plan, but I'd think of something. I backed up, ready to take a running leap the second a cloud came close enough to reach.

Which was when the petals appeared.

They tore through the air, pushed along by a fierce wind that kept changing direction. A blast came barreling toward me and I threw up my hand to shield my face. But the petals fell away, dropping to scatter on the grass.

Huh. The wind stopped at the edge of the hill. *Weird.* I studied everything all over again, trying to figure it out. It didn't take long to see that the clouds (like the hill) were encased in bubbles of still air. They kept up their slow drift, independent of the wind blasting around them. Which meant that if you were on a cloud or the hill, those fierce gusts weren't a problem.

But.

If you were jumping *between* clouds, you'd have to jump into the wind. If it was blowing the right way, that was a good thing. It could push you along, helping you get to a cloud that would otherwise be out of reach. But if it was blowing the wrong way, it could knock you off course and send you plunging into the blue. And right now the wind *was* blowing the wrong way, because those petals were being blasted toward me. If I jumped into that gust, it'd push me back when I needed to go forward. And there was no cloud near enough anyway.

That meant there was nothing for me to do but wait for a cloud to drift close and the wind to change. Which was exactly what I was doing when Sasha screamed, "Bell! Behind you!"

I swung around to find the other two were here. Spite was standing at the top of the hill. But Worships . . .

Worships was coming right at me. Her sword was raised and she was shouting about how the sun-god had delivered me to her and she'd cleanse the Test of my presence. . . .

Crap. She was coming to kill me.

Tricks released a burst of something tangy that made me feel as weightless as a leaf in the breeze. I sprinted away from Worships, moving so quick and light that I barely touched the earth. Behind me Worships lost her footing on the wet grass, falling but still spewing hatred: "Treesinger scum! You are not worthy!"

I'd heard those words before, but not from her. *Alasdar.* He'd gotten to Worships, probably through that zealot guard trainee. And now she thought Tomas himself had "delivered" me to her because I had no friends on this hill. Certainly not Spite, who was just standing there (close enough to the action to see me get killed but far enough away to deny responsibility if there was trouble about it later).

I caught movement out of the corner of my eye. Sasha was cloud-jumping in my direction. And Tamsin had gotten to her feet and was clearly and idiotically contemplating doing the same.

"Stay where you are!" I shouted at her.

But I didn't have time for more than that. Tricks's scent had worn off. I'd slowed down, and Worships was charging at me again. She launched herself into the air and all I could see was the sword and the awful fanatical gleam in her eyes.

I twisted, flinging myself to the side as Tricks blasted Worships with pollen. She coughed and spluttered, and I took off, plunging down the hillside. Which gave me an excellent view of Tamsin heroically leaping onto the cloud closest to her. She collapsed the second she reached it, overcome by dizziness. I screamed as loud as I could: "Tamsin, stop!"

But I knew she wouldn't. And Sasha had run out of clouds and had to wait for a new one to get close. She couldn't jump. But she could yell, and she did (although not at me).

"Your grandfather would be ashamed of you, Carina!"

Worships shouted back, between coughs, "You don't know . . . anything about . . . my grandfather."

"I know he was a priest! What would he say if he knew you'd lost faith in the sun-god?"

"I haven't lost faith! You're the one who's allied yourself with a Treesinger!"

Worships wasn't coughing anymore. That was bad. But she wasn't coming after me either. I seized the moment to get all the way to the base of the hill.

Sasha was still shouting: "Tomas himself judged Bell worthy. You *saw* how her hill rose up in the first challenge. What makes you think that you know better than Tomas does?"

"I *don't* think that! I . . . I think . . ."

Her voice trailed off. The air seemed to shift, growing thick and heavy. The Bubble had heard Worships's doubt. But apparently she wasn't doubtful *enough* to die, and it didn't seem to care about candidates killing each other.

Tamsin was lurching to her feet. *Blackbark blood.* She wasn't going to stop. Nor was Worships, who'd gotten over her little crisis of faith and was sprinting in my direction. I was going to have to run and getting chased around this hill didn't seem like it'd end well for me. But there were no clouds close, I had no way to escape—

—and then I did. Because everything faded away and I *saw* what was about to happen. I knew when those gusts of wind would blow, and in what direction. I knew when they'd fall away. I knew how the clouds would align with each other, and the series of jumps that would take me to Tamsin. Except I couldn't be seeing this! It was impossible.

My blood hummed so hard it pounded. Telling me it wasn't impossible at all.

My sight cleared. I was back in the world of the Bubble. But the pattern was still here, beating in my blood. All I had to do was follow it.

I sucked in a breath. Pelted forward. And leaped for a cloud that was too far away.

For a moment I soared. Then I began to fall. Tamsin let out an awful, wrenching wail. But I knew *when* that wind was going to gust. And gust it did, slamming into my back to shove me onto the cloud.

I landed with a gasp. Tricks burbled excitedly: We can fly! We can fly!

"Sort of," I muttered. My heart was thumping against my ribs, and all I wanted to do was cling to this lovely cloud and definitely not throw myself back into the void. But I couldn't stop. Not until I'd reached Tamsin.

I forced myself up, clenched my teeth, and jumped. Then

again, and again, following the pattern that hummed beneath my skin. Except I was often jumping *before* there was wind. Which was terrifying and not just for me. Tamsin and Sasha were both screaming at me to stop.

But I was a Treesinger and I trusted my Ancestors.

I landed on another cloud and waited, knowing that there was about to be a mighty gust of wind in the right direction. Tamsin shouted a warning that the wind was too strong and I'd miss the cloud I was aiming for.

I leaped anyway. An updraft sent me soaring high into the air. And it was too fast and too strong and I *was* going to overshoot.

But the wind cut out and I dropped like a stone onto the cloud nearest to Tamsin. *Thank you, Ancestors!* I surged to my feet and made the final jump across, landing at her side.

She threw her arms around me. "*What did you do?* You could have died. Never do that again!"

I hugged her back. "It's okay, Tamsin. We're okay."

Well, sort of. I still wasn't sure how I was going to get Tamsin to the statue. But one life-threatening problem at a time.

I rested my head against Tamsin and looked over to check on the others. Sasha was cloud-leaping in our direction. Spite was still on the hill, and Worships wasn't, although she wasn't that far from it. *Must've only done a couple of jumps.* And she wasn't jumping at all now. Just staring at me and shaking so bad I could see it from here.

I'd done something that looked impossible. And it would've been, without the help of the Ancestors. But Worships didn't know about Ancestors. She must surely think Tomas himself had reached down with an invisible hand to save my life.

She dropped to her knees, clasping her hands together and

calling out to a god who wasn't there. "Holy Tomas, I'm sorry I doubted you. I'm sorry I didn't believe! Forgive me, please forgive me!"

But the Bubble wasn't built to forgive. It was built to judge. And Worships had just confessed to losing her faith.

There was a rippling in the air. The cloud beneath Worships vanished.

She didn't make a sound as she plummeted into nothingness.

And the rest of us were spat back into the tower.

14

Like before, we ended up scattered across the platform. I lurched to my feet, reaching out to lean against the wall as I searched for Tamsin and Sasha. I found them sitting on the far side of the tower, looking as shaky and queasy as I felt. But they were okay. And Alasdar . . . wasn't here. No priest was. Only moon-sisters, swarming around the candidates in swirls of white robes.

One came over to me, and pressed a little bottle into my hand. I recognized the smell wafting out of it (a restorative) and sat down to drink, trying not to gag on the bitter taste. Then I handed the bottle to the sister and closed my eyes so the room would stop spinning while I waited for it to work.

A voice spoke, aimed at my moon-sister helper. "I will tend to Bell. See to the others."

My eyes flew open and I tried to get up. At least I pretended to. I had no intention of actually standing but Bernadise would expect me to make the effort.

"Stay where you are," she commanded. "You require time to recover."

The high priestess was all dressed up in her formal robe (silver and covered with glittering moons) and looking even more displeased with the world than usual. She shook her head at me. "Foolish girl. Did you not realize something was wrong? You should have asked for the help of the moon-sisters."

I pretended confusion. "We weren't supposed to be in the Bubble this morning?"

"You were not. But"—she sighed—"I can see how you might have misunderstood. This has been a *most* unusual Test." She glanced around at the other candidates. "No one is injured. Good. You should all recover quickly." Her gaze focused on me. "How are you feeling?"

"Better." Which was true, and saying otherwise would just get more foul-tasting medicine shoved down my throat. Then I realized why she was pleased everyone would get better quick. "We're going to the Cave *now*?"

"Oh yes. There has been quite enough of a delay."

That didn't give me much time to tell Tamsin and Sasha how to beat the thing. I tried to get up again, for real this time. But Bernadise pressed me back down and leaned in close. "There is something about the challenge I must tell you, Bell. You understand that it involves dreams?"

I nodded, *very* curious to see where she was going with this.

She leaned closer still, lowering her voice until it was barely above a murmur. "It is my belief that candidates can direct what they dream. All you need to do is focus on what you wish to dream about immediately before you fall asleep."

I let my mouth fall open while on the inside I rolled my eyes at her. *Unbelievable.* She was *still* trying to get information on the grove sickness.

"You mean . . . I could dream about Falling Leaves?" I whispered.

"Yes, and it might be possible for you to uncover new insights. The Cave will allow you to reach knowledge held at a deeper level of your consciousness." She sighed. "I should not be telling you this, of course. But I know how difficult it has been for you over the years, when you could not provide me with any answers that would assist in curing the sickness."

Yeah, because she'd *made* things difficult for me when she didn't get the answers she wanted. But I looked down and away, like I was ashamed of having failed her. Then I met her gaze and lifted my chin. "If there's something to find, I'll find it."

"I am sure you will. I look forward to discussing whatever you discover." She patted my shoulder.

And I had to lock my whole body in place to keep from slapping her hand away. Because I'd just realized what she was doing.

Bernadise hadn't warned me how important it was to get out of the dreams, and she knew I wouldn't want to leave a dream of Falling Leaves. She wasn't just trying to find out about the grove. She was trying to get me back under her control. Because it was the sisters who cared for the sleepers. If I slept, I'd vanish into the moon-temple, where Bernadise could do whatever she liked to me. And the thought of being in her power again made my insides turn to ice.

She went off to check on the others and I levered myself to my feet, so cold I was surprised I wasn't shaking. A gentle scent puffed out around my head and I sucked it in deep.

We are brave. Songs will be sung.

The ice melted a little, enough for me to think. Yes, this was a trap, but thanks to the Queen I already knew how to get out of it. I *wasn't* going to be in Bernadise's power, not ever again. I was going to beat the Cave, and whatever insights I got would be mine, not hers. . . . Huh. *Insights.*

Now I felt shaky for a whole different reason. If the Cave could take me to a deeper level of consciousness, I could potentially use it to get into the Silverleaf memories! Except . . . maybe it wasn't the best idea to force my way into memories that had been supposed to come to me slowly, as I grew into my gift?

I thought about that. And decided I didn't care. I needed to know *now.*

Bernadise cleared her throat, drawing everyone's attention. "We will now commence our journey to the Cave. You may leave your weapons here. Those of you in the final three will have them returned."

She strode to the stepper, and everyone followed her down the tower and back through the golden corridors of the Hall. Spite pushed past the rest of us to walk right behind the high priestess, looking as smug as ever. She obviously expected the Cave to work out for her just like everything else had.

I slowed down and Tamsin and Sasha did too, matching their pace to mine. When we were trailing far enough behind, I drew them closer and explained, in whispers, how to beat the Cave.

Sasha cast an astonished glance in Bernadise's direction. "She told you that?"

Um, no, actually. But it was an obvious conclusion to draw, what with Bernadise talking to me outside the Bubble. And I certainly wasn't going to tell Sasha about the Queen. So I nodded.

Sasha still looked shocked. "She's trying to *help* you?"

"She's trying to help herself. She's obsessed with the sickness in my grove, and she's hoping I'll get some insight about it during the Cave that I can tell her about."

Tamsin scowled. "Bet she gets on well with the high priest."

"Oh, they're the best of friends. At least for as long as he's useful to her."

That came out more angry than I'd intended. Sasha was instantly curious. "You don't like him?"

"He doesn't like me. And I don't think Wor—I mean, Carina came up with the idea to go after me on her own. Some of what she was saying was straight out of his mouth."

She gasped in outrage, loud enough that Spite glanced back at us. I elbowed her. *"Hush."*

"We should report him," she hissed.

Tamsin rolled her eyes. "You are *such* a knight."

"What's that supposed to mean?"

"It means report him to who?" I said. "He's the *high priest*. No one would believe the word of a Treesinger against him, and even if they did, what could they do about it?"

"It isn't right!"

"Yes," Tamsin replied dryly. "We know."

Sasha opened her mouth to speak again, caught sight of Tamsin's expression, and went quiet. But not for very long. I was starting to think "quiet" wasn't really for her.

"*How* did you do that thing with the wind?" she asked.

I scrambled for a plausible lie. But in the next moment she came up with an explanation all on her own. "Or did the Bubble do it to save you? Because it has to be against the rules for another candidate to try to kill you."

Yeah. Sure. That'd do. Except I didn't even get a chance to agree with her when Sasha had another idea. "Or was it because it wasn't working properly? Like how it was ignoring you two?"

What was she talking about? "It wasn't ignoring us!"

She frowned, her gaze flitting between Tamsin and me. "But it was—you must have noticed! At the start, when we pressed the word? It worked when I did it."

"I figured we all had to press it."

Sasha gave a thoughtful nod. "Maybe. But . . . that doesn't explain later. On the field?"

"What about the field?" Tamsin asked.

"I *felt* the moment it was going to break right before it happened. It was as if I'd crossed some invisible line. Except"—she looked at Tamsin—"you were ahead of me, so you should have triggered it first. Only you didn't."

Huh. I went over what had happened in my mind. Tamsin *had* been ahead. But it was only when Sasha had walked up beside her that everything had come apart.

Sasha chattered on. "It's so strange—as if the two of you weren't even there. I think it must have been malfunctioning. The Cave wasn't working yesterday, you know, although they must have fixed it now."

As if we weren't even there. . . . I had a sudden thought, so shocking that I missed a step. I recovered fast, slapping a bland expression on my face. But in the next moment, Tamsin reached the same conclusion I had. And stopped dead in the middle of the hallway.

I grabbed her arm and pulled her onward. "Come on. The Cave's not so scary."

She started walking, casting an urgent look at me that said

she hadn't stopped because of the Cave. I returned her look with one of my own, then flicked my gaze toward Sasha. She nodded, understanding. We couldn't talk right now about what both of us knew.

The Bubble had been ignoring *Treesingers*.

Out loud, I managed, "Maybe we should all think about the kind of dreams the Cave might try to tempt us with. So we're prepared, you know?"

"Good idea," Tamsin said, a little overenthusiastically, but it got the point across. Sasha subsided into silence, and we all walked on without saying a word. Tamsin and I still couldn't talk to each other, but at least this gave us both some quiet to think.

What the heck was going on? The Bubble hadn't ignored us the first time we'd gone into it! The worms had chased us down and our hill had sunk along with the rest. But this time had been different. Would we even have died if we'd fallen? Maybe not, although I wouldn't have wanted to try that. And I'd certainly have died if Worships had caught up with me. But she wasn't part of the Bubble. Sometime between yesterday and today, someone had messed with that thing to . . . protect Treesingers? No, to protect *me*, because no one knew about Tamsin.

Who'd been trying to help me? Who even could? The priests didn't seem to understand the Bubble at all—unless maybe it was just Alasdar who didn't. Other priests might know a lot more. . . . Eldan?

Ahead of us, Bernadise stopped. Tamsin, Sasha, and I hurried to catch up as she swung around to face us, gesturing to the stairs behind her. "At the base of this stairway lies the Cave. Once inside, you will be exposed to vapors that will encourage deep, meaningful dreams." She paused, subjecting each of us to a slow, measured glance. "We shall see which three of you triumph over what you encounter in your sleep, and who will sleep until the reign of the next Queen."

That last sentence was accompanied by a faint, contemptuous smile, as if she'd be astonished if any of us made it out, which was a very Bernadise way of doing things (the strong would prove her wrong and the weak would rightfully fail). She turned to start down the stairs, and I tore my thoughts away from the Bubble. It was the Cave I had to be thinking about now.

We followed the high priestess down steps lit only by the soft glow of brightstone until we arrived at a heavy door. There were whitestone moons everywhere here, pressed into the brightstone. Half-moons, quarter moons, full moons . . . Everywhere except for the door, which was plain except for a single indent of a circle.

Bernadise walked over to it. "Once you go through, the challenge begins. You will find a lever inside. Pull it to be released from the Cave when three of you wake—and one does not."

She lifted her medallion, pressing it into the circle, then took it away again. There was a soft click and the door rolled to the side, sliding into the wall.

Sweet-smelling air swirled out. And the four of us surged into the Cave.

15

As expected, the room was windowless. In the center of the floor was a hole covered by a grate, with a white orb floating above it. Vapors rose up through the grate, only to be sucked into the orb and released again. Except the vapors that came through the grate were a colorless shimmer in the air and the ones that came out of the orb were silver. The sisters were taking something that came from the earth and changing it for their own purposes.

The vapors were surrounded by white chairs, arranged into a loose circle. Each one was curved into an S shape and looked *really* comfortable, all soft and padded. . . . Yeah. I was already sleepy.

Spite charged ahead and reached a chair first. Tamsin, Sasha, and I stumbled over to fall into chairs on the other side of the grate. I focused as hard as I could on Mum and Granny, and all the Silverleafs. *Show me their memories. Show me the things they know that I don't.*

Then my eyes drooped shut and I was asleep.

For a moment there was only the peaceful dark. Then . . . vines?

They twined together to form a tunnel that sprouted with green leaves and red flowers. And there were doors. *Lots* of them, spaced out along the viny passage. The doors were dreams, I just knew it the way you know things sometimes in—well, dreams. And with any luck, at least some of them were Silverleaf memories.

The vines beneath my feet grew warm and then hot, sending me dancing from side to side. I couldn't stay here. I had to go through a door. But which one?

"Tricks? What do you think?"

They are all the same!

"I know, that's why I asked!" I cast a frantic glance around, trying to find something, anything, that would distinguish one door from the other. But Tricks was right—they were all the same.

Then one of them suddenly shifted in color, turning smoky black. That was enough of a sign for me, and anyway my feet were burning so I couldn't stay here any longer. I dove forward, wrenching the door open to throw myself inside.

I became someone else. Only I wasn't Mum, or Granny, or any other Silverleaf.

I wasn't even human.

Talks Sweetly was back.

He was strolling through my veins, mingling with the humans. He was no more one of them than I was. But he wore a human form.

I liked the humans. I had not expected so many to answer my call, but I was not displeased that they had come in such numbers. At least some amongst them would make an excellent crew when they had learned enough to comprehend the true nature of what I was.

Talks Sweetly thought that educating humans was a foolish waste of my time and resources. He said, *They're not suited to symbiotic relationships with other life-forms.* He said, *They're too limited to grasp the* existence *of life on worlds other than their own.* I disagreed, although I knew I was hardly objective on the matter of their potential, for I *must* have a crew. Without one, I could not continue my search for my mother and the rest of my clutch. I'd gone as far as I could alone. When the humans had learned enough, I would reveal to them my true nature. My true name, though I did not object to being called by the one they had given me. But they must know all the truths of who and what I was, in order to make the choice of whether to be *crew* or *not crew.* I hoped some at least would choose *crew* and join with me to travel the stars.

Talks Sweetly was moving closer to the heart of me. *Perhaps I should refuse to see him.* I had contemplated doing so before. Except he had come to trade. It was hard for us Vaulters to refuse a trade, and though I did not like him, liking was not necessary to trading. There were only two rules for exchanging the sparklies my kind found upon our travels. The first was that whomever we traded a sparkly to would not use it to cause harm to innocent life. The second was that whatever we received must be of greater value than what we gave up. Talks Sweetly had offered me much for the sparkly he wanted, but nothing that was of greater value than the sparkly itself.

But he would have another offer. He always had another offer.

He had reached the heart of me now. I let him in. As always, he began with smiles and gentle words. Then he sighed a mournful sigh. "You drive a hard bargain, Journeys Far."

"It is a valuable sparkly," I said. "A *rare* sparkly."

In truth, there was no way of determining how many of these sparklies the Ancients had made before they had departed all those centuries ago. But it was a known thing that what they'd left behind was hardly ever found anymore.

"And," I reminded him, "you came to this world seeking it." He did not need reminding of this, of course. He just liked to pretend that he did not want the sparkly as much as he did. But I knew, and he knew, that he had traveled long and far in search of this particular sparkly, following rumor and story until he'd found me.

"It is valuable," Talks Sweetly acknowledged. "But you must remember it may be of little use to me. It may even kill me."

That was a truth. More than a truth—it was a certainty. Or so I thought.

The sparkly Talks Sweetly sought was called pathway. A passage to the higher plane of existence where the Ancients had gone, embodied within beads of crystal. The Ancients had scattered their pathway across the stars as if breaking up a necklace, sending beads flying out across worlds. All so that the "bright of spirit" might follow them. And while there were many interpretations of what "bright of spirit" meant, most thought it required that someone be fair of mind and big of heart (like the Ancients themselves). Those who possessed a sufficiency of brightness ingested a bead and joined the Ancients. Those who did not ingested a bead and died.

I did not believe Talks Sweetly was "bright of spirit," and the fact that he thought otherwise indicated a profound failure to comprehend himself. But his likely demise mattered little to me. He was very far from being innocent life, so his death would not breach the rules of trade. But until he offered something of proper value, my pathway would remain locked safely inside me with all my other sparklies.

Talks Sweetly reached into his robe and produced something with a flourish. He was fond of flourishes.

But this time what he was offering was indeed of value.

He held up a green orb, tipping it so the light caught the swirls of silver in its surface. "You know what this is?"

I did know. Talks Sweetly had a heart compass. Called so because it would guide you to your heart's desire. Perhaps. It was said there were those who'd followed a heart compass for hundreds of years and never found their desire. It was also said the entire notion was a myth and a heart compass was little more than an interesting bit of gemstone from a long-dead world.

Talks Sweetly spoke softly. "We all lost something. In the war."

A blatant attempt to manipulate me. He knew of my desire to locate my clutch. He knew they'd been taken by soldiers. The only reason I had escaped was that I had been out exploring much farther than I should have ventured. My mother always warned me that my curiosity would get me into trouble. Instead it had saved me. But I would rather have been taken instead of being the one left behind.

"As you can imagine, I am reluctant to part with something so valuable," Talks Sweetly said. "It is why I have not offered it before now. I confess, I was hoping not to have to. But I will give it up. For all the pathway beads you have."

That was far more than was needed for one person to ascend, and I did not know what he would do with the rest. Perhaps it could harm innocent life and breach the rules of trade? But no, because there was nothing to be done with pathway except ingest it, and only the "bright of spirit" could follow the Ancients. All others would die.

But that was not the only potential breach. The heart compass might not do what the legends said it could. It was foolish to bargain on the basis of the mere possibility that the legends did not lie. I might not be receiving something of greater value than what I gave up.

For once I did not care. I would seize any opportunity, however unlikely, to locate my clutch and find my mother.

"Your bargain is accepted," I said.

Talks Sweetly set down the compass and I drew it into myself. Then I opened a passage to where I held the sparklies and called up all the pathway I had, sending beads floating into his hands.

As he grasped hold of them, his face changed, becoming something I did not recognize. Something far more dangerous than I'd ever believed he could be. In the same moment, a wave of unpleasant energy poured out from the compass that I had taken into my being.

I had made a catastrophic error.

I burst out of the door and back into the passage, so angry with myself I could barely breathe. How could I have been that *stupid?* I should never have given him the sparkly, never. . . . I clutched at my head. *That. Wasn't. Me.*

"Tricks?" I whispered. "What *was* that?"

But she just flooded my mind with questions. Who are Vaulters? Who is Talks Sweetly? I think he is bad!

"I don't know!" But a smooth-talking other-worlder who convinced people to part with valuable things? Talks Sweetly hadn't looked anything like the pictures of Tomas, but I'd bet that's who he was. "Talks Sweetly might be the sun-god."

Do you think the Vaulter is okay?

"I hope so." But it seemed like Tomas had hurt him badly. *And then he gave some pathway to the Birth tree and it's somehow poisoning her.* . . . Um. I could see no reason for him to do that, or why this pathway stuff would even hurt the tree (it couldn't be because she wasn't "bright of spirit"—no one was fairer or more bighearted than trees). Besides, the memory had felt a bit distant, as if I was seeing something that had happened a very long time ago. There was a lot more to this story than I knew yet. Although things were starting to make a bit more sense now that I understood pathway was both a bead of crystal *and* a passage that could be walked, what with eating it possibly taking you to some kind of higher realm. Except . . .

"Tricks, *why* would the Silverleaf trees want me to eat pathway? It's going to kill me or take me somewhere else!"

It is very mysterious!

She didn't know. I sighed and stared at the doors, thinking hard. I wasn't getting stuck in dreams (maybe because I was going into other people's memories), which was good. It hopefully meant I could go in and out of dreams as often as I wanted without getting trapped. But I still had to find the right ones. And the vines were warming up again.

I shifted from foot to foot, concentrating on Silverleafs and pathway and the Birth tree. "Can you help, Tricks? I've *got* to get to a Silverleaf memory!"

She didn't say anything but I felt her adding her strength to mine. There was a sharp cracking sound, somewhere far beneath my feet. That didn't sound good, but I didn't care, because one of the doors lit up with the shape of a silver tree. *Victory!* I plunged through it.

And became Alethea Silverleaf.

My heart was like a fire, guttered out. Nothing there but embers and ash. Excepting that I burned still. I didn't reckon on ever being cold again, not with this rage to warm me up. And I wasn't the only one it'd be warming. Generations of Silverleafs would feel the blaze of this anger. The pain beneath it, too.

It cut and cut, that pain. Always would. I should've died with the Nexus. No fault of mine that I hadn't. Never asked to be saved. I had been, though. Now I had to go on, like all the Silverleafs after me would. Until the man calling himself a god of the sun was dead, right along with the woman who claimed the moon. Maybe they'd die screaming. Like the Nexus trees. That'd be a good thing. But I wasn't going to be choosy about how they ended. Dead was dead.

Truth was, sun-man was dying already. But he wasn't going quick. So said the god who'd fought at my side. Who'd saved me when I didn't want to be saved.

Elodie said, sun-man and moon-woman wanted to get to some higher plane they weren't "bright enough" to reach. But they'd figured they could get a look into it without needing to go there. Allora had taken a speck of a pathway bead and a speck of Tomas and bound the two together. An experiment. Clever woman had been trying to fool the pathway into thinking Tomas was a part of it. If it'd worked, it would've opened up a window onto that other place. Let them get a peek into the knowledge of those Ancients who lived there. But it didn't work, leastaways, not how they'd hoped. The view Tomas got was small and cloudy, and the price was high.

He had to keep on eating those little specks of pathway now. El said his "system was dependent." But the pathway knew he was no bright spirit and it was eating him back. Except the amount he was taking in was so tiny that it was all happening slow. He'd last for generations and generations yet, and for as long as he had pathway in him, he couldn't be killed by anything else. And if he found a way to hold it, to "stabilize his system," he'd be here forever.

141

Footsteps, behind me. Walking up this ridge that I was standing on so I could get one last look over Mistfall. If I turned, I'd find her watching me out of eyes that were brown like the earth. Although they could've been any color she wanted. Her human shape was just a cos- tume she wore. But she was real, and she was still hoping. I could feel it.

I waved her forward and ended her hope. "I'm going with the ones the Risen are taking away. My place is with my people." *Not with you.* "You'll be going somewhere else."

"I'm not going anywhere else! You think I'd leave you—leave Treesingers—to deal with Tomas and the Risen on your own?"

"Someone's got to chase after Allora."

She breathed in sharp. Said nothing. Too surprised to speak, I reckoned. Too scared, about what I was asking of her.

Allora had left this world altogether. Gone elsewhere and taken much of their pathway with her. Given Tomas enough to keep him fed while she went looking to steal the power they needed to hold it. They'd tried to get that power from the Nexus after one of their technological devices had told them about those trees. All the life of Mistfall had flowed into Nexus, to be sent back out again to where it was needed most. Sun-man and moon-woman had figured a tree that could hold life like that could hold pathway too. They hadn't counted on the trees fighting back. Nexus would rather die than help those two. The Nexus *had* died. Now Tomas was taking some Treesingers back to Radiance, hoping we'd one day grow more Nexus, while Allora was off hurting other folks and maybe finding what she needed if she did enough hurting.

"Allora's got to be stopped."

"You think I can do that? You know I'm no good at fighting, Thea. Look how I failed here."

I stared right at her. No forgiveness in my face. "Do better."

142

She went small. A butterfly, folding up her wings.

I sighed. "No help for it, El. We've both got to be different."

We were outsiders, her and me. I was a wanderer and a warrior amongst a peaceful, home-loving people. She was a butterfly amongst stern folk. Enforcers, her people were. Charged with keeping order across the stars. Not so good at keeping order amongst their own, it seemed. But Elodie said there'd been a war. Over long ago now, but there were worlds in chaos still, and her people were stretched thin.

"I won't be wandering anymore," I said. "Won't be looking up at those stars and thinking about what's out there. Won't be fighting either, leastaways, not directly. It'll be a hidden kind of fighting Tree-singers do, in Radiance."

"I can't."

"You can. Old One says so."

She didn't say anything to that. Nothing to say. She'd never met the Old One, but she'd heard me speak of the very oldest of the trees on Mistfall. A farseeing tree.

"I say so too," I added. "Use your strengths. You're good at getting folks to listen to you. I'm thinking Allora must've made herself a lot of enemies, in her time. Might be, they help you. Even if they don't . . . you can be more, El. We both can be."

"I know you can." She raised up her head. "And as for me, I don't know. But I'll try, Thea. For you. And for . . ." Her voice went husky. "For Ronan."

The little brother, long dead. She'd never gotten over him dying, any more than I was going to get over losing the Nexus. Some wounds just don't heal.

She spoke again. Brighter, this time. "You're right that she has enemies. If I can bring enough of them together, I might be able to defeat her! And then I can come back here."

She was hoping, still. Wasn't in her nature not to. But the Old One, who saw so far and so much, had already told me the fight would be long and hard. Elodie would likely be chasing Allora for more seasons than I had on this earth.

I said it as gentle as I could: "I'm thinking maybe this will be the last time we'll speak in this life."

She cried, of course. Big, noisy tears. She cried easily, Elodie. Laughed easily too. I didn't do either, much. But we were friends. Both of us feeling like we'd known each other always, not just the little while since she'd come to warn us about the gods. I'd never had a friend before. Always been too different to make one amongst my own folk.

I was going to miss her. Every day and always. No use telling her that. It'd only make her cry worse. I'd tell her something else when she could hear me. Something she'd like.

When her sobs became sniffles, I reached out. Took her hand. "The Old One would say we're always this close." I pressed her fingers in mine. "Being as we're only ever as far from someone as there's a way to be reaching them, and there's always a way. She reckons, love crosses worlds."

Truth was, I hadn't thought much of those words when the Old One first said them to me. Made more sense now. Seemed to make Elodie feel better too. She even smiled, a little. Then her smile went away.

"I'm sorry, Thea. About the seed. I really thought I'd saved something."

"Don't be telling me sorry," I said. "You did your best. You ever doubt that, I want you to hear my voice saying otherwise."

She nodded. Smiled again.

I looked away. Felt badly, for lying to her. She had saved something. She'd rescued a Nexus seed, the last and only one. But I'd told her the seed was weak. Couldn't grow anything from it. Wasn't true. But that seed was part of a Silverleaf secret now. And Silverleaf secrets were for Silverleaf women and Silverleaf trees.

I'd asked the Old One once if I could walk that pathway, talk to these Ancients, and come back with a way to kill sun-man quick instead of slow. But the Old One had said it would take a tree and human together to do that. Human, because we moved light and fast across the earth. Tree, because they didn't. They were rooted in this world. Connected. Humans could leave this world, but once we did, we'd forget about it. Trees, though—trees would always remember. They could come back.

Human and tree together. I'd thought of that when Elodie gave me the seed. Then I'd taken it to the Old One and asked her to plant the seed. But not in earth.

The seed was in my blood.

Old One said, being one with the Nexus would make Silverleafs more like them. And Nexus were born knowing all that'd been known by the trees that went before. Silverleafs would start to have knowledge of Silverleaf generations too, only not born knowing it. We'd have to go walking our memories. And Nexus didn't grow quick, even in dirt. But that tree would be stronger in the daughter I'd have one day than in me. Stronger in her daughter than in her. All the way to the Silverleaf who'd be strong enough to go and come back.

Elodie leaned against my shoulder. I rested my cheek against the top of her head. Looked up at the sky. It was early evening. Light still, but a few stars were out and more were coming. Like I'd told her, I wouldn't be gazing at them anymore. Wouldn't be dreaming of going with her to places elsewhere. I was never going to be traveling those stars now.

But my descendants would.

16

I staggered into the passage, choking on sorrow and rage. I was filled with too many feelings and too many thoughts. Nothing made sense.

Everything made sense.

We are Nexus, Tricks whispered.

"Yeah." My voice sounded strange. Not as husky as it should be. *Because it's my voice, not Alethea's.* I held out my hand, staring at it as if I could see through my skin and into my blood. The secret of the Silverleaf women. Human and tree together. That meant . . . that meant . . .

I didn't know what it meant. I didn't know anything.

I sank to the ground, putting my pounding head in my hands and trying to think. And the first thought that came was that pathway had nothing to do with healing the grove. Except it did, because Mum had thought *the* Silverleaf could fix Falling Leaves. *Why* had she thought that? I prodded at my worn-out brain until it gave me an answer. The Ancients. They'd made pathway, so they must know how to fix whatever it had done to the Birth tree.

Something rattled behind me. One of the doors had lit up with a silver tree and was shaking in its frame. A memory, trying to get my attention. But I had all the memories I needed, didn't I? It was hard to think. Hard to do anything.

The door rattled harder. I hauled myself up, lurching over to yank it open.

And fell into being my granny.

If you wanted something done right, you'd best be prepared to do it yourself. This world was full of dreamers and fools. Leana was both, thinking she'd be able to come here tonight when she was so tired from what folk were calling the grove sickness. My daughter would be sleeping now and she wasn't going to be waking soon. Those herbs I'd dosed her with were strong. Stupid woman should've known I was up to something, the way I asked her so sweetly if she wanted tea and then went all quiet when she said no, as if I was heartbroken there was nothing I could do for her. She changed her mind quick then. *Oh, Mum, please bring me the tea—I'm sure it'll make me feel better.* Lying to her mother, because she knew as well as I did that the only thing that might make her feel better was carried in our blood. And neither of us was the one who could do what needed to be done with it.

The streets of Radiance were quiet. Nearly midnight, so there weren't many of the Risen bastards around and the few who were about weren't going to see me. Not in my rippler suit, which bent the light, making this Treesinger woman nothing more than a shimmer in the air. Useful thing, my suit. Should be, too. Sixty-two years I labored over it, gathering the fallen petals from the only flower that a rippler bush makes in a growing season. Building up an immunity to the toxins so I could wear the thing. All because the Nexus told me a long time back that there'd come a day when I'd need this suit.

Today was that day.

The moon-temple rose up ahead. Leastaways, the wall around it did. I got out my clinger moss, pressing it to my hands and feet. Only took moments to be up that wall, over the top, and down again. When I landed on the other side, I felt something. A pulling sensation, like Bell tugging at my hand. *This way, Granny. This way!* I followed until I found myself at a nothing-looking door. Looked ordinary enough, but it had an energy on it that made my skin go prickly and hot. If Allora was using some of her other-world gadgetry to close a door, there must be something special behind it. I was in the right place.

There was a humming in my blood. *Wait.*

Would've liked to try that door. But I wasn't going to argue with the Nexus. So I took myself off to the side and got to waiting. And thinking, about my granddaughter.

Didn't like leaving her. But I didn't have a choice about it. The grove was going to have to go dormant. It'd be left to Bell to wake us up again. Because she was *the* Silverleaf, I knew it all the way to my bones. Good thing the Holdfast blood hadn't made her soft. Such needy folk, Holdfasts. Always sharing their feelings and the like. I hoped I'd taught Bell better than that. She'd want her strength to do what had to be done. Especially with Allora being back.

Had to have been her who put that pathway in the Birth tree. One of her experiments. She must've come sneaking into the grove from the sky in spirit form under the cover of that big storm a few months back, though the first Leana and I knew of it was when the tree got sick. Leana figured moon-woman was wanting to see what happened if she gave pathway to the oldest tree in Radiance, a tree that was the strength and heart of a grove. Wanting to see if maybe a *grove* could hold pathway, and use that learning to help Tomas do the same.

Just went to show how little the so-called gods knew about trees. Every one of them was bright enough of spirit to go following after those silly Ancients if they'd wanted to. But trees didn't go chasing better lives elsewhere. They made everything better where they were. Our Birth tree was fighting being dragged off by pathway and it was tearing her apart.

There was a sound. A crackling, spitting noise, like an angry fire. A big mass of green came swirling down from the sky, hissing with sparks. I'd never seen her in this form. I'd never seen her in any form, not with my own eyes. But Alethea had.

This was Elodie.

She should be ashamed of herself for letting that moon-god get away from her. I'd have liked to tell her that. But she couldn't see me in my suit, and I wasn't going to show myself. Best none of that family pay any attention to Silverleafs.

In the next moment something appeared in her colors. Looked like a little black cube. A glowing wave came out of it and the door went flying open. Elodie went through and I followed after. Stairs next, and another door, and another wave. That took us into a big room, all books and potions and evil. A laboratory. The table in the middle was stacked with glass tubes filled with shining liquids.

And something else.

A tiny, red, spiky shape, blurry around the edges. Hard to properly see. Such a little thing, to be something so big. Because I knew it right away.

That was a pathway bead.

If I was young and foolish I'd have shouted for joy. I knew now why

149

I was here. I was going to take that pathway. Didn't know how yet, but I'd get it and hide it away for Bell so she could go visit those Ancients when she was old enough.

I wanted to grab it right now. But blood thrummed. *Wait.* In the next minute, something came barreling in. Another mass of energy. White, this time. Carrying some kind of blade.

White energy spoke, voice a buzzing in the air. *I hoped you would be foolish enough to come here, Elodie. You cannot touch my pathway. And without your allies you cannot stand against me.*

Green energy bit back. *My allies may not be here, but they have ensured I am well supplied, Allora.*

A silver ball appeared. Didn't look like much. But Allora cried out at the sight of it. Sounding scared, which was a good thing. Elodie threw the ball at the pathway, and sparks poured out all over it.

The sparks disappeared. Pathway was still there. Looked a bit different, though. Not blurry anymore. *Shield,* I realized. That pathway had been protected by something and now it wasn't.

My head went fuzzy and my eyes went funny. I was seeing, but I was seeing *ahead.* Everything that was about to happen was laid out like a blanket on the ground. There was going to be one chance for me to do what I'd come here to do. I'd need to be quick, though. Quick enough to get across the room and back again in the space between one heartbeat and the next. Excepting it was impossible to be that fast. Leastaways, it was for most people. Not for a Matriarch. But drawing on Falling Leaves would drain it of strength and myself along with it. I'd get weaker, quicker. So would the grove.

No choice. Nothing else to be done.

I called on Falling Leaves. Let power fill me up. And waited.

Allora dove for Elodie. But she wasn't where she'd been a minute ago. She was on the other side of the room, sending green energy crackling out.

This was my moment. I tore past them both. Grabbed the piece of pathway, tucked it into my suit, and was away again. All between the space of one heartbeat and the next.

The energy struck. Everything on that table shattered into nothing. Pathway was gone. Destroyed. Or so they'd think.

Allora screamed and snarled and spat, lunging for Elodie.

She made her escape with Allora chasing after her.

I strolled off with my prize.

I tumbled back into the hall, cackling with glee. I had the pathway! Taken it right out from under the noses of those would-be gods. Fooled by a human, they'd been, although they'd never know it. But I did. I laughed and laughed. Then I realized I couldn't stop and started to panic.

I slapped my hand over my mouth, choking off the laughter until it finally went away. Well, almost. Little giggles still kept spurting out. But it was hard not to laugh when I was so floaty and light. I'd found my answers to . . . something. Questions I couldn't even remember right now. But that didn't matter. None of it mattered. Vaguely it occurred to me that this bubbly feeling might not be a good thing.

I looked around the passage. It was all . . . holey. There were gaps between the vines and pale light was shining through, as if this place was breaking at the seams. And that wasn't the only thing that was weird. Something was missing. Something was *gone*.

"Tricks?"

No answer. I patted my head. She wasn't there! "Tricks? Where are you?"

Still no answer. Maybe if I went through one of the holes I'd find her?

I took a step toward the light. Which was when there was a desperate shout from behind me. "Bell, *stop!*"

I spun around. "Tricks, where have you been?"

Only it wasn't Tricks. Not at all.

I blinked in surprise. "Scruffy Risen boy! What are you doing here?"

He skidded to a halt in front of me. "You can't go into the light, do you hear me? You have to stay . . ." His voice trailed off as he looked around. "No, you can't stay here for long either. This interface is breaking down. But you've got to go somewhere while I find you a way out."

He seemed *amazingly* real for a figment of my imagination. I reached out to trace the line of his cheekbone. He sucked in a sharp breath and caught my hand, holding it in his. "Bell. What are you doing?"

"You feel real," I said. "But you can't be. This is all inside my mind."

"I'm not—" He stopped, shaking his head. "No time to explain. Just listen to me. I don't know what's happened, but you've all been asleep too long. The Queen is coming to stop the challenge."

"She is? Bernadise won't like that!" A giggle escaped me, then another. "I'm sorry, it's just everything is so . . . funny!"

"I think the signals in your brain are misfiring," he told me. He sounded grim, but misfiring signals struck me as hilarious and I laughed again. Then I noticed something behind him. "Maybe that's the way out!"

He twisted to look at the new door that had appeared in the wall. Only it wasn't like the others. It was made of brightstone and etched with a picture of a blazing sun. It looked like the doors in the sun-temple. But I hated the temple.

I eyed the door doubtfully. "I don't think that is the way out."

"No. It isn't." And he muttered something under his breath.

"What does 'neural entanglement' mean?" I asked.

"It means that I don't think that's one of your memories," he replied. "I think it's one of mine. But . . ." He looked around again. "You can't stay here."

He was right about that. The light was eating the passage. Uneasiness threaded through me. For the first time, I was worried. "You think I should go through that door?"

"I do," he said. "And while you're in there, I'm going to create an exit for you. But when you see the way out, you have to take it. Promise me you will." His grip tightened on my fingers. "I need you to come back to me."

Kieran sounded scared. I didn't want him to be scared. "I promise."

He smiled. A worried smile, but the warmth of it still lit up the hints of hazel in the black of his eyes. I smiled back.

Then he let me go, and I went to the door.

And stepped through into a familiar room.

17

I *knew* this room. I'd been here before. I just couldn't remember when.

I peered around, taking it all in. A desk and a couple of armchairs. A thick rug beneath my feet. Heavy bookcases, stacked with books. I'd definitely seen those before, hadn't I? Why couldn't I remember?

There was movement behind one of the armchairs. A much younger Kieran straightened up from where he'd been retrieving a red book off the floor. I grinned at him. He stared right through me like I wasn't there. He couldn't see me. This was *his* memory, he'd said. And it wasn't the same as the other memories. I was just a witness here.

I moved into the corner so I'd have a good view of whatever was going to happen next. Kieran reached into his pocket to pull out a tiny, sparkling ball. He dropped it onto the book, but instead of rolling off, it sank in, disappearing through the crimson cover. Then Kieran strolled over to put the book on the shelves before heading back to slouch into the armchair.

There were footsteps outside. Kieran slouched further. And a man burst into the room.

154

I stared hard at the newcomer. I knew him too. Except I couldn't remember his name. At least not all of it. But it was Talks . . . something.

The man slammed the door and stalked across the room to tower over Kieran. "What. Have. You. *Done?*"

"Nothing much, brother," Kieran answered breezily. "Just wrote a little story. You're always telling me I should be doing more with my life."

"You told them we're not gods!"

He rose to his feet. "Because we're *not*."

Memory crashed over me like a wave, leaving me gasping. My room! I was in *my* room, in the tower. With Talks Sweetly. *Tomas.* And Kieran . . .

Kieran was Ronan.

Kieran was *Ronan!* How could I have not known who he was?

"But we *are* gods!" Tomas snapped. "At least, we are to these lesser beings. Why should they not serve our ends?"

"Other life does not exist for you and Allora to—" But he broke off, shaking his head. "Nothing I say will matter. You know, I used to think the war changed you. But it just gave you the opportunity to be who you really were all along. Elodie always understood you better than I did."

Tomas snorted. "I should think you'd have more sense than to listen to her! Have you *read* her testimony? I might object to your literary efforts, but at least it's not sentimental drivel."

He began to turn away. Ronan's gaze flicked to the red book and he spoke again, drawing Tomas's attention. "She calls you a mimicker, you know. One of those invertebrates that pretend to be flowers to lure in glowflies. El says you can be charming and funny and even kind. But it's never real. It's just the way you hunt."

Tomas opened his mouth to reply. But he didn't get a word out before light blasted from the book. It made a shimmering shape like water floating in air, and out of the shimmer came a red-haired woman holding a white blade. She launched herself forward, aiming for Tomas's unprotected back. But she'd hesitated before she'd moved and he was *fast*. He twisted out of the way and lunged, grabbing the weapon from her hand and shoving her away.

"A sensor gate, Elodie?" he snarled. "And an unraveler? The assembly has you well supplied, I see. Are the two of you really the best they could do?"

"You know the war decimated our numbers," Elodie shot back. "And you're *our* family. Our responsibility to deal with."

Tomas switched his furious glare from her to Ronan. "This is why you both came to this world, isn't it? Not to see me. To spy on me. To *stop* me."

Ronan shrugged. "Someone has to."

"You *disappoint* me, brother." Tomas's lips twisted into a bitter curl. "Not simply your betrayal, but the sheer futility of it! What did you hope to achieve by this? You know I cannot be killed with pathway in my system. Or . . ." He turned his gaze back to Elodie, studying her face. "Captured, is that it? Wound me badly enough that I could be taken? To where—those fools on the assembly?"

Elodie raised her chin. "They know, Tomas. We know. About the things you and Allora did in the war. The thefts. The experiments. The assembly has sentenced you both to death for the suffering you've caused. But failing death—yes, they'll settle for imprisonment."

He laughed. "They'll have neither. And I think they'll find Allora difficult to subdue, here in our city of gold."

Ronan hadn't taken his gaze off the . . . unraveler? in Tomas's hand. He was going to try for the knife.

Elodie knew it too. She drew herself up, curving her lip into a sneer. "Radiance brings *Allora* strength," she said. "But all that energy just keeps you functioning, doesn't it? What with the pathway slowly consuming you. Allora has a power generator. You have a life support system."

Ronan leaped for the blade. But Tomas knew he was coming. He swung around.

And threw the unraveler.

Elodie let out a high, desperate scream as the knife plunged into Ronan's chest. I tore across the room, dropping down by his side as he crumpled. His face was twisted in pain. But his eyes were fixed on his sister.

Then Tomas was on him, yanking out the knife. Ronan let out a choked cry, and I swung my fist at the sun-god. Uselessly, of course. It just passed right through him.

Blood was bubbling from Ronan's mouth, but he was still trying to speak. I leaned in to listen. He was gasping a single word, over and over. *Run.*

I yelled it for him. "Run, Elodie! He's going to kill you too."

But she was frozen in horror, staring at her little brother. And Tomas was pacing leisurely toward her, so certain of victory he wasn't even bothering to rush.

"Go!" I screamed at her. "I'll stay with him—he won't be alone, I promise. Elodie, you have to run!"

I didn't know if I somehow reached her or if she realized what Ronan was trying to say, but she grabbed for the book, and the light was back. Tomas charged at her but this time he was too slow. Elodie vanished into the light, and the book winked out of existence.

The sun-god let out a frustrated growl. Cast a single glance at where Ronan lay dying on the floor. Then stalked out without another word.

I hovered my hand over Ronan's. "You're not alone," I said. "I'm here. I'm here with you." But I wasn't sure he'd have been able to hear me even if I'd actually been in the room. His eyes were cloudy and the edges of his body were . . . melting? No. *Unraveling.*

Light flared, again. I looked up, thinking Elodie was back. She wasn't. The light was coming from a shining door that had appeared in the middle of the room.

The way out.

No. And for good measure I shouted it at the door. "No!"

Ronan was still alive. Still suffering. But this had all happened nearly two hundred years ago and I'd made *my* Ronan a promise. *I won't leave you.*

I howled out my grief and my anger.

Then I lurched to my feet and launched myself through the door.

Beyond it was only blackness. I was nowhere.

But I could hear a voice.

Tamsin. She sounded frantic. "Wake up! You have to wake up!"

Then Sasha, as frantic as Tamsin but saying things that made no sense. "The Gleam was just trying to talk to me. He didn't mean to hurt you. . . . Please wake up!"

I tried to move toward them. It felt like I was walking through syrup. I kept going, dragging my limbs onward. My friends were scared. And I'd made a promise.

One step. Two steps. Three . . .

My eyes opened and I sat up, gasping.

I was in a totally unfamiliar space. No, I was in the Cave. Looking straight across the room at Spite, who was deep in sleep. Tamsin was standing on one side of me, Sasha on the other, and everything smelled of—lemons?

Tricks yelled in my head. *You wouldn't wake up! I called you and I made a big smell and it woke Tamsin up but you wouldn't wake up!*

That explained the lemons. "I'm sorry. It's okay. I'm here. I'm . . ." Well, dizzy, actually. I put my head in my hands, shutting my eyes on a world that was insisting on whirling around me.

"Breathe, Bell!" That was Tamsin. "Give yourself time to adjust. It's disorienting when you first wake up."

She wasn't wrong about that. I didn't even know where I was—no, I did. *The Cave, remember?* And I was . . . I was . . . a Silverleaf. But which one?

You are Bell *Silverleaf,* I growled at myself. *You are in the Cave with Tamsin and Sasha and Tricks. And . . . and . . .*

And Ronan was alive.

That thought sent a mixture of joy and relief surging through me. The joy made me want to laugh and the relief made me want to cry and if I didn't get a hold of myself I'd end up doing both at once. I breathed through the feeling, letting it settle into a steady, warm glow of happiness. That, I could manage. Anything else was beyond me right now. My whole brain felt tender and fragile, strained and stretched from too much information. *Really* important information. But I couldn't think about any of it in this moment, because it seemed like if I did, my mind would split apart.

Tricks released another burst of scent, something sweet and soothing, and her own presence faded into sleep. Guess she'd exhausted herself trying to wake me up.

"Bell?" That was Sasha. "You're all right, aren't you? He didn't mean to hurt you."

She'd said something like that before. I cracked my eyes open, relieved to find the room had stopped spinning. "*Who* didn't mean to hurt me?"

159

"The Gleam." She sat herself down on the end of my chair. "He put something into the vapors. But he's taking it away now." She waved at the hole in the floor. The vapors coming up from the earth looked a little . . . green? I remembered they'd been clear before. But as I watched, the green faded away.

"It was something to make a stronger connection with a Gleaming so he could talk to me," Sasha explained. "He's been trying to contact Gleamings—that's what those flashes we've been having were. But whatever he put into the vapors made it hard for us all to wake up."

I blinked at her in total confusion. "You're saying the Gleam is here, somewhere? In the earth?"

"I don't know exactly where, but yes. Except don't you already know some of this? He said he spoke to you, too!"

"He did not—" Connections fired in my brain and I let out a yelp, doubling over and clutching at my skull.

Tamsin flung her arm around me. "Bell! What is it? Tell me what I can do!"

"It's okay," I managed. "I'll be all right in a moment. I just need . . . everyone to be quiet . . . for a little while."

They went silent, and I leaned into Tamsin, letting everything join itself together.

Someone *had* spoken to me. Or at least I'd had a memory from an other-worlder, the one who'd been tricked into giving up his pathway. The Vaulter. And he seemed to be some kind of living ship? Because he'd wanted a crew and humans had been able to walk through his veins. Lots of humans. The ones who'd answered his call. The Gleamings? Except they hadn't been walking through the veins of any Vaulter. They'd lived in the . . .

Realization sparked, sharp and painful.

The Gleam *was* the Vaulter. And the Vaulter was the Beneath.

My brain quieted once I'd made that link. Still painful, but bearable. I blinked my eyes open and straightened up.

"You okay?" Tamsin demanded.

I nodded. "Just . . . lots to process." Then I looked over at Sasha. "Can you still talk to the Gleam now?"

Her eyes went unfocused as she concentrated. Then she shook her head in frustration.

"It's like I can *feel* him, only right at the edge of my awareness. But I can't speak to him. Not like before."

"What did you talk about?"

"History, mostly," Sasha replied. "He's been sleeping for a long time. Recovering. The sun-god hurt him. He *never* left us, he was *hurt,* and so many of us converted to that—" She broke off and drew in a long breath. "Anyway. He wanted someone to fill him in. But . . . he didn't think much of what the Gleamings have being doing." Her gaze slid away from mine. "Or *not* doing. Especially over the Mistfall invasion. He asked why didn't we try to stop it? And the only answer I could give him was that we didn't want to risk our power." She looked over at me, then at Tamsin. "I should have said this before, but I'm saying it now. I'm sorry. The Gleamings were wrong not to stand with your people against the gods."

Oh, the Gleamings were wrong about a *lot* of things (so many things). But my hyperaware brain hadn't missed that she'd directed that apology at both me *and* Tamsin. "You know Tamsin's a Treesinger."

"That's my fault," Tamsin said. "I was shouting all kinds of things at you, trying to get you to wake up. Stuff about Treesingers."

"I won't tell anyone," Sasha said. "You can rely on me—" She stopped, shaking her head. "But you can't, can you? Because

161

Treesingers have never been able to count on the Gleamings." She lifted her chin, a determined glint in her eyes. "I'll *show* you that you can rely on me."

"Well," Tamsin said, "you're going to have heaps of time to do that." She nodded over at the snoring Spite. "About twenty-five years, in fact."

Yeah, because we were the *final three*. I supposed that should make me hugely happy, and it would later. Right now I just felt hugely relieved that we'd made it through. Not to mention so tired it was hard to keep my eyes open. I really needed some sleep, the kind with no dreams at all.

I looked over at the door. There was a lever next to it, just like Bernadise had said. I opened my mouth to say we should get out of here—and heard the noise from outside.

Tamsin did too. "Is that *shouting*?"

The three of us got up, making our way over to the lever. Tamsin pressed her ear to the door. "Seems like they're arguing about . . . *breaking down the door?*"

Oh. Because we'd been in here too long. "I think maybe we've been sleeping for ages. They must think there's something wrong."

Sasha grinned. "Let's show them that there's not." She pulled the lever.

The door slid slowly back to reveal a *lot* of people. Bernadise (looking very unhappy to see me awake). The Queen. A bunch of guards. And workers, armed with hammers as big as Bashy. They let out a cheer when they spotted Tamsin.

My gaze locked onto the Queen's. Images began to flash through my mind, one on top of the other. A brown-eyed woman who'd befriended Alethea Silverleaf. A hissing swirl of energy who'd fought Allora. But the picture that dominated all the others was the one of a red-haired girl who didn't want to leave her dying brother. I'd told her I'd stay and then I hadn't, and connections were sparking so rapidly my mind was on fire. It was all too painful and too much.

"I'm sorry," I whispered. And passed out.

18

I was floating, drifting in a pleasant haze.

Someone had given me something warm and soothing, and the pain was gone. The sparking connections were still there, but they'd settled gently into my consciousness. A network of threads, making a web that stretched across time and space and generations.

I'd been born into something that had started long before me. Over two hundred years before, in fact, when Tomas tricked the Vaulter . . . what was his name again? *Journeys Far.* When Tomas had tricked Journeys Far into handing over his store of pathway. That had led to the Mistfall invasion and, eventually, the sickness in Falling Leaves. And in between and around that, other things must have happened that weren't in the memories of my family. Where had Allora gone after she'd left here, and what had she done? Escaped Elodie, but not without a fight, because Allora had talked of Elodie and her allies coming against her. And where was Tomas? Hopefully curled up somewhere, slowly dying.

But while all of that was important, none of it was what mattered the most. *I know how to fix the grove.* I just had to locate and eat a pathway bead and hope I *was* the Silverleaf so I could ascend to a higher dimension and persuade a bunch of Ancients to help a Treesinger out.

Okay, when I said it like that, it sounded difficult. But it was still more information than I'd had yesterday.

Someone was speaking. More than one person? I was hearing a far-off conversation, the voices too soft for me to identify, although one of them sounded familiar. *Tricks?*

She spoke: We are well. We are safe. Then, smugly: We know many things.

A sense of contentment washed over me. There was nothing to do except stretch out my leaves to the sun and enjoy the moment.

Only there *were* things to do.

I clawed my way back to wakefulness, opening my eyes to find myself staring at a little bottle of blue liquid atop a familiar set of drawers. I was in my bed in my Testing Hall room, and I must've been sleeping for a while, because the view through the window told me that it was night outside. But I had no interest in what was outside. All I cared about was the person sitting by the bed.

He looked pale. Tired. But *here.*

I lunged up, flinging my arms around his neck. "You're alive."

He gave a surprised grunt and put his arms around me, holding me very gently as if he was scared I'd break. "Ah. I thought it might be that memory. Sorry."

I turned my head against his shoulder and closed my eyes, breathing him in. *Ronan.* My Blue. Then I forced myself to let him go, scooting back on the bed even though all I wanted to do was lean into him like I would into the warmth of a fire on a cold day. But there were things to be done and I had to do them alone. That was the Silverleaf way. Uncle Dar's voice suddenly echoed in my memory. *Secret keepers and show-offs.*

We were *not.*

Ronan was looking at me. I'd been quiet for too long. I scrambled for something to say and realized there *was* something I wanted to know. "How's Tamsin? Sasha?"

"Fine. *Very* unhappy at being separated from you. Elodie said she thought that if it hadn't been for the guards, Tamsin might have struck her. And Sasha is apparently making a complaint, although I'm not sure who to."

Sounded like they were completely themselves and absolutely okay.

An awkward silence fell. The room felt like it was filled up with all the things I couldn't say. But that was Silverleaf stuff. I could still talk about us. "I'm so sorry I didn't know you."

He shrugged as if it were nothing, when I knew exactly how much it must've hurt. Because I knew how I would have felt if he hadn't known me. "You never met me in an embodied form before."

I didn't see why that mattered. "*You* knew me."

"Ah, but the natural form of my kind is energy. It's how we see the world—the spirits of the life around us, not the bodies they inhabit. And I knew what your spirit looked like."

Because bodies were just a costume they wore. That made me feel a little better. And I guess I had known him, in a way, because I'd felt so comfortable around him. I still did. I just hadn't understood why.

"Besides," Ronan added, "I didn't know you until I was

standing right in front of you." His mouth twisted. "I got involved in the Test because Elodie enlisted my aid to help the Treesinger candidate. I didn't know that candidate was you. Not until we met."

I realized something. "You were the one who messed with the Bubble!"

"I was going to do it before anyone went into that monstrosity. Then the high priest changed the order—it's lucky you weren't killed!" He shook his head in frustration. "If anyone should be apologizing, it's me. I should have *found* you, Bell. Instead I just . . . stumbled across you. But I promise you, I was looking as best I could."

"I know," I said. "At least, I knew you were coming back. But— Ronan, where did you go?"

"I was—" But he stopped, frowning in thought. Then said, "Before I answer that, I need to explain a few things. About unraveling." He looked calm. At ease. But he wasn't fooling me. I'd heard the horror in his voice when he said "unraveling."

I shifted closer as he started to speak. "Like all life, my kind goes through cycles of renewal and decay. But unless we do something to expend all our energy at once, it takes a *long* time for us to exhaust our life force. When we finally do, we die and enter another cycle. That's a natural death. Being killed by an unraveler blade is different. It breaks our energy into tiny, disconnected pieces. Scatters us into the abyss."

I shuddered at the thought of him turned into nothingness. "But you came back."

"I shouldn't have. Not as myself. It's possible that after a long time—thousands of years—the pieces of energy that *were* me would have become something new. But I should never have been able to return as myself, as it were."

"Then how did you?"

He smiled faintly. "You, I think."

"*Me?* How?"

"That I don't know. I died. I was nothing. And then I wasn't. Or at least a part of me wasn't. A tiny fragment became . . . aware."

A single blue spark. Floating in a white nothingness. But, wait, just a fragment?

"What about the rest of you?"

"There was no rest of me. Not for a while. The pieces that had been me were in the abyss. But the fragment was . . . elsewhere."

"With me," I said. "The Ancestors—my Ancestors—brought me to you. And I took you out of the, um, abyss. It looked like an empty white space to me, and I saw you as a blue spark. Except I thought *all* of you came with me!"

He shook his head. "That would not have been possible. It was something of a miracle that even a single . . . spark? could return to awareness of myself as I had been." He leaned forward, resting his elbows on his knees and lacing his fingers together. "But that spark was the reason I came all the way back. It was still connected to the rest of me. A lifeline, out of the abyss. As it lived, I began to be drawn back together." He scowled. "Then my sister interfered."

"Interfered how?"

His mouth tightened. "When one of my kind dies, those close to them sense their passing and rebirth into a new cycle—and there came a point when I was sufficiently complete that Elodie could sense my return. Which was when she came and got me."

I couldn't understand why he'd be angry about that. "She took you out of the abyss? Isn't that a good thing?"

He shook his head furiously. "The abyss is a kind of . . . between space. I was able to grow there because of the lifeline of the spark, but I didn't have to be whole. But once I was out, *all* of me was pulled back together. I couldn't control it."

A terrible suspicion was brewing in my head. "Ronan, you didn't . . . you didn't stay in that void for me, did you?"

He looked away. Kept silent for a moment. Then: "I would have left eventually. When you were safe."

"*You would have left eventually?* You should've gotten out the second you could! I saw that place—it was horrible. I would *never* have asked you to stay there."

"You didn't have to ask me! You were in danger. The energies around you—they were bad. If the spark of me that was with you was gone, you'd be alone."

"And you'd be alive. *Properly* alive, instead of hanging around some . . . in-between space. Elodie was right to make you leave!"

"No, she wasn't!"

For a second the two of us just glared at each other. Then he threw up his hands and said, "Once I was fully myself, I was new. Weak, and embodied." He shook back his sleeves, revealing blue bands on his wrists. "These increase my strength—I stole them from Elodie's collection of devices after the Glass, so I could prove to you who I was. Because she refused to prove anything to you, even though she easily could ha—" He broke off, shaking his head, and I realized that was what they'd been fighting about. Elodie must've thought that if I knew who he was, I'd leave the Test. He'd certainly asked me to, maybe hoping I'd recognize him. *Run away with me.*

"Even *with* these," he added bitterly, "I don't have my full power. If I hadn't actually met you, it could've taken me years to find you."

"You *still* should have gotten out, Blue!"

He blinked. "Blue?"

Oh. "Um. It's what I called you, at first. That was before I knew who you were. Sorry."

"Call me whatever you like." He tilted his head to the side, watching me. "And answer me honestly. What would you have done if our positions had been reversed?"

"I would have—" But my voice seemed to choke itself off before I could say "gotten out." I just couldn't tell such a big lie. Not to him.

I admitted defeat. "I would have left eventually."

He threw back his head and laughed.

I liked to see him laugh. He'd liked to see *me* laugh, back when he'd been taking me to the Glass. I knew why now. And I couldn't stand to think of him not knowing what he'd been to me. Not knowing what he *was* to me.

"You were always with me, in the temple. I don't know what it looked like to you?"

"Bad energy," he replied promptly. "Big, swirling clouds of malevolence, and you in the middle of it. And I think you were hurt, once? Because you were leaking energy very fast."

"That was when I almost died." He sat bolt upright at that, but I shook my head before he could ask for details. I didn't want to talk about Alasdar right now. "It doesn't matter how. The point is, you saved my life that day. You and the Ancestors."

"Fair trade, I think. You and your Ancestors saved mine."

I edged forward and reached out, tangling my fingers in his. "I was in my own kind of void, in the temple. You were my lifeline, too."

He didn't say anything. But he was watching me with the warmth that brought out the hints of hazel in his eyes. I shouldn't move closer. I did anyway. Close enough to feel the heat of his body, and see the pulse jumping in his throat.

Close enough to kiss him, if I wanted to. And I did want to.

He bent his head toward mine.

And then the door swung open and Elodie strode into the room.

19

I jerked away, letting go of Ronan and scrambling back. Elodie looked between the two of us and shrugged dismissively. Then she sat down on the end of the bed. "You're better. Good."

"How nice of you to be concerned about her," Ronan drawled. "Did you know she almost died in the temple?"

"I did not," Elodie answered coolly. "But it would not have made a difference."

"Of course it wouldn't." His lip curled, and the mocking edge to his voice grew savage. "It didn't have to be her who was sent into your little Test. Any Treesinger could be Queen."

"That is not what I meant and you know it!" Her gaze went to me, and she held out her hand, almost pleadingly. Except I didn't think it was me she was pleading with. "There was nothing I could do to get you out, short of marching on the temple with the guard. That would have started a war the Risen guilds didn't want. They'd have lost no time in uniting with *both* temples to remove me as Queen if I'd done something so reckless." Her attention shifted back to Ronan. "You must see I could only act once I had their support."

"What I see is that the sister I knew would have done what was right," he bit out. "Not what was politically expedient."

There was an airless silence as the two of them stared at each other. But it was Elodie who looked away first. It dawned on me that they hadn't been back together for long, and before Ronan had died, his sister had been the red-haired girl who couldn't kill Tomas. He'd returned to someone very different. Seemed as if he'd liked her a lot better before.

I was furious with her too. Only it wasn't for leaving me in the temple. I had something much bigger than that to be angry about.

"He doesn't understand why you're so different," I said. "But I do. I know Alethea Silverleaf asked you to change."

Elodie's face drained of color. "How—"

"The story's been passed down in my family," I told her. "So I get how you turned into a person who made a cold choice. I could even forgive it—*if* you'd done what Alethea wanted you to. You were supposed to stop Allora. But you didn't. And now she's infected Falling Leaves grove with pathway."

"It's a little more complicated than that—"

Ronan made a derisive noise. "Why don't you tell Bell what happened and let her judge for herself?"

She pressed her lips together. "Very well, then. . . . After the Mistfall invasion, I chased Allora across the stars. Just as Alethea had asked. Pursued her for decades, until I caught up with her a little over three-quarters of a century ago. We fought a battle that exhausted us both and killed some of my allies." She lifted her chin. "But I destroyed all of the pathway she had."

All of the pathway she had. Only that wasn't all of their supply.

"Except Tomas had some. Because he has to keep eating it or he'll die. And—he can't be killed as long as it's in him?"

Elodie nodded. "Correct on both counts. Pathway puts him in a state of flux, existing between this world and another. He cannot be ended while in that state. But I could not access his portion of pathway. It was hidden in the sun-temple, buried behind protections against my kind."

"You could have tried to find a way," Ronan said. "But you didn't believe they'd use it for anything other than feeding Tomas. So you didn't make it a priority."

"It was all the pathway they had left!" Elodie snapped. "It made no *sense* for them to use any of it for an experiment. And yes, I had other priorities, and rightly so. What do you think would have become of Treesingers if I hadn't devoted the better part of a century to wearing the faces of devout Risen girls?"

I had no idea what she meant by that. Ronan saw my confusion, and explained: "Elodie has been taking the place of the candidates who win the Test."

"For how long?" But the second I asked that question, I knew the answer. Because things had started to change for Treesingers during the reigns of the last three Queens. "You've been Queen for *seventy-five years*? What happens to the girls?"

Elodie gave an irritable shrug. "I alter their appearance and memories. They live out their lives in another kingdom with no knowledge of who they were before." Her lip curled. "You need not concern yourself with their fate. They would certainly have no concern for yours."

Seventy-five years. The repeal of the laws that had made Treesinger lives miserable, the ever-widening gulf between the crown and temples, even the slow rise in popularity of the *Testimony of the Dawn* . . . it had all been Elodie.

She spoke again in a low voice. "I admit I was wrong about what they'd do. I can only think that as their supply dwindled and Tomas was facing the very real prospect of his own demise, they grew desperate enough to try anything, however unlikely it was to yield a result."

"Why didn't you *stop* Allora?"

"I did! Just not in time. I destroyed their pathway the moment I realized it was out of the sun-temple. But by then Allora had already introduced it into the grove."

"And," Ronan put in, "Tomas must *still* have some or he'd be very ill by now."

"I don't see how! I was sure I got it all—whatever he has left could only be a tiny amount—"

"You cannot be sure of that, sister. But by all means continue to dance around them both rather than confronting them directly."

I looked from one of them to the other. "The way you're talking about Tomas and Allora, it sounds like they're *both* here. In Radiance."

It was Ronan who answered, gently. "They are. Allora returned here after the battle in the stars, at the same time my sister did. And Tomas . . . Bell, he never left."

"He *never left*? But the priests say—" Oh. I stopped, realizing how ridiculous I sounded. "That was a lie."

"A lie the priests believe," Elodie said. "After Mistfall, Tomas couldn't keep performing the kind of miracles the Risen had come to expect from him. He was badly wounded in the battle with the Nexus. His 'departure' was nothing more than theater. He simply changed his appearance and has been playing the part of a priest ever since. Just as Allora plays at being a sister."

Two would-be gods. Hiding in plain sight, inside the temples that fed them energy. Allora's power generator. Tomas's life support system. Connections flared, and I had a sudden, sickening moment of revelation.

I knew who they were. I licked dry lips, and whispered, "Allora is the high priestess, isn't she? Bernadise?"

Ronan nodded. "Yes. And Tomas—"

But I held up a hand. "Stop. Don't say it. Please." Because as long as he didn't say the name—as long as no one did—I could pretend. I could make believe that Tomas was Alasdar. I *wanted* him to be Alasdar. Because Alasdar was a mean, stupid bully, and I hated him and always had.

Except Tomas wasn't like that. He was clever. Charming. Even kind. *But it's just the way he hunts.* I forced out the words. "Tomas is Eldan."

Ronan was watching me, eyes narrowed in concern. "You knew him. In the temple."

"Yeah." All this time, I thought I'd been brought to the sun-temple because Bernadise was there. But it had been because they were *both* were. The sun and moon gods, working together. Each of them desperate to get their hands on the only Falling Leaves Treesinger to recover from the "sickness," because they thought it might help them hold pathway.

What was it Bernadise had said about Alasdar? *A brutal dull-ard of a man. Although useful, on occasion.* She'd used Alasdar to get me into the temple. Except she'd never had total control of him. And when he'd been forced to let me go—when an unworthy Treesinger had gotten into the Queen's Test—his fury had broken through whatever hold she had. And Eldan . . . the way he'd come to see me. The way he'd pretended he was *helping* me by making a deal with the sisters . . .

But he'd always been pretending. My almost-friend. He'd made himself the one person I could turn to when I was worn-out from Bernadise and her "guidance," or Alasdar and his fists. One kindly old man to share secrets with, if I had any to share. He'd had a *lot* of fun manipulating me. And he'd taken something from me that Bernadise and Alasdar never could. Because nothing they'd ever done to me had made me feel so . . . small as I did now. I'd sneered at the Risen for years for being so easily fooled and it turned out I'd been just as stupid. *Here's some cake and sympathy, it'll only cost you your soul. . . .*

I was breathing too hard and too fast and dark spots were appearing in front of my eyes. Soothing scent burst around my head, and blood thrummed in a steady, calming beat. Then Ronan was at my side, pressing the little bottle of blue liquid to my lips. "Drink, Bell."

I did. It was the warm and soothing substance I'd had before. "What *is* that?"

"An all-healer. From elsewhere."

Other-world medicine. *Effective* other-world medicine. I took the bottle from him and drank the rest. Then I handed it back to Ronan and glared at Elodie. "Why do you let them just *walk around?*"

"Well, there's a good question," Ronan said. "It was one of the first things I asked her."

"And as I said to you, I don't *let* them do anything," Elodie snapped. "I fight them as best I can. Tomas cannot be killed with pathway in his system, and Allora is strong."

"But not unkillable," Ronan pointed out. "An unraveler blade would end her—"

"You know those things are next to impossible to obtain. And the assembly certainly won't give me another, not after we lost the last one." Elodie heaved a weary sigh. "I expect I could have done more, had I not been Queen. But . . ." She turned the full force of her gaze and her expectations on me. "That is about to change."

Oh, okay. This was why she was so obsessed with me getting that crown. I was supposed to carry on her work. There was no one she could trust more to look after Treesingers than an *actual* Treesinger, leaving her free to go off and fight the gods.

And on that thought, the connections in my mind sparked one last time. Drawing my attention to something I'd almost forgotten. A nonsense song, from long ago.

I lifted my chin and squared my shoulders, but I also let defiance leak into my face (like I'd take on the queenship, but I'd do it my way and she needn't think it was because of her because it wasn't). And the truth was, I'd take the crown if I could get it. But I had something far more important to do.

Because I knew where to find the pathway that Granny had stolen.

20

Turn to the right and step some more. . . .

The song *was* directions. Mum must have hidden the pathway that Granny took (no surprise it was Mum who had done the hiding when Granny had drained her energy getting hold of the stuff). And there was only one place Mum would have put something she was trying to keep safe from the gods and the Risen. A place they didn't even know still existed.

The pathway was in the Beneath.

I was *so* close to it. And with that realization came a sudden twisting of my stomach. I couldn't mess with the Silverleaf destiny by using up the pathway and then dying, or leaving and not coming back. I had to be sure I really *was* the one before I ate it.

But surely when I held the pathway, I'd know. I just had to get it.

I let my shoulders sag, slumping back against the wall. Then I made my eyes droop before opening them wide, blinking like I was fighting to stay awake.

The Queen took the hint. "You need more rest." She rose to her feet. "The vote will be held in the morning. I believe the traders are the likeliest to vote for you, along with your own people, of course. If they do, it will result in a tied vote."

For a second my worn-out brain didn't understand what she was saying. Then I realized—Treesingers and (maybe) traders for me, workers for Tamsin, and knights for Sasha. That left only the crafters, and their vote would go to either Tamsin or Sasha (probably Tamsin, because the worker guildmaster had voted against disqualifying Mimic). Which would give two of the final candidates two votes each. And it was the Queen who broke a tie.

"You will have a chance to make a final presentation tomorrow," Elodie said. "And you will have extra time, since you were deprived of the opportunity to deliver your original speech. Focus on the traders. In the meantime, I shall do what I can to sway them in your direction."

I gave a sleepy nod and added a yawn. She walked to the door and left. Ronan didn't.

When her footsteps had faded into the distance, he said, "You can stop pretending to be tired."

I sat up. "You knew I was faking?"

"I *am* the god of lies," he reminded me with a superior smile. But then he dropped the smirk and added, "Also, Tricks told me you were probably going on an adventure." He heaved a mournful sigh. "Without me."

"*Tricks* told you?" I remembered the voices I'd been hearing before, a far-off conversation. "You can understand her?"

He shrugged. "I'm good with codes. That's how I reprogrammed the Bubble. And language is a kind of code."

I tried to glare upward. "Tricks?"

We are two. But with Ronan we are three.

"What's that supposed to mean?"

Three is better than two. Then, defiantly: *With Tamsin and Sasha we are five. Five is better than three.*

Tricks thought I should bring the lot of them along with us. Granny would tell me that was the wrong thing to do. *Generations* of Silverleafs would tell me it was the wrong thing to do. But I couldn't ignore the steady beat of my blood beneath my skin. The Ancestors. Or what I'd always assumed was the Ancestors. But now I realized that the thrumming of blood was what the Nexus had felt like for Granny. I called out in my mind, *Nexus? Is that you?*

And the room around me disappeared.

I was . . . well, I didn't know where I was. Inside myself, somehow. I was standing in front of a tree, and although I'd never seen one in real life, I knew a Nexus when I saw one. Branches sprawled in all directions, covered in dark green leaves and hung with round, black seeds. The Nexus was tall. Wide. But not nearly as tall or wide as they would one day be, although they towered over me. They were still young.

I took a step forward, reaching out to rest my palm against the dark gray of their bark. "Hello, Nexus." And they had to know who I was, but it seemed polite to introduce myself anyway. "It's me. Bell Silverleaf."

Images pounded into my head, a barrage of pictures coming too fast for me to process. The Nexus was talking in the green language, but they were speaking too quick and with way too much complexity for me to understand. I clutched at my head. "Slow down!"

The images stopped. For a while there was nothing. Then the

pictures came back, but much simpler and moving slower. As if the Nexus was trying to communicate something to a little kid. I supposed I was a little kid compared with a Nexus (even a young one). They knew a *lot* on account of being born knowing what all the trees before them had known.

The sequence of pictures ended, then started again from the beginning. The Nexus was repeating themselves. Just as well, because I still didn't quite understand. But after another run-through, I realized the Nexus was telling a story. A story that didn't seem to have anything to do with pathway or the grove or the gods, but okay. Like my uncle Dar, trees often came at things from a sideways angle, but there was always a connection somewhere. Sometimes the connection wasn't clear to humans until years after the initial conversation, but that was trees for you.

I spoke out loud as the pictures repeated again, making sure I had the story right. "A long time ago, someone opened a door. . . ." Pain spiked in my head. I already had it wrong, although I wasn't sure how. . . . No, wait, I was. *Time.* I'd been talking about time as the Risen did, as if it ran in a line. But trees didn't think about time that way. Tree time moved in circles, patterns of life changing and connecting, and it all happened in the now.

I tried again. "Someone opened a door, and it happened a long time ago and it happened today and it will happen tomorrow, because there is no past, present, and future?"

A sense of satisfaction radiated out from the tree, so I kept going. "The door let something into the world—no, into *all* worlds." Because all life everywhere was connected, even if humans couldn't track those connections. But a Nexus could. "Something bad. And the bad thing would die if people didn't feed it. But we do feed it. With . . . with . . ." Images flashed. "Hate. Being selfish. Being greedy." And a thousand other things, but it all amounted to the same thing, so I said the word. *"Imbalance."*

The sense of satisfaction grew, and more images flashed. But this time the pictures were of me. First as a little kid, with Granny teaching me how to listen to Falling Leaves grove. Then talking to Tamsin, trying to teach her some of the ways. Then leaping from cloud to cloud, trusting my Ancestors to guide me. And, okay, it had to have been the Nexus who showed me which way the wind would blow, since they could see everything in the now, but same thing, really. Trees were my Ancestors too.

Treesinger things. The Nexus was showing me doing Treesinger things. And it was just like I'd said to Tamsin—being part of a grove meant trying to keep everything in balance, making sure all the life had the same chance to be who they were supposed to be.

I opened my mouth to ask how all that connected to pathway. But before I could get a word out, a long, thin branch snaked down and tugged at my shoulder, turning me around.

In front of me was a gray space filled with floating black balls that looked a bit like Nexus seeds. Some of the balls were glowing. Healthy. But others were dim. Cracked and broken. *Worlds.* The Nexus was showing me worlds. The ones that were in balance and the ones that weren't.

Then a crack in one of the broken worlds mended itself, and it glowed bright. The glow spread out, and some of the other worlds began to mend too. Not as much, but a little. And I understood. Fixing the balance in one place helped *all* the places.

I had a sudden, horrible moment of insight. "You want me to *mend* the Risen?" I swung around to glare at the Nexus. "I won't!"

The Nexus said nothing. Just stood there, being gentle and kind and patient.

"You want to talk about imbalance?" I growled. "Their whole society is built on it! Traders matter less than knights, and crafters less than traders, and workers less than crafters, and Treesingers less than anybody."

A soft, sorrowful breeze blew through the leaves. The Nexus agreed. But then another image flashed through my mind. Myself, and the crown. I wanted to say I might not be Queen, but it didn't matter. I knew what the Nexus was trying to tell me. I'd either be wearing the crown or right next to it. They thought it was an opportunity.

I snorted. "You think I can change them?"

A new picture. Five seeds thrown into a pool of water. The seeds were little. But the ripples they made were big, reaching all the way to the edge of the pool.

I sighed. "You think *we* can change them. Me, Tricks, Ronan, Tamsin, and Sasha."

I'd thought before that Silverleaf history was a web that stretched across time and space and generations. But what I hadn't realized was that the Nexus had been moving the strands of that web. Connecting energies together. Connecting people together. The Nexus had big plans. But I didn't want to talk about fixing the imbalances of the world. I had a question and I needed to ask it, even though the answer might break me apart. I had to know, once and for all.

I forced out the words. "Nexus? Am I *the* Silverleaf?"

Pictures flashed. Me. Mum. Granny. "It can't be all three of us!"

But the second I said that, I realized that it could. Because this had never been about one Silverleaf, to the Nexus. It had never even been only about Silverleafs. Mum or Granny could've walked pathway and come back. But the Nexus hadn't told them that.

Because I was the Silverleaf the Nexus had been able to connect with the other threads they needed to make the pattern of a future they wanted to come to pass.

My family had been trying to kill a god. The Nexus was trying to heal all worlds.

And I could help them, or not. The Nexus would never force me. I could still choose to do this alone.

But I didn't want to.

And with that realization, I was back in my room.

"Bell?" Ronan looked terrified. "Are you here?"

"Yeah. How long was I, um . . . ?"

"Staring vacantly into space? About five minutes. It felt a lot longer." He sagged into his chair. "But Tricks said you were okay. *Are* you okay?"

"I'm fine. Can you go get Tamsin and Sasha for me? I need them."

He scanned my face and must have been satisfied with what he saw, because he left to go get the others. I reached up my hand to Tricks, who wound around my fingers. Five is better than two.

Which was her way of saying *I told you so*. But her voice wasn't as confident as usual. And I realized she wasn't surrounding me with people just because it was what the Nexus wanted. Tricks was worried.

"We'll be okay," I whispered. And hoped I was right.

In the next moment the door opened again and Tamsin and Sasha came charging in, carrying their weapons. They abandoned them on the floor to rush over, both speaking at once. Mostly asking if I was all right.

"I'm better, promise," I reassured them. Then I waved to the bed. "Sit down. I've got a *lot* to tell you."

They sat on the bed, alternating between casting concerned glances at me and suspicious ones at Ronan. Well, that seemed like a good place to start. I nodded at him and said, "Sasha, Tamsin—meet Ronan. God of lies."

He swept an elaborate bow.

"He's not a god," Tamsin spluttered. "He's the Queen's nephew. And anyway the god of lies is dead!"

"I'm the Queen's brother," Ronan replied, throwing himself into the chair he'd been sitting in before. "Pretending to be a nephew from an obscure branch of the family was just a convenient way to get me into the court."

Sasha put it together. "Her brother . . . Are you saying the Queen is *Elodie?*"

"Yeah," I said. "Um . . . let me start from the beginning."

But I couldn't make any more words come out. Everything in me was screaming that Silverleafs didn't give up Silverleaf secrets. Except the things I knew hadn't ever been only Silverleaf secrets. They were Nexus secrets too, and if I didn't trust the Nexus then I was no true Silverleaf. And besides, I wasn't only a Silverleaf. Holdfasts found strength in sharing.

I sucked in a deep breath and forced out words. The more I spoke, the easier it got, until the story flowed freely. About Journeys Far and pathway. The gods and the Nexus. And the grove sickness.

Now and then they interrupted me to ask a question or get me to explain something again. I talked and talked, until finally everyone ran out of questions and I ran out of story.

There was a long, thoughtful silence.

Ronan was the one to break it. "Pathway is dangerous. Poorly understood, even by those who've studied it for years. And I don't like the idea of you trying to travel it. But if you think this is the way . . ." His lips quirked into a smile that warmed his eyes but didn't hide the worry. "Then I'm with you, Bell."

"We all are," Tamsin said. Sasha nodded agreement. And Tricks sent petals exploding around my head.

I looked at them all. And maybe it was the Nexus speaking, but I could almost see the connections shimmering through the air. The way they made me stronger. The way they made all of us stronger. I felt very . . . Holdfast.

I grinned at my friends. "Let's go save the grove."

21

Falling Leaves.

We'd sneaked out of the Hall and through the streets to get here. Now I just had to get us inside.

We stood in front of a tangle of gray, thorny vines that soared up into the night, enclosing the grove in a spiky dome. They were part of the grove dormancy, which meant they weren't growing anymore. But they weren't growing any *less,* either. Cut off a thorn and it came back, and pretty quick, too. Up close I could see that some of the thorns were smaller than others, which probably meant the sisters were still sawing them off. Studying dormancy, like they studied everything about Treesingers.

I jammed my palm onto a thorn, hissing as it sliced into my skin. I needed the grove to recognize me, and tasting my blood was the only thing that was going to work. It was too deeply asleep to be reached in any other way. Especially since I wasn't a Falling Leaves Treesinger anymore, not since Granny had separated me from the grove. But I *had* been, which meant I should be able to get inside.

Blood seeped out, dripping onto the vines. I felt a rush of heat and eased my palm off the thorn. The wound was closing over. The grove still knew me. In the next moment, the entire tangle shuddered, and vines slithered back to make a hole.

I held out my good hand in the direction of the others. "We have to make a chain. Go through together."

Tamsin's fingers closed over mine. Sasha held on to her, and Ronan on to Sasha. We stepped into the opening, walking through the thick tangles. One step. Two. Three. Four, five, six . . . we were inside.

I let go of Tamsin, turning away from her and everyone else as the vines slid back into place. Sasha said my name, but I didn't answer. It was left to Tamsin to murmur, "Give her a moment."

I was grateful not to have to say any words myself. I didn't have any words. I was home. But I wasn't. Because it wasn't supposed to be like this.

The whole place was glowing with a soft white light. Here and there I could see the shapes of animals sleeping. No humans, because they were farther in, curled up inside the Dewdrop trees. Everything was quiet. Too quiet. And the trees and plants were gray and dull. Falling Leaves was drained of color and life.

Tricks huddled into my hair, flattening herself against my scalp. I reached up to pat her leaves. Then I sucked in a breath and started forward, calling over my shoulder as I went: "Follow me."

My voice came out clipped and hard and shorn of emotion. A dead giveaway that I was in pain. *Stupid.* Except that I was with friends and had no need to lie. But I still didn't like to hand out truth by accident.

I walked on, keeping my eyes fixed on the earth. I didn't want to look around, and I didn't need to. Memory was enough to guide me. I moved along one familiar trail after another until I reached the Tangler tree.

It loomed up in front of us, its roots coiling and twisting like snakes. The roots were taller than me. Taller than Tamsin, even. Tangler trees were enormous. I made an effort to sound more like myself as I spoke. "We need to go in here. I'll guide you all through."

Now I was unnaturally loud and way too cheery. I'd overcorrected, and I could practically feel the concern radiating from Ronan, Tamsin, and Sasha. I ducked into the roots before anyone could ask if I was okay.

The glow was dimmer in here but I knew where I was going. I wound my way deeper, then deeper still, until I arrived at the passage into the earth.

"There's a way down right in front of me," I said. To my relief, I sounded normal. Well, mostly. "I'll go first. Just wait a little while between people going in, or we'll all land on top of each other."

I crouched down by the opening to the tunnel and pushed off the edge, sending myself sliding down soft moss. For the space of a minute or so, everything was dark. Then light shone from below, and I tumbled out into the Beneath.

I jumped to my feet and got out of the way so the next person could come down. I was standing in a black crystal cave that had a bunch of tunnels running off it (most of them caved in). Pretty much all of the Beneath was like this. Partly whole and partly not. Even some of the thin lines of blue that ran along the walls were broken, split into pieces. But all those lines shone, making it bright enough to see.

Tricks chirped hopefully, Hello, Journeys Far!

No answer. I walked over to rest my hand against a wall.

"Journeys Far? It's me, Bell Silverleaf. You talked to me before. Showed me how the sun-god took your pathway."

Still no answer. Just like every other time a Treesinger had talked to the Beneath. And we'd been pressing our hands against walls and giving thanks for safe passage every time one of us came down here for nearly one hundred and fifty years. We'd thought the Beneath was caves, of course, but caves were alive just as all things of earth were. No way to know we'd been trying to talk to a sleeping other-worlder. But he was awake now, and *still* not answering. Maybe he didn't want to talk? Although . . .

I studied the blocked passages and bits of crystal littering the floor. If this was all one giant being and parts of him were in pieces, maybe he *couldn't* hear me. Or maybe he could, but couldn't talk back. He'd used the vapors to connect with me and Sasha in the Cave, and there were no vapors here.

Someone shouted: "Weapons coming!" In the next moment, Bashy slid down the passage, followed by Sasha's sword. I ran to drag both out of the way as Tamsin followed, then Sasha and Ronan. The three of them got to their feet and stared at the Beneath. And just as Tricks and I had, Sasha immediately called out to the Gleam. She didn't get any answer either.

Sasha shook her head in frustration. "I can *sense* him, stronger than before! I think maybe he's aware that I'm here? But . . . he can't seem to speak to me."

"He's—well, a bit hurt." I waved at the chunks of crystal. She made a choked, distressed noise.

"Vaulters are resilient," Ronan told her. "Old, legendary beings. Next to impossible to kill. They'll recover from virtually any wound, given long enough."

That seemed to cheer her up, so I didn't point out the obvious, which was that the Vaulter had been wounded for over two hundred years, being as this damage had happened when Tomas came. But maybe that wasn't very long for a Vaulter.

Tamsin cast a doubtful glance around. "Are you sure Journeys Far doesn't mind us being here?" she asked. "Because I don't think I'd want a bunch of people stomping around my insides."

"It's not like that for them," Ronan answered. "Vaulters are a little like ships, but ones that sail through the stars and not the seas." He shrugged. "Or so the stories say. Vaulters are a rare species. Not like my kind, who are everywhere. Or at least we were. The war thinned out our numbers considerably."

Sasha was still staring at the broken bits of crystal, her gaze sad. "It's why the Gleam ended up here, isn't it? What was the war about?"

"Power," he answered. "Resources. There was a dispute between worlds, over something valuable. The conflict grew from there, raging across species and planets. Lasted for generations, and nobody actually won. It just burned itself out."

"Seems kind of pointless," I said.

"Many wars are." He sighed, and looked over at me. "Where to next?"

That was a good question. I walked back to where I'd first landed in the Beneath, repeating the words to Mum's song in my head.

One step, two steps, three steps, four
Turn to the right and step some more

Four steps from the entry and a turn to the right put a tunnel directly in front of me, and it wasn't one of the collapsed ones. "This way!"

I continued to play the song in my mind as we all trailed down the tunnel.

When you reach the place of eight . . .

"We're looking for a 'place of eight.' Except I don't know exactly what that means. The directions aren't very clear."

Each of us began to examine our surroundings in search of anything that fit the clue. Which meant we inched along *really* slowly. I was starting to think I'd misinterpreted the song when Tamsin said, "Look! Right here."

She was standing by the wall, where one of the blue lines split apart. Into . . . I counted. Eight strands. "That's got to be it."

Step left and left and then step straight.

"We have to go left." But there was no left, at least not here. The passage forked into two just ahead, though. Close enough. I charged down the left branch and when the passage forked for a second time, I went left again.

That put us into a wide tunnel that broke into three in the far distance. I pointed. "When we get there, we go straight. And then we're almost to the pathway!"

We'd reached the next fork. I went straight, and everyone else followed. Except Tamsin, who'd stopped. So we all stopped as well. "What is it?" I asked.

She hefted Bashy and frowned. "I don't know." She lifted the hammer higher, holding it next to her ear. "It's almost like it's . . . buzzing? Seems to be getting louder, too."

Ronan shouted, "Throw it away, Tamsin. Now!"

Tamsin reacted fast to the panic in his voice, sending Bashy hurtling down the tunnel. Blue lightning shot from Ronan's fingers, arcing through the air to break Bashy into pieces.

The whole thing had only taken a few seconds. But it was a few seconds too long.

In the moment before the hammer shattered, a horribly familiar shimmer poured out of it, and two people came tumbling into the Beneath.

The sun and moon gods were here. And Allora had the unraveler in her hand.

Ronan breathed a single word at the rest of us: "Run."

Then he went striding toward them.

He was no match for both of them together, especially not when he wasn't fully recovered from returning to life. And, okay, none of the rest of us were a match for them either (particularly since Tomas was unkillable). But five was still better than one. And I was *not* leaving Ronan to die.

Nor was anybody else. Tamsin surged forward almost as quick as Ronan had, putting herself in front of Sasha and me even though Sasha was armed and she wasn't. *Blackbark blood.* Sasha moved to follow her, but I grabbed hold of her arm.

She tried to shake me off. I tightened my grip. *"Wait."*

I don't know what she heard in my voice, but she went still. Waiting. Even though I hadn't told her why. I couldn't have told her why, because I didn't know. But the Nexus was pounding in my blood and I knew our best chance at getting out of this depended on me standing right here for now and Sasha staying with me.

Allora cast a frustrated glance around. "It is not here." She directed one of her disapproving stares at Eld—no, Tomas. "You said you'd programmed the gate to activate in the presence of pathway."

"I said it would activate in the *vicinity* of pathway," Tomas corrected her. "Believe me when I tell you there is pathway here. Somewhere up ahead."

Allora twisted to look past us and down the tunnel beyond. She licked her lips with an awful, creepy hunger. Then her gaze fell on me, hardening into contempt. "When Elodie was so anxious to free you from the Cave, I knew you must be working with her. After all I have done for you. After all *we* have done for you!"

Tomas touched her arm. "It is not entirely her fault she was led astray. My family have always been guileful." He gave a sorrowful shake of his head. "But, Bell, I do wish you had felt able to confide in me before allying yourself with them."

I wanted to rip his lying face off. But the Nexus thrummed out a warning. I couldn't show him my true feelings. Not yet. He wouldn't be showing me his true face either, not when he thought he still had a shot of manipulating what I knew out of me. And he *did* think that, because believing otherwise would mean believing that everything about me had been a lie. And he'd never accept that he could be deceived by a mere human.

Okay, sun-god. Let's play.

I choked out words in a broken voice: "I didn't tell you about sacred things I was sworn to keep secret. You didn't tell me *anything* about who you really were. And I thought you cared about me!"

"I *do* care about you. And I wish now I'd been more forthcoming. I fear I left you vulnerable to manipulation." His gaze switched to Ronan, and he heaved a heavy sigh. "I don't know what lies my brother has been feeding you. But, Bell—you and I have been friends for a long time. You might not have known I was the sun-god, but you do know *me*." His lips quirked into a gentle, hopeful smile. "Whatever he's said, it isn't true. And there's still a place for you with me, if you want it."

Oh, he was good. But so was I. And I had truth to give substance to my deception, since the humiliating reality was that everything *hadn't* been a lie. I let my all-too-genuine hurt at Eldan's betrayal show in my face as my gaze flicked rapidly between him and Ronan. Buying time. Because the Nexus was trying to tell me something.

The pounding beneath my skin increased, and my awareness split in two. At one level, I heard Tamsin snap at Tomas, "You were *never* her friend" and Sasha hiss in my ear, "You can't believe him, Bell!" I saw Ronan cast a quick, urgent glance back at me, which I had no difficulty interpreting as *Stop messing around with lies and get out of here.*

But at another level, connections flared, too fast for me to follow until Tricks released a scent so sharp it was almost bitter. I inhaled and my brain seemed to speed up, recognizing the importance of things I'd seen and heard. Bringing everything together.

The thorns being cut off the vines that surrounded the grove.

The medicinal salve Bernadise had invented to treat Eldan's "wasting sickness." A salve that *constantly* burned his skin.

The way the Metaphorics had started wearing their medallions *beneath* their robes at about the same time I'd come into the temple. They must have been copying their leader, because if I was right, he *had* to wear his medallion next to his skin.

Those thorns hadn't been cut off by random moon-sisters. It was Allora. And then she'd used them to make some kind of solution that she'd been putting into the medallion that Tomas wore. Something that soaked continually into his skin. It must keep the pathway in him dormant, like the grove was dormant. So he could exist without eating any, and it wasn't eating him. Which meant if that medallion was gone . . . Actually, I didn't know what would happen. Except it couldn't be good for Tomas. We'd have a chance.

But I had no idea how. . . . No, wait. I did. And my heart pounded even louder, but now it was in excitement.

We might just make it out of this after all.

22

The Beneath snapped back into focus.

I let the confusion fade from my face. But I made sure to sound a little uncertain as I spoke to Tomas. "I won't join you. I . . . I can't." It was important that he believe I wasn't totally convinced I was doing the right thing, although I had no idea why. But I was a Silverleaf and I trusted the Nexus.

"I'm so sorry to hear that, Bell." His attention shifted to Ronan. He spread his hands wide, tiny yellow sparks dancing across his fingers. Not attacking, yet. Just being menacing. "You know you can't defeat us, brother. Why waste your energy?"

Ronan's lip curled, and his hands crackled with blue. Like Tomas, he did nothing more. But everyone in this tunnel knew an almighty fight was about to break out. Including Allora, who was eyeing me suspiciously. She was rightly distrustful of me, and that was going to be a problem. I only had one chance to do what I needed to do and I couldn't have Allora getting in my way.

Tomas spoke again, all softness and persuasion. "Stand aside,

Ronan. There's no need for this to become violent. I truly don't wish to kill you."

"Oh, I know you don't," Ronan drawled. "If I die here, the secret of how to survive an unraveling dies with me. *How* you both must be wondering about that."

That drew Allora's attention, with an echo of the same longing she'd shown for the pathway. Although it was nothing compared to the hunger in Tomas's face. Because he hoarded knowledge like pebbler-mice hoard stones. Not everything about Eldan had been a lie, either.

I took advantage of the moment to lean in and whisper to Sasha, "I need you to distract Allora. But don't do anything until I say so, okay?"

She nodded as Ronan spoke again. "How about this, brother? You stand aside, and I'll spare your life." He cast a quick, pleading glance at me, still wanting all of us to run, and added, "It's a better chance than you gave me, the last time we fought."

Tomas didn't bother answering. At least not with words. Electricity burst out of him, crackling at Ronan. But Ronan had already moved, flinging himself to the side and sending blue sparks cascading back at Tomas.

I hissed at Sasha, "Now!"

She hurtled toward Allora, yelling and brandishing her sword. Allora fired a blast of white sparks but her aim was off, thanks to Tamsin hitting her arm with one of the chunks of crystal she was throwing with impressive accuracy. I dove for the floor, looking for my own bit of crystal. I needed exactly the right one. . . . There! As my hand closed around it, Tricks released a scent that flooded my limbs with unbelievable strength and I leaped up, plunging into a battle I could no longer see.

Everything around me had changed into a mass of possibilities, a muddle of potential that shifted and changed . . .

. . . and aligned, to reveal a single, lovely opportunity.

I raised my arm and threw, pouring every scrap of my hope and desperation and newfound strength into the shot. The crystal chunk barreled through the air, heading for a target it should have been next to impossible to hit. Well, impossible for anyone else.

But not for a Silverleaf, a Traveling, and a Nexus.

The crystal hit home, striking the medallion Tomas was wearing under his clothes and shattering it into pieces. Possibilities winked out of existence, leaving me standing amongst a storm of sparks and blinking at Tomas. He was dead pale and swaying on his feet. The protection of his medallion was gone, and the pathway was eating him again. I bet it was hungry.

Somebody shouted, "Bell! Watch out!"

A wave of white energy was coming right at me. Allora. Blue sparks roared into it, absorbing most of the wave. But not all of it.

Then someone slammed into my side, shoving me to safety. And the wave hit them instead.

Sasha flew backward, sword falling from her hand as she crumpled into a heap against the wall. The tunnel filled with a furious barrage of blue and I tore after Sasha, getting to her a second before Tamsin did.

She was alive. Shaking, but her eyes were half open and aware.

"Go . . . ," she coughed. Blood ran from the corner of her mouth. "You have to go, Bell."

"I'm not going anywhere." But Sasha was. She was dying.

Tamsin knew it too. She pressed Sasha's shoulder gently and whispered, "You did good." Then she reached for the sword. She could do nothing for Sasha. But she might be able to do something about the gods.

There was a rush of air as Tricks leaped from my head to Tamsin's, showering her in petals and scent. Tamsin inhaled and her eyes widened. Then she grabbed that sword and went pelting away with a shout that was almost joyful, moving so fast she was a blur in the air.

I gripped Sasha's hand. "You hold on, Sasha. Just hold on."

"'S okay." Her voice had gone dreamy. Content. "Did good. Tamsin said so. Helped . . . and others will help . . . now the Gleam is back. Knights will change . . ."

"I don't want those other knights! Listen to me, Sasha! You're not just any knight, you hear me? You're *our* knight."

That actually brought her back, a little. "Really?"

"Really. And there's only one of you. So you had better live. Promise me you will."

She was focusing now, or trying to. "Promise. Now . . . go."

I didn't want to. But I was no help in the fight, and anyway the only way to truly end this was if Tomas could be killed.

I cast one last glance back at the battle. Tomas was firing bolts of electricity, but they seemed pale and weak compared with what he'd been able to do before. Ronan was subjecting him to an onslaught of blue, forcing Allora to defend him. And Allora was powerful, just as Elodie had said. With one hand she was generating sparks that clashed with Ronan's; with the other she slashed at Tamsin with the unraveler. But Tamsin herself was a whirlwind, dancing in and out with the sword.

I willed them all to survive. Then I turned my back and ran, filling my mind with the song.

Now you're almost done, my love
Just once more left . . .

The tunnel split ahead of me. I went left, and kept on running. And running, for what seemed like forever. Finally it branched again, breaking into passages that went off in every direction.

I stopped, breathing hard. All the passages looked the same! This couldn't be right. I'd taken a wrong turn somewhere. I wanted to scream in frustration and fear. But the only sound that came out was a whimper.

Then I noticed that one of the passages was rising upward. It was a gradual, gentle curve, but it was there.

And then, above.

23

I tore along the tunnel. It rose up and up. Twisted to the right. And ended.

I stumbled to a stop. There was nothing here except for some bits of crystal scattered across the floor! If I'd miscalculated I was never going to find my way to that pathway, at least not in time. The Beneath was huge.

The Beneath was alive.

I stared down at the crystal, breathing through the panic that threatened to choke me and forcing myself to think. Mum wouldn't have left something as important as the stolen pathway sitting out in the open. She'd have covered it up, with (let's say) a stack of rocks. Someone had taken it, and no Treesinger would've been in this out-of-the-way dead end.

"Journeys Far!" I called out. "It's Bell Silverleaf. I'm the Treesinger you talked to. I want to bargain for your pathway. I need it to stop Tom—I mean, Talks Sweetly."

For a moment there was silence. Then a voice thundered from

the walls. "You think you can deceive me? My senses might not be working as they should, but I can feel *him* through the Gleaming child. You have both betrayed me! You brought him here!"

"We did not!" I yelled back. "Talks Sweetly tricked us—you must have seen it!"

But as I said those words, I realized that he hadn't. I was sure now that he couldn't see or hear into all of his veins, not even through his connection with Sasha. I hurried to explain. "He hid something in my friend's weapon, a kind of gateway that let him in. None of us would *ever* help him."

"Why should I believe you?"

"Because he's my enemy too. Tomas—that's what Talks Sweetly calls himself now—invaded my homeland and slaughtered my people. You know that's true, Sasha told you . . ." My voice trailed off as I realized I was just babbling bits of information he already had. I needed to give him something else. I tried again. "My family—we're guardians. We look after the Nexus trees, and Tomas killed almost all of them trying to hold the pathway. Silverleafs have been fighting him ever since. How do you think you even got it back? My granny stole it from him, and my mum hid it here."

"So you say," he replied coldly. "And what was returned was only a tiny fraction of what was taken."

"The rest was destroyed. Or eaten, by Tomas. My friends are fighting him *right now*. Sasha got hurt bad doing it—you must be able to sense that!"

"She does seem . . . farther away," he conceded. "But I will not give Talks Sweetly pathway to save her. I cannot."

"That's not what I'm asking, and they wouldn't want me to!

Listen to me—I can walk it and come back. I'm going to use it to ask the Ancients how to get rid of Tomas for good."

There was a rumbling in the passage, and I realized he was laughing. "Impossible!"

"It's not, I promise you it's not. I've got this . . ." *Um, magic tree?* The Nexus didn't seem like something he'd understand without a lot more context. Which I really didn't have time to give him.

I also didn't have a choice. "The Nexus trees I talked about before, they are—"

He interrupted me. "I am familiar with what is rooted in your blood. It was they who disturbed my contemplative cycle and directed me to the means to contact the Gleaming child—and you. I admit, they are a power."

The Nexus, again, pulling threads across time and space. "Then you know I can do this! *We* can do this, the Nexus and me together."

"I know they have faith in you. But that does not mean their faith is justified. The likeliest outcome is that pathway will kill you as it has so many before. Or you will leave and never return. Such a slim possibility is an insufficient trade."

I wanted to scream that everyone might be dying and I needed that pathway right *now*. But that wouldn't do any good. And— Wait, "insufficient trade"?

That meant he *would* trade, if I came up with the right price. Maybe something rare—next to impossible to obtain. . . . "How about I throw in an unraveler blade?"

"An unusual sparkly. Difficult to acquire. But you do not appear to have one."

"I can get one."

"What a resourceful human you are! Come back when you have."

I bit back a growl of anger. "What *do* you want, then?"

"Ah. Now that, little Treesinger, is a most pertinent question."

There was a grinding noise. And the ground opened up beneath me.

I let out a yell as I plunged into total darkness. Then light shone from below, and my descent slowed. I floated down to land in front of a single massive crystal, black and glittery and lovely. I'd never been in this cavern before. But I recognized it from his own memory. This was his heart.

Journeys Far spoke again. "You will have observed that I am damaged. Unaware, in many parts of my being."

"Yeah. I know the Risen destroyed you—well, tried to. In Tomas's name." Because that was what Sasha said had happened.

"How very like him, to claim a defeat as a victory! No one destroyed me, Bell Silverleaf. I went deep to evade Talks Sweetly, who would surely have come for my other sparklies once I was fully incapacitated by the infection he introduced into my body."

Oh. Journeys Far had sunk *himself.*

"However," he continued, "matters did not eventuate as I had anticipated."

"Because you got hurt?"

"The hurt is nothing. A simple matter to repair. Or it should have been. But while I have fixed some of the damage to my systems, I cannot do more while the source of the infection remains somewhere inside me. With my senses failing, I have . . . a limited realm of awareness. I cannot determine its location."

I saw now where this was going. "You want me to find the heart compass? Because that might take a while."

"You are quite correct. I suspect it will require more than one human too. But the Gleaming said the people of trees are many."

I got it now—he wanted me to make a promise on behalf of Treesingers. Except he was asking for something we'd do for nothing. Only he didn't know that.

I opened my mouth to promise—

—and the Nexus roared.

I couldn't get a word out, not with the Nexus storming through my body. They spoke in an angry whirlwind of images that I had no difficulty in translating: **If you deceive him now, you are no better than Tomas!**

I shouted back inside my mind, *If I don't he might not give me the pathway and everyone will die!*

In response they threw my own words back at me: **You want to talk about imbalance? Their whole society is built on it!** Right after that came another image. Glowing worlds, and broken ones. Then my words again, and the picture, and the words . . .

Stop! I shouted in my mind. *I get it.* The difference between broken worlds and whole ones was whether the people in them held themselves accountable to balance. And it wasn't enough to be a little bit accountable. It was all or nothing.

I was a liar and I wanted to lie.

But I was a Treesinger and I had to tell the truth.

The Nexus faded, subsiding to a soft thrumming under my skin. I could speak again, and I did. "You're asking for something you don't need to ask for."

"I think I know what my requirements are!"

"That's not what I mean. You see, Treesingers have been traveling through your—um, veins so we could move around without being seen by the Risen. You helped us. Generations of us."

"You are saying that your people are indebted to me?"

"Yeah. We actually tell you that, every time we come through. Guess you can't hear with your senses damaged. But the point is, you don't need to trade with any of us for help. We'll just . . . help."

Silence. Then: "I fear you are a poor bargainer, Bell Silverleaf. Telling me this is not to your advantage."

"I know," I replied glumly. "But my Ancestors would've been ashamed of me if I hadn't."

"Ah. I do know a little about trying to live up to the expectations of your Ancestors." A regretful sigh echoed through the cavern. "But we have no trade, person of trees."

We didn't and everyone was going to die and it'd all be my fault. I tried desperately to think of something, anything, I could offer him. And then a connection flared, drawing my attention. The memory I'd experienced, of when he'd lost the pathway.

I didn't need to offer him anything at all. I just had to remind him who he was.

"Give it to me anyway," I said. "Trade it for the chance that I can do what I say I can."

"Why would I do such a thing?"

"Because," I told him, "you're *Journeys Far*. You go where you shouldn't, just to see what's there. And maybe I'll eat the pathway and die. But if I don't—if this works—then you get to be a part of something no one's ever done. Also," I added in a moment of inspiration, "I'll come back with some tales to tell. Wouldn't you like to know what's on the other side?"

Rumbling laughter again. But friendly instead of mocking this time. "You are a bold and foolish human who is *far* more likely to fail at this endeavor than to succeed. But . . . I do believe I'd like to see you try."

There was a whooshing noise, and part of the wall slid away to reveal a dark hole. After a moment something came floating out, bobbing on air. *Pathway!*

And Journeys Far said, "Make both our Ancestors proud. If you can."

24

I raced across the cavern. Grabbed hold of that spiky red bead. And swallowed it down.

The world splintered into pieces. So did I.

I was nothing. Just fragments, floating in space. Or maybe I was stars. No, maybe I was worlds.

But I was too many and too much. So many worlds. So much life. It was chaotic and confusing, and I didn't know what to do. Maybe if I got some distance, things might be clearer? I separated myself from all-that-was and moved away, trying to see everything at once. But it didn't work, and I began to drift apart.

I was lost.

And I heard my mum's voice:

Everything returns to the earth. . . .

My nose filled with the rich scent of the dirt of Falling Leaves. I fell into it. Becoming earth. Going home.

But everything returns from the earth too.

Something drew me upward. I turned into a sprig that would

one day be a tree, shooting out of the soil. Other trees loomed around me, young, old, and in-between. I felt stupid, and a little embarrassed. Only an idiot would try to understand the whole of something by moving *away* from it. Treesingers understood our groves by getting close. By looking after them, as they looked after us. Except I didn't see how that applied to all life everywhere— Oh. Wait, I did. Alethea Silverleaf had said it, long ago. *Love crosses worlds.*

Which probably meant I was supposed to care about everyone and everything. Easy enough to care about trees, animals, plants, and such. Or beings from elsewhere like the Vaulter. Tomas and Allora, though? I wasn't sure I could do that.

Good thing it wasn't up to me.

The Nexus began to sing. It was a song I'd never heard before, and it was about . . . well, lots of things. Birds flying. Beetles scurrying. Leaves dancing on the wind. And so many other life-forms. Some from here. Some from elsewhere. But the Nexus didn't care about familiar or strange, or even bad or good. At a larger level, life was just life. And the Nexus loved it all.

The song wound its way into my brain and heart, and I *changed.* Became a little bit gentler. Kinder, and more patient. A little bit Nexus. And they became a little bit me. Our connection got bigger and deeper until I could see like they could, tracking the threads that held everything together. And they could run quick and light like me instead of being rooted to the world.

We traveled the stars, following one thread of connection after another. We went faster and faster and the song got louder and louder until I was dizzy with it. My vision blurred, turning everything into a fuzzy haze. And when it cleared again, I was somewhere else.

I was surrounded by trees. Except these weren't normal trees.

Their colors were impossibly bright and they glittered around the edges, leaving trails of sparkles in the air as their leaves waved in the wind. This was a weird sort of forest.

Except it wasn't. It was my forest, where I'd lived always. Nothing weird about it. Although hadn't someone been singing a moment ago? If they had, I couldn't hear them now. And I didn't want to stand about listening, not when every cell in my body was buzzing with possibilities. I was light enough to fly. So I did.

I shot upward, skimming the treetops as I dipped and whirled through the air. Vaguely it occurred to me that there was something I'd forgotten. Something important. But it couldn't be *that* important or I'd have remembered. Anyway, I'd remember whatever it was eventually. There was no need to worry. There was never any need to worry, here.

A flutter from below caught my attention. I zoomed down, landing on a flat rock by a stream. The water was making a lovely gurgling sound, and I lost interest in the flutter. Instead I dipped my hand in the water, marveling at the feel of it burbling past against my fingers.

The flutter came again. "Hello, child."

A black-and-white bird was perched on the other side of the stream. Their eyes were ringed with red, which meant this was a very old bird. I gave a deep nod. "Hello, Elder Mudlark."

The Mudlark laughed. "You see me as a bird? Everyone makes this place their own, but I don't believe I've had feathers before. I am He Who Dreams Largely. But you can call me Mudlark, if you like." He hopped closer. "Do you remember how you got here?"

That was a weird question. "I've always been here."

"It feels like that, doesn't it? But you haven't, you know. You were once somewhere else, just as I was."

I frowned. That wasn't right. It couldn't be right, because there wasn't anywhere else. Only this perfect place, where I could do anything and be anything. Where I wasn't weighed down like I had been . . . Huh. *Like I had been before.*

I *had* come from elsewhere. "Where was I?"

"I don't know. Nor is it for me to say if the knowledge has already left you. Besides, there is no need for thoughts of somewhere else! It is better here."

There was no arguing with that. I sat back, tipping my face to the warmth of the sun. Only the hazy sense of contentment I'd had a few moments ago was lost. Something was tugging at my mind. Something to do with wherever I'd been before.

I sighed. "Do you know where you came from, Mudlark?"

"Sometimes I do. It is like a dream that I don't like to think of. There was a war, I think."

That seemed familiar. "There might have been a war where I'm from too." But I wasn't sure that was right. "Or maybe not. Maybe there were . . . trees?" One tree, at least. Gray. Big branches. Black berries—*the Nexus!*

Memory returned, so quick my head spun and my stomach lurched. I could hear the Nexus again now, a low humming in my blood. Singing softly and patiently of Treesingers, and groves. Waiting for me to hear.

I staggered to my feet. "I've got to get back!"

"Back to where?"

"Home—but before that, I need to find the Ancients."

"You are speaking to one, child."

The Ancients were birds? But of course they weren't. *Everyone makes this place their own. . . .* I suppose it made sense that I was seeing Ancients as beings that could fly. "I need your help. On my world, a very bad person has some pathway, and it's eating him but it's slow. I need a way to end him quick or he'll—"

He interrupted me. "Calm yourself. None who are not bright of spirit can eat pathway and survive."

I shook my head. "He's found a way to hold it by mixing . . ." But I stopped, realizing I didn't really understand what Allora had done. "Okay, it doesn't matter how. The point is, he's using it to understand bits of your knowledge, and trust me, he's bad. And he's working with someone who's just like him. They invaded my homeland and killed my people, fed pathway to the Birth tree of my grove and poisoned it—"

"Pathway is not a poison!"

"It is if you give it to someone who can cross to the other side but doesn't want to."

"Doesn't *want* to?" Mudlark sounded bewildered. "Everyone wants . . ." Then he stopped. "No. Not everyone does, do they? There was one amongst my kind who did not wish to come with us. I had forgotten that. It is so difficult to hold on to memory here. But these others you speak of . . ." He made an anxious hop from one foot to the other. "You bring grave tidings, child. This news requires a congress."

And he threw back his head and trilled.

There was a sudden storm of wings as birds of every shape and size appeared out of nowhere, settling onto the ground and into trees. They all started speaking at once, and I couldn't understand a word. But I sensed confusion and doubt. They weren't sure whether to believe me. And it seemed like this congress thing could go on for a while. Probably forever.

There was never any need to hurry, here.

I shouted, "Hey!" When that didn't get their attention, I yelled louder. "*Hey!*"

The trilling stopped. All the birds looked at me and it didn't seem like they were pleased at being interrupted. Except for Mudlark, who bobbed his head encouragingly. "Speak, child."

I thought fast. The Ancients weren't sure whether to trust me, and I didn't think it was just because I was a newcomer. They didn't like the idea of pathway not working how they'd planned (even though it seemed as if some enterprising bastard trying to corrupt a passage to a higher realm was a completely foreseeable thing). But there was nothing to be gained from telling powerful beings that they hadn't been anywhere near as clever as they'd thought.

"Isn't there a way for you to test me or something?" I asked. "So I can prove what I'm saying is true?"

Mudlark flew across the water to perch on the rock at my side. "You can share your understanding of this person you say is misusing our pathway, if you choose. But I warn you, it will be difficult."

"I'll do it."

He tilted his head to the side, watching me out of one bright eye. "Then, child, you must think of the person with the pathway and hold out your hand."

I concentrated very hard on Tomas and stretched out my palm. Mudlark leaped forward and pecked it. Blood welled up, and pain spiked. Only not just through my hand. This pain was through my whole body, and, wow, it *hurt.*

I doubled over, gasping. It felt as if my insides were being dug into by tiny beaks. I wanted to scream at them to stop, but

I couldn't. Everything now depended on me (a world-class liar) passing a test of truth. I gritted my teeth and endured as the birds took the things I knew about Tomas. Only they didn't just want knowledge. They wanted my experiences. My feelings.

They went deeper. It hurt more. I toppled to the side, curling up into a ball. And I realized something horrible. *True liars never lie to themselves.* But I had. I hadn't let myself really feel how bad things had been, in the temple. I'd had to pretend so I could go on. But now the pretending was gone and only the pain was left. The birds went after that too. They opened up wounds I hadn't even known were there and pecked away at the insides. It was *agony* and this time I flat-out screamed, rolling across the hard rock and howling.

Then it was over. No more pecking. Just me, whimpering pathetically. I forced myself to stop whining and focused on breathing, steady and slow. When I thought I could manage it, I sat up. *Very* carefully. I was tender and sore from the inside out.

The birds were all watching me still, but their feathers had gone flat and dull. They believed me.

Well, okay then. Glad that hadn't been for nothing.

They began talking softly amongst themselves, making distressed cooing noises. And I didn't have the energy just yet to interrupt them and repeat my request for a way to kill Tomas and heal the grove. I crawled over to a tree and rested my back against it. I felt—well, in quite a lot of pain, but also weirdly empty. As if I'd had a bunch of splinters lodged deep inside and now they were gone. Those birds had cleaned out my wounds.

The cooing noises changed. Became sharp and screeching. An argument? Mudlark was certainly trying to make a point. His wings twirled and his little claws stabbed at the earth as he bounced around. Then he started shrieking, making a really *big* noise for a small bird. The others seemed impressed (or maybe it was just that nobody could outshriek him). One by one, they fell silent.

Mudlark fluffed out his feathers and strutted back and forth, as if daring someone to speak. No one did. Satisfied, he fluttered over to me.

"We are grieved to discover what has been wrought with our creation," he said. "More than you will ever know. But we cannot give you a weapon, child."

After all that, they weren't going to help me end Tomas? "You—"

"But," Mudlark added quickly, "we have another solution. Because we *can* take back what we gave."

He leaned over and spat something out. A familiar red, spiky crystal. Only it shone impossibly bright, like all the colors here.

"Take it," Mudlark said. "It is what you will need, to do what you must."

I wasn't sure how giving me *more* pathway was going to help, but I wasn't going to argue. I reached across to pick it up. But the moment I touched it, the thing dissolved, sinking into my skin. A whisper shivered through me. Like wings, beating in my blood.

"This is pathway in a purer and more concentrated form than anything that exists in your world," Mudlark explained. "You can use it to draw other, lesser manifestations of pathway to you. They will long to be part of it, like leaves returning to the tree that gave them life. And once you have all of the pathway, you will be able to release it in a way that harms no one."

I worked my way through that. "You're saying I'll be able to take the pathway from Tomas? And the Birth tree?"

"Exactly so." Mudlark sounded smug. It was obvious this was his idea. And it was an excellent idea. I mean, okay, taking the pathway wouldn't kill the sun-god, but it meant he *could* be killed. Plus, I could definitely cure the grove. A grin spread across my face and I shouted on the inside. *We did it, Nexus!*

The Nexus didn't say anything. But I had a sense of them reaching out to lay a branch upon my shoulder, like they'd done once before. Only not in guidance this time. It felt more like they were trying to comfort me.

The way you would when someone was about to get really bad news.

It dawned on me that the birds were casting sorrowful gazes in my direction. Including Mudlark, who looked sadder than the rest put together.

"What aren't you telling me?" I demanded.

"There is a price to the journey back." Mudlark flattened himself against the ground and added, very softly, "No one was ever meant to return, you see."

He hadn't actually named the price. But I knew. *Crap.* "I'm going—" My stupid voice broke. I swallowed and tried again, forcing out the words. "I'm going to die."

"We fear so," Mudlark replied. "We believe returning will take too much of your life force for you to survive. You will have some time, on the other side. Long enough to do what you must do, we hope. But not much longer. And"—he flattened further—"there is more."

"More than being *dead*?"

"In this life, or any other, you won't find this place again. The way will be closed to you."

He sounded like he thought that was much worse than dying.

I suppose it was, from his perspective. "That's okay," I answered, more steadily this time. "I have somewhere else to go."

"You could stay," Mudlark suggested. "You would be happy here, child. Everyone is."

Because they all forgot. Maybe I'd forget too. Maybe even the Nexus would if we were here long enough. That didn't mean it was the right thing to do, for me or the Nexus. And I didn't have to ask them if they wanted to stay, because I already knew what their choice was, even though my death was theirs too because there was no other Silverleaf to carry on the bloodline. But trees and Treesingers didn't leave our groves behind.

"I have to go, Mudlark."

He sighed mournfully. "I thought that would be your answer." Then he brightened, bobbing up. "Memory does not last here. But elsewhere, it endures. Even across lives. We will give you something to carry with you."

With that, all the birds burst into the air, diving and whirling to surround me in colors and feathers and song. I began to float, carried upward by the beat of their wings and the joy in their voices. Possibilities shone and stretched around me. I could do anything. I could be anything.

And then it was gone.

I wasn't flying anymore. I was falling. Tumbling through space to land on a hard surface. And my life was slipping away, running down my arms to fall from the tips of my fingers. I wouldn't have been surprised to find myself lying in a pool of blood. But I wasn't. There was just me and a floor of black crystal.

I was back in the heart of Journeys Far.

He spoke. "You have returned, Bell Silverleaf! Did you speak to the Ancients?"

"Yeah." I blinked, a bit woozy from the sudden shift between glitter forest and Vaulter. Except the forest was fading now. All that remained was the sense of endless possibilities. But that was a feeling for another world.

I began to haul my stupid heavy body upward. Everything here was so weighty. The air itself seemed to drag against my skin.

Journeys Far spoke again, in a quieter voice. "You are sick. Very sick, in a way I cannot help with. Not even with my medicinal sparklies."

"'S okay," I told him. "I got what I wanted. I can stop Talks Sweetly." I'd made it onto my hands and knees. Now I sat back and reached out to steady myself against the wall, ready to get to my feet. I had no idea how long I'd been gone, but the others had *better* still be alive. That thought triggered another. *Medicinal sparklies.* "I'll make you a trade, Journeys Far. The unraveler in exchange for you using your medicine on Sasha and any of my other friends who are hurt."

I waited for him to point out that I still didn't actually have an unraveler. Instead he said, "A fair deal, Bell Silverleaf. I accept."

His voice was gentle. I glared. "Do not feel sorry for me!"

"*Sorry* for you? Sorry for one who has walked pathway and returned? One does not feel sorry for a being of legend, Bell Silverleaf." He made a snorting sound, as if the very idea was ridiculous. Then he added, "I remind you it was part of our original deal that I would hear tales of what lies on the other side. I do not expect such stories now, of course, with Talks Sweetly still to deal with. You must return and tell me later."

He was asking me not to give up. "I'll do my best." And it wasn't a lie. I was clinging to this existence, trying to hold on to something that was leaving me behind, and not just because I still had things to do. I wanted to live.

I staggered upward. It was getting easier to move as I got used to this world again. "Journeys Far? If I don't make it, will you tell my friends . . . my family . . ." I stopped. How could I put everything I needed to say into words? In the end I went for the only thing that really mattered. "Tell them I love them. And I would've stayed, if I could."

Then I lifted my chin. Trying to look brave, so when Journeys Far told the story of this moment, no one would get upset thinking about how scared I'd been. "Send me back. I'm off to make our Ancestors proud."

The ceiling opened above me and air rushed around my body. I shot upward, landing in the dead end I'd been in before. I immediately took off running, but I was *slow*. Except I wasn't. It just felt slow because I couldn't move at the speed of thought anymore. And life was continuing to leak from me, running down my face. Okay, those were tears.

I brushed them away. I did *not* have the time to be upset. I snarled at my emotions, shoving them aside and focusing on what was ahead. I had far more important things to think about than my own stupid life. And anyway . . .

My lips curved into a painful smile. I'd found comfort in Mum's long-ago words, after all. *Everything returns from the earth. . . .*

Anyway, I'd be back again.

25

Everyone was still alive.

I was crouched by Sasha's side. She was unconscious but breathing. Hanging on, like she'd promised.

No one had noticed I was back yet, what with the battle going on ahead. The tunnel was filled with flashes and crackles of light, making it hard to see exactly what was happening. But after a minute or two of staring and squinting, I'd worked it out.

The sun-god was protecting himself with some kind of barrier. The barrier itself was just a shimmer in the air, but I could make out its shape from the way Ronan's blasts flowed around it instead of striking Tomas. Allora was at Tomas's side, sparks pouring from one hand and the unraveler glittering in the other. Tamsin (with Tricks still on her head) was battling Allora's sparks with a sword that now crackled with blue energy (Ronan must've charged it up). And Ronan himself was firing bolts at Allora when he wasn't blasting Tomas. It was fast. Chaotic. And basically *everybody* was in my way.

I had to touch Tomas to take the pathway from him (and I couldn't even have said how I knew that, but I did). Which meant, first, I had to find a way through the fight. That I could do, with the help of the Nexus. But, second, I had to get Tomas to drop that shimmer-shield. And I didn't see how— Oh. Yes, I did.

There was one last lie to tell.

I opened my wardrobe of falsehoods and put on the clothes of Eldan's star student. A girl who was hurt that the old man hadn't told me who he was but who loved him regardless. A girl who'd still turn to him in a moment of panic and confusion. Such as if I'd gone and eaten this strange stuff called pathway and had no idea what to do next.

When I had the lie right, I called on the Nexus. It hummed in my blood, and I knew how I needed to move to get through the battle: when to swerve left and when right; when to duck and when to charge. I just wasn't sure I could actually do it, because I didn't have Tricks with me to make me faster and more coordinated.

But then I felt . . . something. A fluttering beneath my skin, like the beat of wings. And right along with it a lightness and quickness in my body. The enhanced pathway? Or maybe Mudlark had given me something extra. Whatever it was, I'd take it.

I tore into the fight, weaving and dodging my way through the frenzy of battle with the reflexes of a fierce little bird. When I got close to Tomas, I adopted a bewildered expression, stretching out my hand.

His eyes widened in shock (he could sense I had pathway in me). Then his features twisted with a desperate hunger (he wanted to know why I could hold it). But there was also the tiniest bit of doubt in his gaze. For a horrible second I thought this wouldn't work. Except the sun-god was no true liar. He'd been deceiving himself for generations and was way too convinced of his own superiority to believe I could be a threat.

The shield vanished. Tomas grabbed my hand and pulled me to him. He spoke in Eldan's voice as the shield re-formed, sealing us in. "My dear girl, what have you done? My brother has led you into danger—but worry not! We'll sort this out together."

I gazed up into his face and let the lie of the humble Treesinger fall away. Giving him a single second to appreciate that he hadn't trapped me in here with him.

It was the other way around.

The pathway I carried surged up to become a thing of claws and teeth.

I hissed, "Alethea Silverleaf says hello."

And I ripped the lesser pathway from Tomas.

He let out a long wail of rage and pain and fear. The shield flashed out of existence. And the Nexus thrummed, expanding my awareness so I could see everything that was happening at once.

Allora flung herself toward Tomas and me, one hand brandishing the unraveler as white sparks shot out of the other, aimed at my unprotected back. But a ferocious blast of blue knocked her sparks away. In the same moment, a crackling sword wielded with immense force came down on her wrist—

—and sliced right through.

Allora screamed even louder than Tomas as her hand (and the unraveler) dropped to the floor. A wave of energy blasted out of the stump, sending Ronan and Tamsin flying backward. And a strand of gold streaked out of Tomas to grab hold of Allora. The rope of light dragged her across the ground until she lay huddled beside us, clutching her arm to her chest.

Tomas clamped one hand down on her shoulder. But it wasn't to help her. It was to take her energy for himself.

The sun-god roared, gripping his pathway as he fought me with everything he had (and with everything Allora had). He couldn't get back what I'd already taken. But I couldn't wrest any more of it away from him either. The two of us were locked into a tug-of-war, and I was getting weaker by the second as my life trickled away. *I can't do this!*

Then, from nowhere, I heard Tricks. Faint, but clear. Sending me strength with her words. Songs will be sung.

Yes, they will. I gritted my teeth, seized hold of the pathway, and *pulled.* Tomas tried to get it back. Except my will was stronger than his. He'd never had to truly endure. Never had to carry on day after day with not much hope of anything ever getting any better. But I had. He'd made sure of it. Now I used that strength to take the only thing he truly cared about. I tore the pathway from his grip, bit by painful bit, until I had it all.

I snarled my triumph as he sank to his knees, whimpering. Then I realized Allora was gone. My head swiveled left and right, trying to find her before she could come after me. Until I noticed the fading white strands scattered across the floor. She was *really* gone. Tomas had taken everything she had, and when their kind exhausted their energy, they died.

The sun-god stopped whimpering. Mostly. He was trying to get to his feet, except he kept falling over. Yeah, he'd be a while. I glanced back to check on the others. Tamsin was sitting up, and Ronan was leaning over Sasha. He looked up to give me a quick nod (she was still alive) and then came striding in my direction. *Everyone* was okay, and the moon-god was dead, and the sun-god was defeated, and I hadn't let my Ancestors down. I hadn't let anyone down. I was so giddy with relief, I could've laughed. But there'd be no stopping the giggling once it started to come out.

Tomas managed to stand. And glare. But not at me. His gaze was focused at a point over my shoulder. "You think . . . to kill me . . . brother? You don't have . . . the strength."

The god of lies arrived at my side and he had the unraveler in his hand. But he didn't do anything with it. Just gave me a look that said he was leaving this decision to me. And I waited for the Nexus to come pounding through my blood, because they'd probably want to spare Tomas. Even though Tomas had killed all the other Nexus. Even though Tomas would come after me and everyone I loved once he recovered, and pathway or no, he still had powers no human did. But the Nexus was silent. This choice was mine.

"You . . ." Tomas was speaking again, to me this time. "Traitor. Fool. After all I did for you . . . tried to teach you . . ." His voice trailed off into a fit of coughing.

He looked so weak. So pathetic. And while I wouldn't have exactly described myself as gentle or kind or patient, I wasn't who I'd been before I'd blended with the Nexus. That had changed me. Made me different.

But I was still a Silverleaf.

I took a last, long look at Tomas the Incandescent. Would-be god, fake father figure, and all-round evil bastard. Then I nodded at Ronan.

The unraveler went spinning through the air to strike the sun-god in the heart.

Tomas's eyes widened in disbelief. His mouth opened to speak. But all he did was howl as his body came apart. Slowly at first, and then faster and faster, breaking down into tangled strands of yellow energy. The howling noise continued long after he had no face, right up until he was nothing but a pile of loose threads. Then those threads disappeared, one by one, and the sun-god was finally silent.

The sun-god was dead.

I blinked, staring at the space where he'd been. Where Allora had been. The only thing there now was the unraveler. A deep sense of satisfaction seemed to shudder through my bones. As if generations of Silverleafs were saying, *Well done.*

Or maybe it was just Alethea.

I hurried forward to get the unraveler, my mind already jumping ahead to healing Sasha. Then Tamsin shouted, "Bell!"

And I knew from the heartbreak in her voice that something terrible had happened.

26

I ran back down the tunnel, thinking this had all taken too long and Sasha was dead. But she was still breathing. Then I thought there must be something wrong with Tamsin. Except she seemed okay too, sitting upright and cradling something in her arms. Something that looked like Tricks. Only it couldn't be. Tricks was green and bright and alive.

Whatever Tamsin was cradling was gray and still.

I dropped to my knees at her side, gasping. I couldn't seem to get enough air into me. Tamsin was babbling: "She flew off my head when that energy wave thing hit us, I thought she was okay at first, but she must've been hurt, really hurt . . ."

Songs will be sung. The words that had sounded faint. Because Tricks had been dying. That strength she'd sent me had been her last.

I dropped the unraveler and reached out to take her. Tamsin was making an awful wailing sound. No, that was me. I choked it off, but I couldn't stop the hot tears pouring down my cheeks. I wasn't sure I wanted to. Tricks deserved tears.

"Bell?" That was Ronan, standing at my shoulder. "She's gray, just as the grove is. There's nothing that could be done to wake her?"

I shook my head. Tried to speak, and couldn't. My voice had shut down with grief. I swallowed and tried again. Words came out this time. "There's a spark of life left in her, but only because she's part of a bigger tree. The spark will go to the tree when she's taken back there. She's gone."

I wanted to hunch over her and sob. I couldn't. Life was still flowing out of me. But for the first time it didn't seem like such a bad thing that I didn't have long. Because as Mum had always told me, Treesingers were connected to the people we'd loved, even across different cycles of existence. Tricks had just gone to that next cycle ahead of me. *I'm coming, Tricks.*

I lifted her to my hair like I had when we'd first met, only this time I tangled her into my curls so she wouldn't fall. Then I took everything I was feeling and pushed it away. Not far. It was too big to go far. But enough to function. Because I *had* to function, just a little while longer. "Tamsin? I need you to do something for me."

"Of course. Anything. And I'm sorry about Tricks, I'm so sorry. . . ."

"It's not your fault." I reached across to put my hand on hers. This was the last conversation we'd ever have. I didn't want her to be sad, or at least not any sadder than she had to be. "You couldn't have saved her, Tamsin. But you *can* help Sasha. Listen to me now—I need you to take her to the heart of Journeys Far, along with the unraveler. I promised him he could have it in trade for helping her, but I can't take it to him." *Because I'll be busy dying.*

I obviously wasn't going to say that out loud. "I've got to go cure the grove."

Her face lightened. "You can *cure* the grove?"

"Yeah. The Ancients told me how." I almost said I'd tell her all about it later, but I managed to squash that sentence before it left my mouth. No outright lies. Not in front of Ronan, because there was a good chance he'd know I was lying.

She scrubbed at her eyes and lifted her chin. "How do I get to the, um, heart?"

"Follow this tunnel. Go left at the first fork and then at the next take the passage that rises up. You'll get to a dead end. Call out to Journeys Far when you reach it. Have you got that?"

"Got it."

I hauled myself up, watching as Tamsin grabbed the unraveler and went over to Sasha. And I didn't say: *You were the first friend I made after I left the temple.* Or: *I wouldn't have made it through the Test without you.* Or even: *I'm sorry we won't be Treesingers together.* I didn't say anything at all. I just hoped she knew.

Tamsin lifted Sasha into her arms and took off down the passage.

I turned and went the other way.

Ronan fell in beside me, matching his steps to mine and saying nothing. He knew I didn't want to talk. I suppose I should've sent him away as well. But I didn't have a convincing-enough reason to make him go. Okay, that was a lie. I could've thought of something. But I was selfish and weak. I didn't want to be without him at the end.

We made our way back through the Beneath and into the grove, following the trails to the Birth tree. Her twisting branches reached up and out above us. Once, they would have made a huge canopy. But now her lovely green leaves were gone and her bark was gray instead of black. *Not for long.*

I sank down and pressed my hands against her trunk, closing my eyes. I could feel the pathway pulsing through her veins, and I reached for my own. It wasn't claws and teeth this time. It didn't need to be. It was just a call, long and gentle. The pathway in the Birth tree began to flow in my direction—

—and stopped.

I called louder. The pathway *still* didn't come. It was almost as if the Birth tree was holding on to it— Oh. She *was* holding on to it. She didn't want me to get hurt.

It's okay, I told her. *I'll be okay.*

No answer. But I sensed defiance. She was asleep, but her deepest instincts were telling her I'd once been a Falling Leaves Treesinger and she had to protect me from this terrible thing she was fighting.

Panic rose up inside, choking off my breath. I was getting weaker by the moment and I had to cure Falling Leaves while there was enough life left in me to do it. I grabbed for the pathway, only to have the Birth tree snatch it away.

Let it go! I shouted. *It can't hurt me, I promise!*

Which was true. But it didn't sound true to the Birth tree.

A rush of images flew through my mind, too quick for me to interpret. But that was okay, because the pictures weren't for me. I don't know what the Nexus said to the Birth tree, but whatever it was, it worked. The pathway began to seep toward me, a trickle at first, and then a stream, and then a mighty wave. And with it came something else. A rush of gratitude—and sadness. She knew I'd never grow into my leaves in this life.

I was suddenly overwhelmed by a sense of *home*. I could smell the richness of the earth and the lighter scents of berries and flowers; feel the wind rushing through trees; hear the voices and laughter. I drank it in, knowing this was the closest I'd get to the grove when it was awake. It would take Falling Leaves a week or more to come out of dormancy.

Then the sense of the grove faded away, leaving just me and the pathway. Except I was *bursting* with it. It felt like my skin was stretching trying to keep it all in. Mudlark had said I'd be able to let it go safely, but I didn't know how.

An image flashed into my mind. Little flames, everywhere. People. Trees. Animals. Life. Worlds and worlds of bright-of-spirit. And I understood.

I reached out to the pathway inside me and said, *Break*. It did, coming apart until it was nothing but tiny fragments.

Then I reached out to the Nexus, and together we scattered pathway across the connections that stretched and shone between life and worlds, sending a fragment to every bright-of-spirit. It wasn't enough to take them to the other side. It was just enough to be . . . well, a hope, I guessed. To feel some of what I'd felt, those endless possibilities, that moment of being lifted up by the beat of wings and the joy of song. A world where something better was possible.

We pushed the pathway out until I had none of it left in me. Okay, maybe one tiny little bit (just enough to be a hope). But otherwise I was empty and exhausted. So was the Nexus. But they were content, drifting into a sleep from which they wouldn't wake. I'd have liked to do the same. But I couldn't let go of life just yet.

I forced my eyes open and lurched up, stumbling. Ronan caught hold of my arm and helped me to stand. He glanced from me to the grove with a dismayed expression. "It didn't work?"

I yawned. "It worked. It'll just take a while for Falling Leaves to wake." I pulled Tricks from my hair, holding her against Ronan's chest.

"You have to take her," I told him. "Give Tricks to the Matriarchs, so they can get her back to her tree. Promise me."

He put his hand over mine. "Of course, but—this has to be done now?"

"No. Later. You have to promise."

"Later? But you could . . ." His voice trailed off as fear flashed across his face. "I promise. Bell. What's wrong?"

But I had no intention of getting into a pointless conversation about me dying. Instead I did what I'd wanted to do from the moment I found out who he really was. I rose up onto my tiptoes and kissed him.

The grove vanished. Everything vanished. There was nothing but the scent and the feel and the taste of him. I was suddenly, gloriously awake and aware, and as near to flying as I'd been since I left the world beyond.

Then it all went away. He and I were standing apart from each other, surrounded by blackness.

I swiveled. "What the— Where did everything go?"

"Nowhere," he answered. "We're still where we were before. We're communicating mind to mind. Like we did in the Cave."

Oh. I reached for him, but he caught my hands in his. "Explain to me what's happening, Bell."

Looked like I was going to have to talk about this after all. "I'm dying. From traveling the pathway."

233

"What? *Why?*"

"Because no one was ever supposed to come back. The Ancients said it would probably kill me. And it is."

Comprehension dawned in his eyes. And we were in the grove again.

He broke the kiss. I growled in disappointment. But then he bent to nuzzle my neck and I snuggled into him, filled with a delicious warmth. Dying really wasn't so bad.

Ronan spoke against my ear. "What did the Ancients say, exactly, about returning?"

I struggled to remember. "That it was going to take too much, um, life force. 'S okay, though. Worth it, to get rid of Tomas."

He sighed, his breath stirring my curls. "My family has cost you everything."

"Mpfh," I replied. I didn't want to talk about Tomas, or Allora. I didn't want to talk about anything. He got the message and gave up on speaking to leave a trail of kisses across my skin. The warmth turned to a molten heat that coiled through my blood. And I didn't know if it was so intense because I was dying or if it would always be like this. Seemed unfair that I'd never find out.

Ronan spoke again, very softly. "My beautiful liar. I really can't let you die here."

Talking, still? "Don't have a choice."

"Oh, but I do." And there was a laugh in his voice. I'd remember that later, that he'd been laughing. That his eyes would have been lit up with hints of hazel. That he wasn't scared or sad. And then he pressed his lips to mine and I stopped thinking at all.

The world dissolved into heat and light and now I really was flying and so was he. We floated upward like sparks from a fire. For the space of one heartbeat I was stupidly, ridiculously happy.

And then I was alone.

I was standing all by myself in the grove, totally shocked yet totally aware of what had happened. Because I was surrounded by little sparks of blue that were winking out, one by one.

It had taken too much life force to return, I'd said. So he'd given me his.

And I wasn't the only one he'd saved.

Something green and bright moved in my hand. Tricks scurried up my arm, flattening herself into my curls. *What happened? Whathappenedwhathappenedwhathappened?*

The last of the lights disappeared. "We're alive," I whispered.

And Ronan was dead.

27

Songs will be sung.

A song *was* being sung. Only not in celebration. Tricks's voice rose and fell in mourning. It was a long singing. A great honor. I told Ronan that, in my head. But of course there was no reply and there never would be again. This time he was really gone.

I was curled up at the base of the Birth tree with my eyes shut. I had no plans to go anywhere else for a while. Or ever. But after a while there was another sound. Footsteps.

"You were *dying*?" someone yelled. "You were dying and you didn't tell me?"

Tamsin. And right after her, Sasha: "The Gleam said you were better. Are you better?"

I cracked my eyes open and stared up at them. "I'm better."

I wondered how Journeys Far had known I'd recovered. Then I remembered the Nexus could speak to him. They must have told him I was all right. I yelled at the Nexus in my head. *Did you know this was going to happen? It was supposed to be me!*

The Nexus answered softly, *We will all be here again.*

I supposed they thought that would be comforting. And maybe it would be, later. But not now.

Tamsin dropped down beside me. Sasha too, and she looked much better. The medicinal sparkly had done its work.

I closed my eyes again. Willing them to go away. But they didn't. Instead Tamsin spoke, sounding delighted. "Tricks! You're okay! Where's Ronan?"

Oh. They didn't know. It seemed impossible that they couldn't feel his absence from the world, but that was just stupid. They'd never been connected to him like I had.

"He's . . ." The word got stuck in my throat. I forced it out. "Dead. He saved me. Saved Tricks. And it killed him."

"Oh, Bell," Sasha breathed. "I'm so sorry."

Tamsin reached across to rest her hand on my shoulder. For a moment everyone was quiet. *Good.* Maybe they'd finally leave me alone.

Then Tamsin said, gently, "We can't stay here. You know that, right?"

I did *not* know that, and I lifted my head to glare at her.

She gestured to the vines above. "It's hard to tell with how thick those vines are, but it has to be morning. Or near to. One of us is supposed to be voted Queen today. And if they can't find us, they're going to come looking."

I wanted to shout that I didn't care. But they might look *here,* and I didn't want anyone searching around Falling Leaves. The grove needed to be left in peace to wake in its own time.

I gave a grudging nod and stood. Except I didn't. I tried harder, forcing my weary limbs into action. This time I managed to rise. Okay, I needed Tamsin and Sasha to help me, but once I made it to my feet, I could walk on my own. Well, for as long as I concentrated on not tipping over. No surprise that it was hard for me to find my balance when Ronan and I had been leaning into each other for years. Now he was gone, and I wasn't, and I'd be replaying his last moments forever. *My beautiful liar. . . .*

I stumbled my way through the grove and into Radiance. The sky outside was light. Tamsin had been right—it *was* morning. And that wasn't the only thing she'd been right about.

Halfway to the Hall, we ran into a bunch of the Queen's Guard.

They looked both very relieved and very angry to see us. Well, except for their short, well-muscled leader, who just looked angry.

"I'm not even going to ask where you've been," Muscles growled. "You can explain yourselves to the Queen. Follow me." Then, to the rest of the guards: "Go find the other search parties. Let them know they've been found."

She led us through the streets and back into the Testing Hall. Tamsin and Sasha matched their pace to mine, which meant progress was slow, but all three of us ignored Muscles's efforts to hurry us up. Somewhere along the way, Tricks finished her song and fell asleep. I wished I could. I'd give anything to be unconscious right now. Anything not to feel, even for a little while.

Anything not to have to tell Elodie that Ronan was dead.

Except she'd already know. Because their kind felt when the ones close to them died. I'd have to tell her how, though. I tried to come up with a way to say it that did justice to who he'd been and what he'd done. I was still trying when we turned into a wide passage that ended in a big door with guards standing on either side. The Queen must be behind it. And she wasn't alone, because someone was shouting. *Alasdar.*

"There have been too many strange happenings. A full investigation must take place. I insist that you delay the vote!"

The Queen yelled right back. "I do not answer to you, Your Holiness. And from what I hear, you should be far more concerned about holding on to the high priestdom than presuming to give orders to me. Leave. *Now.*"

The door flew open and Alasdar came storming out, stopping still at the sight of me. He opened his mouth to say something horrible.

Sasha got in first, all haughty and knightlike. "I advise you to keep walking, Your Holiness. One of us will be your Queen, and we three stand together."

Of course that made him even more angry. "That worthless girl doesn't deserve to be here!" He took a step in my direction, spitting with rage. "Treesinger scum, you defile—"

And that was as far as he got before Tamsin took two long strides forward and punched him in the face.

The high priest dropped like a stone. I blinked at the sight of him lying unconscious on the floor with his skinny arms and legs sticking out. It didn't seem real. Maybe because it was hard to feel anything beyond the howling loss inside me. Or maybe because I'd imagined hitting him a thousand times, and this wasn't how I'd thought it would be. I hadn't expected him to look so . . . ridiculous. So small. But that's exactly what he was. Alasdar was just like his god. A small man made big by unearned power.

Except his power was fading while mine grew. And anyway I wasn't eleven years old anymore.

I didn't know why I hadn't realized that before now.

A cool voice spoke. "Dear me," said the Queen. "The high priest has fallen over."

Which was a blatant lie. But the guards went right along with it. "Yes, Your Majesty," Muscles said. "I saw the whole thing."

"Tripped over his own robes," another chimed in, while the third asked, "Shall we lock—ah, *place* him in a room to recover?"

"Please do. And ensure he remains *placed* there until after the vote. So he gets the rest he needs, of course."

The guards bowed to the Queen. She inclined her head in acknowledgment and waved us into the room beyond the door.

We entered a space that was big and bright. Armchairs covered in gilt embroidery were gathered around a low table, and tall windows gave a view across the city. Four other doors led off the room, which meant this was probably a set of interconnected chambers. . . . Okay, none of this was stuff I needed to be thinking about. I was noting useless details to delay doing what I had to do. And that was cowardly.

I looked at Elodie. Her face was calm. Remote. But I could see the fire beneath the ice, the searing grief breaking through. She'd already felt his loss.

Her gaze flicked to Tamsin and Sasha, then back to me. I answered her unspoken question. "They know everything. You can talk in front of them."

"They're dead, yes? Allora. Tomas. Ronan."

Her voice trembled ever so slightly on that last name. Otherwise her tone was flat. As if she were indifferent. But she wasn't and I answered fast, because until I said it, she'd cling to that faint, useless hope. She knew. But she didn't want to know. "Yes."

Elodie whipped around to stare out the window. *I'm sorry.* Except I'd said that to her once before about him dying and it had been pointless then too. Sorry wasn't going to bring him back.

I drew in a breath, readying myself to tell her how he'd died. "Ronan—"

But she held up a hand. "Later." She turned, casting an assessing glance over the three of us. "It's only a few hours until the vote, and none of you look like potential Queens. There's not much time, but my dressers should be able to do *something* with you."

In other words, she couldn't bear to hear it yet. That was okay. I wasn't sure I could bear to tell it. But I would, whenever she was ready. Because she'd loved him too.

The Queen left the room. Wanting to be alone, which I understood. And that was the last thing I understood for a while, because we got swept off by a bunch of people who were *very* concerned about our appearance. I began to drift, disconnecting from the total insignificance of what was happening. What did it matter if we were bathed in scented oils, or if our nails were painted gold and there were strands of gilt threaded through our hair? *Makes us look more queenly, I guess.* Except right now the crown felt kind of insignificant too.

Tamsin and Sasha kept looking at me and whispering together. I told them I was okay. Or I thought I did. But maybe I just said it inside my head.

Finally the "make the candidates shiny" ordeal was over and we were back where we'd started. Only now there was food spread out on the low table. Apparently it was customary for the candidates to have breakfast with the Queen before going to the final vote, or so the dressers had said. Only the Queen wasn't here. Just us (wearing the same swooshy dresses we'd worn into the Glass) and a heap of food.

I stared down at my golden nails, wondering how long it would take to get the polish off. Then I realized Tamsin and Sasha were watching me.

"What?" I asked.

"You were going to eat something," Tamsin said. "Remember?"

Had I said that? Maybe. But I hadn't meant it. "I'm not hungry."

Sasha picked up a pastry and held it out. "Come on, just try this one. It looks *delicious*."

It didn't. But it was obvious they weren't going to let this go. I took the pastry and nibbled at the corner. They both smiled big, encouraging smiles. I put it down. Their faces fell.

I sighed and picked it back up. I'd made it about halfway through the thing when one of the doors opened and the Queen stuck her head through. "Bell. I'd like to speak to you, please. Alone."

I got up immediately. So did Tamsin and Sasha.

"You can't come," I told them, in a low voice. "And you don't need to. I'll be all right. She has to know how it happened, and I'd like to do this now." Because after the vote I was going to hide myself away and fall apart.

They exchanged glances, communicating silently. Evidently they decided I could be allowed to go into the next room all on my own, because they sat down again. I would've told them to stop fussing over me, except that I kind of liked it. Granny would say I'd gone Holdfast.

I went through the door and into a small room that contained a couple of comfortable chairs, a small table, and not much else. It felt lived in, with a pile of books on the table and rumpled cushions on the chairs. This was where she came to be alone.

Elodie spoke as we sat down. "I have unfortunate news."

For a horrible second I thought something had happened to Tamsin or Sasha or Tricks, but I'd just left Sasha and Tamsin, and

Tricks was with me. Then I thought something had happened to Treesingers. My whole body locked with tension, bracing for another blow.

But all Elodie said was "Guildmaster Daylon has struck a deal with the traders to vote with the knights. And I believe the crafters will vote with the workers."

Oh. I wasn't going to be Queen. *Big deal.* The tension drained out of my body. Then it returned as I opened my mouth to tell her about Ronan. Except no words came out. I just didn't know how to start.

She spoke again. "You need not fear telling me the worst of it. I already know . . ." Her voice broke. She drew in a ragged breath and began again. "I already know he was killed with an unraveler."

That was what she thought? "He wasn't! He died saving me. He gave me his life force."

"You are certain of this?"

"Yes." Little lights, blinking out. "I was there."

"My apologies. That was a foolish thing to say. But if he *wasn't* unraveled . . ." She frowned, drumming her fingers against the arm of the chair, then leaned forward. "Bell. I need you to tell me everything that happened. Leave nothing out."

I nodded and looked down at my hands, like I was trying to gather up my thoughts when what I was actually trying to gather was energy. I was tired all the way down to my bones, and now I had to construct a believable lie. Because there were things I *had* to leave out. Like the Nexus.

Except the moment I had that thought, blood thrummed and I knew the Nexus wanted me to share it all.

Startled, I spoke to them in my head. *You want me to tell Elodie everything? Really?*

Pictures flashed, too fast and too complex for me to understand, other than that I was seeing a bunch of connections across time and space. Basically, the Nexus was saying they knew a heck of a lot more than I did. And I wasn't going to argue with them. They *did* know more than me, and anyway it was a relief not to have to do the work of lying.

So I shared. I told Elodie about the Nexus, and the Silverleafs, and Journeys Far. The pathway. Tomas killing Allora, and Ronan killing Tomas. Curing the grove. And Ronan, dying to save me.

I was okay until I got to that last bit. I managed to make it through, but by the end of it I was raw and aching. And Elodie was turned away from me with her head bowed.

After a while she said softly, "Alethea lied to me."

Oh. I hadn't really thought about how that part of the story would affect her.

"She felt bad doing it," I offered. But I had nothing else to say, because Alethea *had* lied and I would've done the same. Silverleafs were liars when we needed to be. Ronan would have understood.

She was silent for a moment longer, then shook herself. "Well. It is hardly the most significant matter before us now. Because . . ." She raised her head, shifting to face me. "I think we may have cause to hope."

She was *smiling*. Not a big smile, but a smile nonetheless, and there was a brightness in her eyes that hadn't been there before. "When my brothers died," she said, "I sensed them going. Allora, too, though I wouldn't describe us as close. But our lives were deeply entangled, I suppose. In any event, it was only she who passed into a new cycle. Not Tomas. And not Ronan."

That was why she'd thought he'd been unraveled, because

when their kind died that way, they weren't reborn. But it didn't sound very hopeful to me! "Doesn't that mean he's trapped somewhere, like the abyss place where he was before?"

"No. *No.* That's not what this is. He *should* have been reborn. The fact that he wasn't means—or at least, I think it may mean—that he isn't gone, yet."

"Not gone yet?" My heart seemed to stop for a moment and then sped up, slamming against the walls of my chest. "Are you saying he might come back? Is that something your people can do?"

"No one ever has," Elodie admitted. "But no one has ever returned from being killed by an unraveler either. The connection between you and him is unheard of, Bell." She sighed and added, "I admit, it is possible that it is merely taking him longer to transition between lives. But I thought I'd lost him once before, and I was wrong. So for my part . . ." Her gaze met mine, and I saw how much she wanted to believe he wasn't gone. "I am not going to mourn him just yet."

We will all be here again. Maybe those words hadn't meant what I'd thought? I reached out to the Nexus and got a sense of certainty followed immediately by doubt. The Nexus knew he'd return, but they didn't know when that would be to me. It might not be in my lifetime, and if it was, it might not be soon.

But not soon wasn't never.

I lifted my chin. "Guess I'm not going to mourn him either."

Elodie's face lit up, which was stupid of her, and my mouth was turning up a tiny bit, which was even more stupid of me. Ronan himself would say that one of the surest ways to make a lie feel true was to have more than one person believe it. Two deluded people didn't make a truth, even if one of them was a Queen. But I didn't care. Like Elodie, I wanted to believe.

I reached out in my mind, calling to someone who probably couldn't hear me (but who maybe could).

Come back, Ronan. Come back to me.

28

The Glass, again. It was shinier than the last time. Or maybe it was just that the whole world seemed brighter right now.

Tamsin, Sasha, and I were standing on the platform in the water, all gilded up with our swooshy dresses and sparkling nails and hair. Elodie was sitting in her chair, wearing her gold ball gown and her Queen face (icy and distant). And all of us were awaiting the arrival of the guilds.

I'd told Sasha and Tamsin about Ronan, and they'd embraced the idea of his return. I guess after dealing with pretend gods, trees living in blood, pathways to higher realms, and other-worlders beneath Radiance, nothing seemed impossible. Which meant I now had three other people believing something that could be a lie, and their collective faith shouldn't make me feel any better. But it did. It was enough to make me wonder if I was being influenced by that bit of the pathway I'd kept. Hope could make you stupid. And yet I *still* didn't care. At least for now, I was going to believe.

Sasha cast a satisfied glance around the Glass. "Did you think, on the very first day, that we'd be here?"

"I thought you'd be here," I answered.

"Everyone thought that," Tamsin agreed. "But after everything that's happened, this all feels . . ." Her voice trailed off as she searched for a word.

"Irrelevant," I said.

But her and Sasha shook their heads.

"It *matters*," Tamsin said. And Sasha directed a cold stare at the empty guild seats, her gaze lingering on the one that was going to be occupied by the knight guildmaster. "Someone has to change things. *Really* change them, I mean."

"And that someone will be one of you." I'd already told them that I didn't have the votes. "Although I guess I'll help you out. If you ask nicely enough."

That was meant to be a joke. But they didn't laugh. Instead they exchanged conspiratorial glances. For the first time, it occurred to me that their whispered conversations might not have totally been about making me feel better.

I opened my mouth to ask what was going on. But before I could get a word out, the doors at the end of the room opened and the guilds filed in.

No Uncle Dar this time, which wasn't surprising. My people could hardly send a substitute guildmaster to the final vote. Instead it was Granny Faran, who was as tiny and birdlike as I remembered. And just as much of a liar.

She was with the knight guildmaster, hanging on to Daylon's arm as if she needed his help to walk. She didn't. Granny Faran could swarm up to the top of a tree faster than anyone else in the groves. And Daylon was laughing at something she'd said, which meant she was being funny and charming and wholly unlike her actual self. She was my own granny's best friend, and people who didn't know them thought they were complete opposites. Really they were each as spiky as the other. But Granny Faran kept her spikes on the inside.

She cast a swift, penetrating glance at me. I tugged on my ear to signal *All okay.* She nodded in acknowledgment, making her way toward her chair.

The Queen reached out to put her hand on the orb that sent sound across the room as the guilds took their seats. "Candidates! Congratulations on reaching the end of the Test. Now is your final opportunity to convince us that you are the best choice to rule. But whether you rule or serve, I know that you will do so with honor."

She fell silent. And the silence stretched on for a while before I realized that Tamsin and Sasha were both looking at me. As if *I* should go first, which was weird because I'd just be filling the air with words that would change nothing. But since it seemed like they weren't going to speak until I did, I adopted my best humble Treesinger tone and said: "I ask that I be judged by my performance in the Test. I know I can trust the guilds to choose the most worthwhile candidate as Queen."

There. That should do it. I waited for Tamsin or Sasha to launch into their big speech. Instead they both took a few paces forward to stand together, a little ahead of me. And Sasha said, "The worker candidate and I wish to make a joint statement."

A *joint statement?* What the heck was that supposed to be?

The Queen spoke over the murmurs of surprise from the guilds. "That is a *most* unusual request. But there is no rule against it. You may proceed."

Sasha drew in a breath and began: "Throughout the Test, the

worker candidate and I have reflected deeply upon the qualities necessary to be Queen. We believe it is vital to be honest, about everything that makes us who we are."

Tamsin chimed in. "Our *family*. Our *history*."

And Sasha added, "Our . . . associates."

I clamped my lips together to stop my mouth from falling open. Sasha was threatening to *expose the Gleamings*? Surely I must have interpreted that wrong. Except from the way the knight guildmaster had suddenly straightened in his chair, he'd reached the same conclusion I had. Only it was such a weird thing for her to do! There was no need for Sasha to make any threats. The knights were already voting for her. And the workers were already voting for Tamsin, who was definitely threatening to expose that she was a Treesinger. Which her stepdad wouldn't want coming out, although it hopefully shouldn't matter that much otherwise (I'd still be a bit worried about the sisters trying to disqualify her, but they were going to have a lot to deal with, what with the disappearance of their high priestess).

"If I or the knight candidate were the Queen," Tamsin continued, "we would *both* be *compelled* to meet the high standards of integrity and honesty that are expected of us."

I worked my way through that sentence twice over before I figured out that they were saying they'd go spilling all the secrets if their guilds *did* vote for them. Were they actually trying to lose the crown? That made no sense. . . . Oh.

Yes, it did, and yes, they were.

"But," Sasha added, "we do not wish to rule. There is one amongst us who is far more worthy of the crown. We are proud to call her our friend. We will be proud to serve her as Queen."

And those two schemers swiveled around to face me—and bowed.

In my head I yelled at them both. *You're blackmailing your own guildmasters into making me Queen? I don't even know if I want the crown anymore!* But with everyone watching and listening, the only thing I could do was try to look overwhelmed with the honor of it all. Sasha and Tamsin marched back across the platform, obviously hugely pleased with themselves, and didn't stop when they reached my side. Instead they positioned themselves a few paces behind me. Just to emphasize how very special I was, I supposed.

A sleepy voice spoke. This will be the best adventure ever!

It won't. But I couldn't say that out loud.

Across the water, the worker, trader, and crafter guildmasters were making outraged spluttering noises. Granny Faran was grinning, and Daylon was staring into the distance, obviously thinking hard.

The Queen swept a stern gaze across Sasha, Tamsin, and me. "Candidates do not choose the Queen! That is a matter for the guilds. Despite this . . . *extraordinary* display, the vote will continue."

But there was the hint of a smile in her voice. She must've realized her true feelings were seeping through, because when she spoke next, her tone was completely emotionless. "As is the usual practice, we will begin the vote with the guilds who have candidates left in the Test." She looked at Guildmaster Daylon, Tamsin's stepdad, and Granny Faran in turn. "Can I assume that you are each voting for your own candidate?"

Granny Faran got in first. "I certainly am! You all know how often I've spoken of the need for more cooperation between our peoples—what greater opportunity could there be than for a Treesinger Queen to work with the guilds for the betterment of us all? And can I just say . . ." She paused to dab at her eyes with her sleeve, casting a knowing glance at me, and I realized she thought this whole thing was my idea. Dar must've told her I thought I could win it. "I'm so touched to see such *strong* and *powerful* bonds of friendship between Treesingers and Risen. We could all learn something from these candidates."

In other words, Bell-the-humble-Treesinger would be anxious to accommodate the wishes of the Risen guilds. Oh, and if they didn't elect me Queen, my very good friends were totally going to carry through on what Granny Faran had obviously realized were threats. Sweet old lady, my arse.

Elodie turned her attention to the knights. "Guildmaster Daylon? What say you?"

He was silent for a moment longer. Then he shifted to make a half bow to Granny Faran. It was difficult to look elegant doing that while seated, but he managed it. "I find much wisdom in your words."

Well, *of course* he did. Because he wasn't an idiot, and he'd already worked out that voting for Sasha meant making an enemy of the next Queen, no matter which of us won.

Daylon put his hand over his heart, like he was as deeply touched as Granny Faran was claiming to be. Overplaying it, but he was a knight, and no one was going to call him on it. "My vote goes to the Treesinger candidate."

"Well, mine doesn't!" Tamsin's stepdad snapped. "I vote for the worker candidate, as is proper for the worker guild." He swiveled toward Tamsin, radiating rage and defiance. She stared back at him, and he probably couldn't read the nuance of her expression from that distance, but she was looking at him in the way she'd once looked at Alasdar. Calculating all the ways in which he could be hurt.

The Queen turned to the trader guild. "Gabie? Your vote?"

But the trader guildmaster didn't reply. She was busy staring at Daylon, and I didn't think she was pleased. Elodie had said traders had agreed to vote with knights and this was not the deal she'd signed up for.

Daylon leaned over to speak to her. "Many will be taking notice of the outcome of this vote, Gabie—and you know as well as I, there are those within the surrounding kingdoms who still doubt the sincerity and speed of reform in Radiance. We have both lost potential alliances because of it. What better proof of change could there be than the election of a Treesinger as Queen?"

Yeah. One Treesinger making it to the top in spite of determined efforts to destroy me did *not* make this an equal society. But apparently the prospect of money to be made in far-off places was a winning argument, because Gabie lifted her chin and declared, "I also vote for the Treesinger candidate."

Elodie didn't even try to keep the smile out of her voice. Or off her face. "That is a sufficient number of votes." She rose, still with her hand on the orb. "I declare Bell Silverleaf to be the winner of the Queen's Test!"

The guildmasters broke into loud applause. Except for Tamsin's stepdad, who didn't applaud at all. And the crafter guildmaster, who was clapping in the half-hearted way you did for someone you definitely hadn't been going to vote for but were stuck with now.

Granny Faran beamed from across the water. Tamsin and Sasha bounced around me. And I just stood there, feeling . . . I didn't know.

Stunned. And a bit overwhelmed. Especially because there were pictures of broken worlds flashing through my mind.

A cheery voice chimed in my head. Five is better than one!

Tricks was right. It wasn't just me who had to try to live up to the ridiculous expectations of a tree that appeared to be basically trying to save the universe. We'd all gotten stuck with it.

The Queen gestured to us to come back across the lake, taking her hand off the orb. We could speak without being overheard, and Sasha did, asking anxiously, "You're not mad at us, are you?"

"I'm sorry if you are," Tamsin chimed in. "But it had to be you who won, Bell. It always had to be you."

I sighed. "I might be the one wearing the crown. But what has to be done is going to take all of us. Nobody can do this alone." I wasn't actually sure we could do this together, either, what with the stakes the Nexus was playing for. But that was a conversation for another time.

They grinned, relieved that I wasn't angry. Then Tamsin stretched out her hand, palm down, and Sasha put hers on top of it. I put mine on top of them both and reached out in my mind to include Blue in this even though he wasn't back yet. A burst of scent exploded around me, and petals showered down. I inhaled and felt . . . confident. Even a little reckless. After all, we five had already found the pathway, killed the gods, and cured the grove. Maybe this really would be a big adventure. At least for us.

Not so much for Risen society.

My lips curved into a smile my mum wouldn't like.

Five. Will. Rule.

Mum's eyes were fluttering. Not open yet. But soon.

Uncle Dar was in the next room, watching over Granny. My job was to watch over Mum. They were the last two sleeping, but the Matriarch wouldn't wake until everyone else did. So it'd be Mum first, then Granny.

I'd spent most of the week since the vote in the grove, talking to Uncle Dar of the things that could only be spoken of by a fire in the quiet dark. Jeffry was here too, part of the team of Treesinger healers sent in to look after Falling Leaves as it came out of dormancy. There was a lot to do, what with getting everyone accustomed to being awake again, but Jeffry still found time to keep checking in on me. I knew neither he nor Dar would be pleased when I left Falling Leaves for the palace. Tamsin and Sasha were already there, except that Tamsin was splitting her time between the palace and Winding Vines, where she was getting to know her Blackbark family. And Sasha was helping us both out by taking on much of the tedious queening duties (Ronan had been right that a lot of it was very boring).

Mum's eyes flickered again. Then blinked. She focused on me, letting out a shocked gasp as she took in the details of my face. The last time she'd seen me, I'd been a lot younger.

I grabbed her hand. "It's okay, Mum. Everything's okay."

She pushed herself up. "How . . . long?"

"Four years."

"Four? Four?" She clung to me, hugging me so tight I could barely breathe. I hugged her right back, feeling warm and loved . . . safe. I'd almost forgotten what safe was like.

Then Uncle Dar's voice came from the next room, sounding slightly panicked. "Bell, I need you to come in here!"

I stood, and Mum tried to, but she was still shaky from all the sleeping. Only she wouldn't let go of me, and I didn't want to let go of her either. So she put her arm around my shoulders and I put mine around her waist, and we staggered forward together.

Voices floated out from Granny's room. First Granny herself: "I'm the Matriarch. I can go anywhere I like."

Then Dar: "Of course you can, but you've only just woken—you're still a little weak. . . ."

"Weak? Weak? I'll show you—"

Mum and I both rushed forward to keep Granny from doing herself an injury and ended up falling in a heap onto the floor beside her bed.

Granny looked down on us and sniffed. "You shouldn't have gotten up yet, Leana. You're still weak."

Dar made a choking noise. Then he and I together lifted Mum to her feet, helping her onto the bed.

Granny focused on me, her brown eyes bright with approval. "Look at you, all grown! I always knew . . ." But her voice slid into silence. She cast a quick glance at Dar, and I remembered that as far as she was concerned, Silverleaf secrets were still for Silverleaf women and Silverleaf trees. So instead of telling me she'd always known I was the Silverleaf, she said, "Come help your granny up! People will be wanting to see their Matriarch."

"They can see you later," Mum said. "You're shaking like a leaf in the wind."

Granny glared at Mum in absolute outrage for daring to point out the obvious. It was clear to us all that she needed more time to recover. Much more time. Except I knew only one way to keep her still.

I'd told Uncle Dar everything, but we'd agreed that I wouldn't tell it all to Mum and Granny right away. Dar had painted a picture of how lovely it would be for the Silverleaf women to enjoy some quiet time together.

I really should have known better.

"You can't go out yet, Granny," I said. "Because I need to tell you how the gods died."

That got her attention and Mum's too. But then Granny's gaze slid to Dar again.

"He knows, Granny."

As I'd expected, she scowled. It was probably best to get the rest all out at once. "There's more. I'm the . . . that is, I'm . . ."

But I just couldn't say the words. So someone else said them for me.

Hello, Bell's mum and Bell's granny. I am Tricks! We are Queen!

Mum looked puzzled. "Queen? Queen of what?"

I swallowed. Squared my shoulders. And confessed. "The Risen. I'm the Queen of the Risen."

Mum let out a cry of dismay. But Granny went quiet. I couldn't read her expression at all. Until she started to laugh.

"Queen?" she gasped between chortles. "You're Queen of those

Risen bastards? Ha! Bet they think you're a good little Treesinger. They're going to be surprised!"

Mum shook her head at Granny. "Don't go giving her ideas. She can't do anything that puts her in danger."

"Never said anything about danger, did I?" Then she muttered under her breath, "Course, if you stir up trouble right, no one will ever know it was you that done it. . . ."

Mum glared. Granny gave the bed a cheery pat. "Come tell me about it. And as for you—" Her gaze switched to Dar. "Go make yourself useful and brew us a tea."

Dar smiled his big, gentle smile at us all and left to get the tea. I hopped onto the bed, snuggling in between Mum and Granny. As if I was still little. As if I'd never left the grove.

But I had, and I wasn't the same as the girl they'd known. I wanted them to know the Silverleaf I'd become. I guess I could've begun that story with the sisters and the priests. With Alasdar, Tomas, and Allora. Except that would tell them what had happened to me. It wouldn't tell them who I was, because I wasn't made out of the people who'd tried to bring me down. I was made out of the ones who had lifted me up. Tricks and the Nexus. Ronan, Tamsin, and Sasha. Journeys Far. The Ancients. Even Elodie.

I started with the one I'd met first. "I once went to a nothing place. And I found the god of lies. . . ."

ABOUT THE AUTHOR

AMBELIN KWAYMULLINA is an Aboriginal writer and artist who comes from the Palyku people of the Pilbara region of Western Australia. She is a previous winner of the Victorian Premier's Literary Award and the Aurealis Award. You can read more about Ambelin and her work at akauthor.com.au.